'More than anything  for my wife.'

Anne sprang to her ment. Never in her wil to hear him say such MacKenzie! If only it

'You are quite mad to suggest

'Very well, I am mad. Mad for wanting you as Mad for thinking we can live together and forget what has passed between your brother and my sister. Mad enough to carry you off in true MacKenzie style and lock you away somewhere until you agree to marry me.'

Anne took a step away from him, unsure of the gleam in those dark eyes.

In two long strides, Roy crossed the space between them and caught her in his arms. She felt his fingers bite into the soft skin of her shoulders. He was not smiling now. His dark features were angry, the narrowed black eyes like pieces of jet. 'Can't you see how I ache to take you in my arms every time we are together? Is it proof you need to tell you how I feel? I'll show you when Roy MacKenzie says he wants a woman—he means it!'

Valentina Luellen was born in London in 1938, and educated in Gloucestershire and London. She began writing at school—mainly because she loathed maths! It took her twelve years of writing before she had a book accepted, but she has now had over 40 stories published. Historical romances are her favourite to write, because she loves researching into so many different countries, learning about customs and costumes and the way people lived hundreds of years ago.

Valentina Luellen and her husband moved to Portugal six years ago when he became seriously ill. There his health began to improve and they now live in a renovated farmhouse on the Algarve with their 21-year-old son, 21 cats, two Portuguese dogs, and around 100 trees—almonds, olives, figs, plums, lemons and oranges —most of which they planted themselves.

Valentina Luellen has written 21 Masquerade Historical Romances. Recent titles include *Love, the Avenger*, *Where the Heart Leads*, *The Passionate Pirate* and *The Devil of Talland*.

THE DEVIL'S TOUCH

BY

VALENTINA LUELLEN

MILLS & BOON LIMITED
15-16 BROOK'S MEWS
LONDON W1A 1DR

First published in Great Britain 1987
by Mills & Boon Limited

© Valentina Luellen 1987

Australian copyright 1987
Philippine copyright 1987

ISBN 0 263 75745 5

Set in Monotype Times 10.8 on 10.8 pt.
04-0587-76571

Typeset in Great Britain by
Associated Publishing Services
Printed and bound in Great Britain by
Cox & Wyman Ltd, Reading

CHAPTER ONE

'FATHER, FOR God's sake! She's your own flesh and blood!'

Roy MacKenzie leaned forward in his chair, his dark features taut with anger at the words which had just been hurled in his direction so unfeelingly. His voice, like tempered steel, cut through the stillness of the room, the fury neither in his tone nor in the glittering black eyes altered the stony expression of the older man standing before him.

'I have no daughter,' his father replied, turning away to stare into the enormous fireplace which stretched five feet along the wall in front of him.

'You have a bonny daughter!' Roy leapt to his feet, his hand falling to the hilt of his sword. He was taller than Ranald by a good five inches, a man quickly roused to anger with a temper his old nurse had always maintained had been bestowed on him by the devil—D'hommil Dhu himself! And when it came to defending the sister he idolised, he was beyond control. 'Her name is Mairi and she is twenty years old. She disobeyed you and married the man she loved. Like a fool I did nothing about it. I'll regret it for the rest of my days, but I wanted to see her happy. Well, now she needs us and we shall not fail her.'

'Bring her beneath this roof again and I'll kill her. She's brought disgrace on our name, sorrow on the house of MacKenzie.' Ranald wheeled on his eldest son. 'She chose to wed Ewen Fraser against my wishes, and I disowned her for it. You were the only one to side with her in her scatterbrained choice—even your brother, Coll, saw the repercussions of her marrying a member of the clan who have been our enemies since we came out in '15. Although events now are beyond anything I had visualised.'

'You can't stand being disobeyed,' Roy challenged. 'Your authority defied by a chit of a girl. She married the man she loved, not some weak-kneed suitor you picked out for her.'

'Ay—for love. And how long did it last? By all accounts, no more than three months. Three short months before she began to tire of him and look about for other diversions. First it was his brother, James. She cared not that he was happily married. She drove him to his death.'

'It was an accident,' Roy snapped, but his father did not hear him.

'Then, when he died, she sank even lower, to stableboys and grooms . . . God knows who else she took to her bed under her husband's nose.'

'You go too far,' Roy snarled, and for one mad moment was prepared to draw his sword on his own father. The two men measured each other in silence, tempers barely held in check. It was Ranald who made the first move and so relieved the tension that threatened to explode into a bitter fight.

Roy was his eldest son, with his own fierce Highland pride and quick temper and because they were so alike, Ranald had been inclined to favour him above his other two children. Had it been Coll standing before him, daring to mention his sister's name, he would have felt the flat of his father's hand across his face for such impudence.

Ranald poured himself a glass of brandy, momentarily pausing before he poured a further glass and pushed it across the table to the silent man watching him. Roy made no move to take it. Ranald shrugged and drank his own without appreciation, allowing his eyes to wander slowly around the panelled walls of the study. His daughter's portrait was missing from the family group. All his ancestors were there, staring down at him from their polished wood frames; those of his wife, too. The MacKenzies of Tigh an Lóin could be traced back to Kenneth, second Earl of Ross.

His daughter's rooms upstairs had been sealed off on the day she ran away and had never been opened since. Her name was forbidden in the house—and yet Roy had dared to speak of it. In so doing, he revived the pain and heartache of the past twelve months and brought to mind the rosy-cheeked, vivacious girl with her large expressive brown eyes and her sparkling infectious laugh.

In a sudden fit of passion, Ranald flung his empty glass into the fireplace.

'Damn you, I should have you whipped,' he muttered and slumped into the nearest chair.

Roy leaned back against the table, his arms folded over a broad, muscular chest. He was perfectly calm now. He had managed to penetrate his father's protective shell and for the moment he was satisfied. Instead of being thrown out of the house, he had achieved a minor victory and was well pleased. As he smiled to himself, the light of the candelabra suspended above him shone full on his features, giving the appearance of a man younger than his thirty-two years.

Ranald MacKenzie sighed and lifted his eyes to the portrait which hung over the mantel. There hung the same handsome features, the thick auburn hair and dark, piercing eyes. There was even the same arrogance in the thrown-back head and folded arms. The hint of ruthlessness in the square-cut jaw. Was it only thirty years ago he had looked like that? Tonight, he felt like an old man!

'Ay, father, we are alike,' Roy murmured, following his gaze.

'Where is she?' Somehow Ranald forced the words out through tight lips. He did not want to hear—yet he had to know.

'So you know she has left him?' Roy was mildly surprised.

'There are those hereabouts who have taken great delight in conveying to me her every movement, together with every little piece of scandal.' Still he could not bring himself to say her name. She was supposedly his flesh and blood, but she had disgraced his name, forfeited the right to be called his daughter. 'She ran off some two months ago, didn't she?' His tone was bitter.

'Did they not tell you that Mairi is in Inverness?'

So near! Somehow Ranald succeeded in keeping his face impassive.

'I care not where she is—nor the bastard child she has with her.'

Roy's eyes glittered dangerously. 'You must pay well to get such up-to-date information,' he sneered. 'What right have you to pass judgment without first hearing what she has to say?'

'I heard enough from Ewen Fraser himself—curse him! You can tell that one has Campbell blood in him just to hear him whine. He came here while you and Coll were making merry in Edinburgh last month. He turned her out of the house because she was about to have a child. Not his, mark you! It could be his brother James's child—he's not been dead all that long—but it could also belong to the stableboy she took up with. God only knows!'

'That's a lie, and Ewen Fraser will admit it to your face before I'm through with him. Turned her out! God, man, she must be past her time now. Alone—with a new-born babe!' Roy ejaculated.

'You will not lay a finger on Fraser,' his father thundered. 'Find her if you must, but don't let me hear about it. And make no attempt to seek out her husband. Do you understand me?'

'I hear, but I don't believe my ears.' Roy's tone bordered on contempt. 'You prefer to believe him rather than your own daughter.'

'I believe Fraser's sister, Anne, who saw Mairi and James together in her room—embracing. She has no reason to lie, for I have heard that, since Mairi married, the two of them have been good friends. I believe James's widow, Frances. The maligned woman heard from his own lips of his infidelity.' Ranald averted his gaze so that his son would not see the anguish mirrored in his pale eyes. 'She is no better than a common whore. She will bring us no more disgrace—neither will you. I'll kill you myself rather than allow you to call out an innocent man over her wantonness.'

'I shall find her, and if she tells me these stories are all lies then not even you will stop me from my revenge,' Roy answered slowly and turned towards the door.

'Find her then, and the devil take you both!' his father flung after him. The thunderous slamming of the door almost drowned his words completely. Muttering a string of oaths he reached for the decanter and his empty glass.

Tigh an Lóin in the Gaelic meant 'the House by the Marsh'. It had been built many centuries before,

beside a small loch which meandered its way through
beautiful wooded countryside a few miles from the
River Orrin. It had been flanked on both sides by
peat bogs, which in those days proved to be a
formidable opposition to unexpected attacks from
enemy clans. It was approximately thirty miles to
Inverness: Roy's destination the following morning.
A journey to be made in bitterly cold weather which
threatened snow before the day was over.

Roy rode his horse like a man possessed, his mind
filled with anger against his stubborn father and pity
for the helpless sister somewhere alone and friendless
in the city. He would find Mairi even if he had to
stay there a month. Not for one moment had he
ever believed the malicious rumours spread about
her. Not when they had first come to his ears four
short months after she had been married, nor now,
when they seemed to be confirmed by her being
turned out of her husband's house to bear the child
of another man.

He had taken his first woman, a maid at the
house, when he was sixteen. Young Coll, now twenty-
six, had been even more adventurous, boasting of
his exploits when he was but fourteen. But Mairi!
She had never looked at a man until she was seventeen and then it had been under the eagle eyes of
them both, for they had jealously guarded their little
sister whenever she ventured away from Tigh an
Lóin. Even when there were parties or New Year
balls and the cream of MacKenzie youth came to
court her, they were always vetted by both Roy and
Coll.

She was no whore. He would get to the truth of
it, and when he discovered who had begun the
rumours and the necessity for them, he would settle
the score once and for all. If it meant killing Ewen

Fraser, for he was in no doubt the man was behind everything, he would do so and risk his father's wrath. It would not be the first time.

A few yards behind him Coll bemoaned Roy's fast pace, swore at him when he refused to slow down and increased his own in an attempt to keep up with him. The two men were somewhat alike in looks, but totally different in temperament: Roy had been greatly surprised when Coll had voiced his intention of riding with him. Like their father, Coll believed the rumours and shrugged off Roy's heated arguments that there was some plot afoot to discredit their sister.

'Suit yourself,' Roy had said shortly, and those were the only words which had so far passed between them. Now, as his brother drew abreast of him, he begrudgingly slowed his mount, aware of the questioning look on Coll's face. 'What are you grinning at, brother?' he demanded ungraciously. He was in no mood for polite talk and Coll knew it, but ignored the sourness of his expression.

'I hope you do not show *her* that face,' he murmured, and Roy's scowl grew.

'Who? What are you blathering about, man?'

'I heard you tell father—before that little argument the two of you had last night—that you intend to open up the house in Inverness. For entertaining?' A wicked grin crossed Coll's face. 'What kind of entertaining?'

'That's none of your business!'

'You're not thinking of installing Mairi there —when you've found her, are you? He'll kill you!'

'My reasons are my own.' Roy was determined not to be drawn on the subject, but his brother was equally adamant that he should be.

'So there is a woman. You sly old *sionnach*. Who

is she? Ellen MacDonald? No, she has eyes for a bigger fish. Not that you aren't a good catch . . . Who else is there?'

'You've never met her.' Roy's mouth had tightened into a tight line of displeasure. 'I've no intention of discussing her, so save your breath. Speculate all you like, you'll never find out who she is from me. This one I intend to keep to myself.'

'Have you bedded her?' Coll asked. For years they had competed for the favours of women who came into their lives. Friendly rivalry, although the game was played with deadly cunning. Coll fell in love with monotonous regularity, but so far Roy had emerged unscathed from his affairs. Now he had a woman hidden away somewhere and Coll was curious!

'She's a lady, not a whore. Forget it, Coll. I'll not be drawn.'

By the time they reached Inverness, Coll was complaining of hunger pangs demanding to be satisfied, but Roy had other plans. He had been given an address where a woman answering his sister's description had recently lodged and he went straight to it. He knew she would be without money, or financial support of any kind, but even he was unprepared for the squalor of the street, the stench of rotting food penetrating his nostrils as he dismounted before the house, set between two taverns. Although it was only midday, there were sounds of great revelry coming from inside both, and several drunks were propped against the walls, sleeping off the effects of their latest disaster.

A bitter smile touched his lips as he witnessed the horror in Coll's expression. A painted whore lounged in one of the doorways, eyeing them expectantly as they approached. Unceremoniously Roy pushed her to one side as she attempted to detain him.

'Stay here,' he ordered Coll. 'And shut her mouth,' he added as the woman began to swear in gutter-language at his rebuff.

His information was that Mairi had a room at the top of the house. He halted outside the last door on the topmost landing and raised his hand to knock, then changing his mind, he put his foot against the door and kicked it open.

A startled gasp came from the ashen-faced girl lying on a makeshift bed in one corner of the room. Roy was instantly aware of the smell of damp and rotting wood. There was only one small window in the room, which made it so dark he could scarcely make out the figure before him.

'Who is it? What do you . . . ' came a frightened voice.

As the voice trailed off, Roy took the candle on the small table and lit it. The light slowly illuminated his hard features. The young girl gave another gasp of shock.

'Roy! Oh, dear God! No!'

He stood in silence, appalled at the conditions in which he found her. Appalled by the creature who came unsteadily towards him, her eyes dilated with horror—and he was stirred to murderous intent. Fraser had brought her to this!

Her dress was clean, but faded. The shoes on her feet were ill-fitting and obviously not her own. The long brown hair, which had once been her pride and joy, fell unkempt about her shoulders.

'I did not hear you knock, brother. Were you, also, hoping to catch me in a compromising situa-tion—like everyone else? How that would please our father. Proof from the lips of someone he trusts implicitly.'

The bitter mockery in her voice made Roy flush uncomfortably. He did not know why he had entered in such a forceful way. Had he been expecting to find her with someone? With a fierce expletive he strode across the room and gathered her frail form into his arms.

'I don't care how many men you have had; you're still my sister and I love you,' he muttered.

He felt her stiffen. Slowly freeing herself from his grasp, she stepped back and she was trembling from head to toe.

'Do you also think I am a whore?'

'Mairi, for the love of heaven! Of course not!' Roy declared harshly.

'Then why do you speak of the men I have had?' She backed away from his outstretched hand. 'You have talked with Ewen and James's widow, Frances. They have deceived you as they have deceived all others. Of all people I counted on you, Roy . . . It seems I was foolish to do so.'

'Fraser spoke to Father and convinced him. Not only him—but James's widow and the sister also.'

'Anne! But I thought . . . Once she was my friend . . . ' Mairi moaned and tears began to stream down her colourless cheeks.

Roy caught her to him, steadied her as she swayed. She was barely conscious in his hold and he realised she was skin and bone beneath the dress. She muttered incoherently as he lifted her and carried her back to the bed. Striding to the door he flung it open and bellowed for Coll.

'Go out and buy a bottle of the best brandy you can find and some food,' he ordered.

'Is she there? Is she all right? Can I come up?' Coll had one foot on the stairs, but Roy waved him back.

'Fetch the bottle, man, she's in need of a stimulant and a decent meal. And be quick about it.

Roy turned back into the room and looked across at the girl who lay still and silent on the bed, her eyes open, filled with apprehension. She was a shadow of the happy sister he had last seen as he gave her his blessing for her wedding and rode with her to the edge of Fraser land, where they parted. From that day to this he had not seen her. Somehow—some way he would seek revenge for what Ewen Fraser had done to her.

A strange sound arrested his attention. A pathetic whimpering coming from behind a tattered curtain which partitioned the room. Frowning, Roy followed the sound, aware of his sister's gasp as he drew aside the sacking. His mind still refused to accept what he knew he would find. From a tiny cot, a pair of hazel eyes so like those of his sister blinked up at him from a cherub face which must have been moulded by angels. He felt a tight knot form in his stomach. So it was true—there was a child!

Almost unconscious of his actions, he reached out and touched the curly hair. Immediately tiny fingers clutched at his and held them fast.

'I think he resembles me—don't you?'

His hand was abruptly withdrawn as Mairi's voice sounded behind him.

'He has your eyes and hair,' he answered quietly. 'And, by his grip, he's a true MacKenzie.'

'Is he?' she demanded, sitting up. 'Are you sure they aren't James Fraser's eyes? His were that colour, and my stableboy paramour had light brown hair.'

'Stop it!' In two swift strides Roy had crossed the room and grabbed her by the shoulders. 'What do you take me for? You may have fallen out of love with Ewen Fraser, that I'll believe, but to take a lover . . . ? Not you. I know you too well. You have not forgotten how it was with our mother—the consequences of her forgetting her marriage vows.'

'I am of her blood—and the blood of the lover she took when she could no longer stand father's indifference to her. Perhaps it is tainted?'

He perched himself beside her, his expression growing reproachful.

'You could have sent word to me. You know I would have come to you if I thought you needed me.'

'I have my pride, although there is very little left,' his sister whispered.

'Has pride come between us then? Before you were married, there was nothing between heaven and earth could do so.'

'You are Father's right hand; he relies on you so much now his health is not good. And Coll is following in your footsteps. I am—a product of another liaison—the other skeleton in the cupboard which he cannot bear to discuss. Oh, Roy, I have been so wretched! Hold me. Tell me you are really here, believing in me, or I think I shall go quite mad.'

Roy held her close, gently stroking her hair, his thoughts far removed from the tiny room and the quivering girl in his arms. After a long moment she caught his hand and held it tight.

'You always used to comfort me when we were children. Thank you.' She took his hand and held it against her cheek. Her skin was as cold as ice. 'You have a gentle touch. This hand has comforted me, caressed the many women you have made love to, wielded a sword that has ended the lives of a countless number of men . . . '

'I shall not tell you the true number,' Roy replied

with a humourless smile. 'But I promise you Ewen Fraser will be the next one to end his miserable life on my blade.'

'Father will never forgive you if you call him out because of me,' Mairi said, with a sad smile. 'You will sever the close bond you have both shared for all these years. And I shall never forgive myself if you are hurt.'

'Fraser? Best me? I know what I'm doing, lass. Don't fear for me. When Coll gets back you will eat your fill and get some good brandy inside you, then we will take you out of this pest-hole.'

Mairi drew back and stared into his dark face. His thoughts were closed to her and she did not like it.

'You have not asked me how—how it really was.' Her voice began to tremble again and Roy caught her hands between his and held them fast.

'When you feel able to speak of it, then tell me.'

'It must be now—while I have the courage. I did not betray Ewen, Roy, either in my thoughts or with my body. Not with so much as a look in the direction of another man. Yet he . . . ' She was silent for a long moment. He said nothing, knowing she must find the words in her own time. 'It was a short month after we were married that I discovered Ewen and Frances, James's wife, were lovers, and had been long before he married me. I was foolish enough to speak to him about it—beg him for an explanation.'

'Beg!' Roy spat. 'You should have demanded.'

'I loved him. A woman in love can still trust and love a man even when she knows he has betrayed her. You have never been in love, so you do not know the torment it can bring . . . '

'Not yet,' Roy murmured, a strange gleam in his

eyes. He had that to come, he thought silently. 'You cannot feel for him still? Not after he turned you out of the house?'

'That was Frances's doing. As most things have been. She was afraid that when my baby was born he would look so much like Ewen that I could prove him the father, despite all the lies she has spread about me. I had told them both as soon as the child was born I was leaving . . . Oh, if only James had been alive.'

'You—and he?'

'No! He was kind to me. He understood what I had to endure—loving a man who possessed no feeling for me. He knew too that Frances had married him only for his money. He told me she was Ewen's mistress before I married him—and afterwards. She was—is—an enchantress, Roy. She controlled the lives of those two men as if she had some evil power over them. I think in the end James grew to hate her, but his love for her was so strong that he could not send her away.

'That night . . . the night James was seen in my room, it was not as you have been led to believe. He came to comfort me when he heard me crying. I was in despair when I realised I was with child. I was going to run away, but where could I go? Ewen caught me trying to leave, and beat me. James had a terrible row with him the next day. They came to blows. From the way he spoke, Ewen made it sound as if he was the injured party. He accused James of being my lover and even threw doubts on to who was the father of the child I carried.

'When James went riding, Ewen followed him. No one will ever know what happened, but when I saw Ewen return an hour later, his clothes were wet and covered with mud. Later that afternoon, James's body was found in a nearby loch. Frances threw herself into a fit of hysterics, accused me of stealing her husband, of driving him to his death. Oh, Roy . . . ' Mairi leaned her head against her brother's solid shoulder with a weary sigh. 'I could go on and on about the indignities I have suffered at their hands, until love died inside me. I feel nothing now . . . not even hate. Loneliness perhaps, and sometimes pity for the gentle man who tried to help me and died at the hands of his own brother. But I will not speak of that now. With the infamy now surrounding me, who would listen? So you see how pointless it would be to call Ewen out?'

'I have every intention of doing just that,' Roy returned, 'but your name will not be mentioned. I have another plan in mind. No, ask me no questions. It is something I must do and I will allow no one, not even you, to sway me from it.'

Looking into his eyes, Mairi was suddenly very afraid at the coldness she saw lurking in their shadowy depths.

A few hours later, having sat by and watched his sister consume half a chicken, washed down with several glasses of brandy—on his insistence—Roy was pleased to see some colour returning to her cheeks. As she rose to attend to the baby, who had begun to whimper, he decided it was time to leave. Coll's mouth gaped visibly as he ordered,

'Open up the house for me, Coll, and see Mairi is given everything she wants. The pair of them will be needing clothes. Send someone out for fresh milk for the child and make sure he is entrusted to someone capable of caring for him. Here are the keys.'

'No,' Mairi said quietly, but stubbornly. 'I will not allow you to go against father.'

'You will do as you are told, my girl,' Roy returned sternly. 'I didn't come all this way to leave you here to rot. You will go with Coll and I will see you later this evening. I have some—business to attend to first.'

'He means he has a woman hidden away somewhere!' Coll nudged Mairi with a grin. 'I do believe our brother has been smitten.'

'You may dance at my wedding feast sooner than you think,' Roy answered, a smile touching his lips, but both saw the humour did not extend to his eyes. He bent and kissed his sister on the cheek, touched the curly head of the babe in her arms. 'I shall see you this evening, Mairi. You will be there, won't you?'

'Yes, Roy.' She had prayed for him to come and find her while she lay in childbirth and during the long days afterwards when her strength had diminished and the desire to live flickered inside her like a dying candle flame. Only the child nuzzling at her breast had given her the will to survive. And now Roy had come for her, to take her away from the squalor in which she found herself, to give her back her self-respect—to give her the love she had been denied for so long. Bright tears sprang to her eyes, but they were tears of happiness. The shadows of fear were wiped from her face as she smiled at him, nodding. 'I shall be there.'

Roy reined in his horse on the outskirts of the town and sat looking up at the first-floor windows for a full minute before he dismounted. His keen gaze caught the slight movement of a curtain. She was there, waiting for him as always. Every decent instinct in him urged him to turn his horse about and ride away and never set eyes on her again, but he could not. A chance meeting four weeks ago had placed in his hands the instrument of his revenge against Ewen Fraser and when he had struck up an acquaintanceship, that was all that had been on his mind. Four short weeks and his desire to see that accursed man dead now battled against his love for the woman waiting for him inside the house. It should never have happened. *He* should never have allowed it to happen, to be so vulnerable as to fall in love.

It was too late to have regrets, he thought, as he dismounted and knocked at the door. The die was cast. He was committed. How he would resolve the new dilemma facing him he did not know at that moment. He loved her and he would have her. He would also kill Ewen Fraser. The consequences of such an action did not bear thinking about. He could lose everything!

He was admitted into the parlour by a servant girl who told him to make himself at home until the mistress arrived. He promptly did so by crossing to the decanter of brandy on the sideboard—placed there especially for him, he suspected—and pouring himself a large measure. He swallowed it quickly, standing before the welcoming warmth of a roaring fire and replenished his glass. He must not allow himself to dwell on what *might* happen. Only what he was sure *would* happen. A marriage! He was mad, he told himself for at least the hundredth time since he had first met her. Quite deranged. Had she not lied about Mairi along with the rest of them? Poor little Mairi, who had once been her friend?

'Roy, you are early, but I am pleased to see you.' The woman who stood in the doorway was tall and slender. She dismissed the hovering maid, meant to act as a chaperon. Roy took the ringed hand extended towards him, warming to the warmth in her own voice, and touched it to his lips in a long, lingering caress that brought a flush of bright colour to her cheeks. Then he stepped back—his eyes slowly considered her from the top of the gleaming tresses which shone with red fire, secured in a mass of curls on the crown of her head. His gaze wandered further, down over the gown of jade-green silk that accentuated every curve of her figure, lingering longer than was considered polite on the firm swell of her breasts above the low neckline and then down on to the dainty leather shoes peeping from beneath the full skirts.

When his eyes returned to her face he found it was burning with fierce colour and the brilliant blue eyes held a hint of anger in them.

'Must you stare at me in that way?' He had looked at her the first time they met in the same scrutinising manner and she had blushed to the roots of her hair. But she could not deny she liked it!

Roy gave a soft laugh and bent to kiss her on the mouth. She jerked back from him and sat down in a chair.

'I did not give you permission for that either. You are too bold, Roy MacKenzie.' The soft tones held mild reproach.

'Perhaps I should go?' He swallowed his drink and put the glass aside. She had never allowed him to take liberties with her, unlike many of the women he had known. Until now, he had not realised how empty and meaningless his existence had been. As he turned towards the door, she said quickly,

'No, stay. You know I did not mean it. I—I have never met anyone like you—so full of yourself—so confident.'

'You may say arrogant, for that is what you mean,

and you would be right,' Roy said smilingly. 'I am. As for confident—with others, perhaps, not you. I have never met a woman like you, Anne Fraser.' He moved to her chair and stood before her, his smouldering gaze on her face. He did not touch her, though he suspected she wanted him to for all her reticence. 'I came early because I must speak with you, and I cannot stay to dinner as we arranged.'

Anne hid her disappointment. She had been looking forward to seeing him again since they last met, seven long days ago. She had made special preparations for the meal and purchased a new gown.

'You make it sound—of importance.' More important than being with her, he easily guessed her thoughts and immediately dispelled her fears.

'It concerns the future—our future,' Roy said gravely.

She gave a little gasp of surprise and looked up at him, questioningly. She had known him only one short month, yet in that time he had turned her world upside down and stolen her heart. Love! She had almost given up hope of ever knowing what it was like to want a man as she wanted this one—this man who by his very name should have been kept at a distance. But she had found him charming, exactly as his sister had described. Sometimes too confident of manner, but after seeing how her brother had thrown away all pride in himself as a man, it was a pleasure to find one who was his own master. If only his sister did not stand between them, would things have been different.

'We—do not have a future—not together, you know that,' she said quietly, and frowned as an expletive exploded under his breath. From the beginning, they had mutually agreed not to discuss the

marriage of Roy's sister Mairi to Anne's brother
Ewen, but it had always hung between them like a
dark cloud heralding the approach of a storm. She
sensed it now, in the room with them, and knew he
was about to broach the subject.

'I will not accept that. Nor will I allow you to
spoil what we can have together. I have accepted—I
must accept that Mairi is no longer the sister I knew.
I like not what she has become, but it is a fact. I
admit I have fought against it, put myself against
my family in her defence, but now it is over . . . I
must forget her, forget what she has done, if I am
to be at peace with you.' Surely God would forgive
him one small lie? 'And that I want more than
anything else in this world. I want you for my wife.'

Anne sprang to her feet, her eyes wide with
astonishment. Never in her wildest imagination had
she thought to hear him say such words. His wife!
The wife of Roy MacKenzie! If only it were possible.

'You are quite mad to suggest such a thing.' She
tried to sound indignant at the suggestion, but failed
miserably. Was it possible he loved her? He had
always behaved so correctly with her, even if it was
after a fashion of his own which left her wondering
if he was not laughing at her primness sometimes.
He did not know the things she had heard and seen
at her brother's house. She was sick of the way
people deceived each other in the name of love. She
was considered an old maid in the circles in which
she moved, because she was twenty-two and still
unwed. She had had proposals, but taken none
seriously and because she was of age, Ewen could
not force a husband on her. As if she would have
let him!

'Very well, I am mad. Mad for wanting you as I
do. Mad for thinking we can live together and forget

what has passed between your brother and my sister.
Mad enough to carry you off in true MacKenzie
style and lock you away somewhere until you agree
to marry me.'

Anne took a step away from him, unsure of the
gleam in those dark eyes. They were dancing with
wicked lights—as if he meant every word. Her heart
quickened with the audacity of the suggestion.

'I am aware of how your ancestors used to get
their womenfolk, Roy MacKenzie, but I won't be
taken like that! I will have a ring on my finger and
go with you willingly to the kirk.'

'When?' He shot the question at her unexpectedly
and she floundered for an answer. Frightened to
consider the consequences of such a foolhardy action.
Marry him! Ewen would have a fit.

'We—hardly know each other. It would not be
proper to wed so hastily . . . ' she faltered. Never
before, in any situation that she could think of, had
she been so unsure of herself. She was stammering
like a schoolgirl.

'Does that matter?' Roy asked, his mouth deep-
ening into a grin. 'We shall have plenty of time for
that kind of thing.'

'We have not—I mean, you have given me no
indication of such feelings before . . . '

'Are you blind?' In two long strides, Roy crossed
the space between them and caught her in his arms.
She felt his fingers bite into the soft skin of her
shoulders. He was not smiling now. His dark features
were angry, the narrowed black eyes like pieces of
jet. 'Can't you see how I ache to take you in my
arms every time we are together? Is it proof you
need to tell you how I feel? I'll show you when Roy
MacKenzie says he wants a woman—he means it!'

She opened her mouth to protest at his roughness

and found it crushed beneath his. She had never been held so possessively by any man before, nor kissed with such ardour. Any man who had dared such liberties before had been rewarded with a stinging slap and the sharp end of her tongue. But this man was different. She had known it from the beginning. She had desperately tried to keep some distance between them, knowing the danger which threatened if she gave way to her feelings. She was completely in his power, of that she was certain. She had no will to resist him as she had done others. Her lips responded to his kiss, betraying what she had been afraid to put into words.

The eager answer Roy tasted on her lips drove him on to press more searching kisses on her mouth, caress her with skilful hands that made Anne inwardly shiver with pleasure and excitement. She had not allowed a man to be so bold with her before. Yet in the arms of this comparative stranger, nothing mattered except this moment.

She wanted to answer him kiss for kiss, touch for touch, and pressed closer against him, her body moulding against his. Roy was abruptly brought back to reality when she suddenly pulled free of him and stepped back, her face growing pale. He stared into the blue eyes filled with uncertainty and understood her expression.

'No. You are right. I'll not take you now. You would hate me for it.'

'It—It isn't that. I—I love you so much, there is nothing I would deny you.'

'Then why?'

She seemed to be fighting some inner battle as she turned away from him and stared down into the fire for several minutes in silence. Then, deciding she must speak, she turned back to him, saying haltingly,

'You speak of—of being married, of being able to be happy despite what has happened between my brother and your sister, the hatred your family bears mine. You make me want to believe it could happen . . .'

'It can,' he insisted. 'We shall make it happen. I swear it.'

'Yet there have been times when you have looked at me and—and . . .'

'Did wicked thoughts show on my face?' Roy grinned at her.

'No . . . It's as if . . . as if you hated me! Yet wanted me also and did not know which feeling was the strongest. Sometimes you frighten me.'

'Never say that! I love you. Ask of me what you will as proof. I'll even go to your brother and ask for your hand if that's what you want.'

'He would have his men cut your throat and then send you home across your horse.'

'He might try.' He smiled slightly. A confident smile which told her he would take many men with him before he died. 'Many a man has tried to kill Roy MacKenzie and failed. I'm not an easy man to be rid of, as you will find out. Few can best me with a sword.'

'Ewen may be the one to succeed,' Anne replied quietly. 'Which is why I am frightened. If—if I deny what I feel for you, I shall lose you. If I accept it and become your wife, I know I shall cause more bloodshed—perhaps the death of my brother—or your own. I don't want the blood of either of you on my hands. I love you both. I cannot choose between you.'

'Then you shall not. Will you not trust me, Anne? I swear to you, after we are wed, I shall not be the one to raise a sword against your brother. If he challenges me, then I will defend myself—but only after provocation. I swear it!' Love had addled his brains, Roy thought as he looked at her and watched the tension slowly fade from her face. Here he had Ewen Fraser almost at his mercy and yet he was throwing away this wonderful opportunity so that he could marry his sister! He knew he would never love another woman as he loved Anne. He could not lose her! He would have another chance to settle with her brother. He would keep his word. He would not be the first to raise a weapon in anger, but neither would he refuse a challenge if it came. And come it would when the Fraser discovered his sister had married a MacKenzie.

'Marry me,' he said quietly. 'At once. We shall tell no one.'

'That is impossible!' Anne cried, but silently she was considering the mad suggestion. Ewen was at home at Eskadale. She would write to him, of course, telling him what was to happen, but by the time he received the news, it would be too late to stop the marriage. No . . . No! He would ride to the MacKenzie house and call Roy out. She would be a widow before she was a wife.

'Don't think of what might happen,' Roy interrupted. He reached out and caught her by the shoulders and the strength in his hands instilled fresh courage in her. 'By the time I take you to Tigh an Lóin, everyone will have accepted the idea. Your brother and my father. They will see we are happy and accept the marriage. We will give them a week. There is a hunting-lodge in the forest near the house—not too near. We shall spend our honeymoon there—totally alone.'

'Roy . . . please, give me time to think?' she pleaded.

'No. Either I walk out of here and make the arrangements—or I go through that door and do not set foot in this house again. Are you willing for that to happen? Are you going to throw away what we have found? Lass, lass, don't do that to us—to me.'

He began to kiss her again and Anne knew she was lost against his kind of argument. She did not want to fight him. She wanted to belong to him—to show him the depths of her love.

'I'm still of a mind to drag you off to the lodge if you refuse me . . . and then our families will have another scandal to contend with,' he chuckled wickedly.

'Yes . . . ' Her lips moved beneath his, giving him the answer he sought. Anne knew that her brother would never forgive her, but she was in love! She had a right to happiness the same as everyone else. 'Yes, Roy MacKenzie, I will marry you—and God help us!'

'There's a small kirk on the edge of town.'

'No, we shall be married here. No one will know. My maid can be a witness.'

'And my brother Coll.' Roy smiled down into now flushed cheeks. 'As you wish. How much time do you need to prepare yourself? I warn you, I am not a patient man. Do not make me wait too long.'

'I have brought sufficient clothes with me from France . . . ' For a moment Anne's eyes were wistful. 'I would have liked to be a real bride . . . in white with my family . . . '

'One day you will stand by my side in the chapel at Tigh an Lóin, with a hundred guests about you,' Roy promised her. 'You shall have your bridal gown and anything else you desire.'

'I shall have you and I shall be content. Let us be

married at the end of next week.'

'Eight days?' He gave a mock groan.

'And you must not be seen coming here again. Should any friends of Ewen call here . . . '

'I'll send word where you can reach me. Send your maid to me if you need to. Come, let me hold you a moment longer, then I must go. There is much to be done.'

CHAPTER TWO

'ARE YOU SURE you know what you are doing, mistress? It isn't too late to change your mind, you know. I can have the carriage ready in fifteen minutes and we can be safely back at Eskadale before nightfall. You don't *have* to go through with this.' Agnes put her head on one side as she asked the question, surveying the smiling, elegant young woman who turned to and fro before her awaiting some words of approval. 'You know nothing about him except that he's a MacKenzie, and that's nothing to boast about, especially in *that* family. They say the Laird of Tigh and Lóin did not father young Mairi, and that's why she has gone bad—it's in the blood.'

Anne frowned at the rumour that she too, had heard. How cruel people could be. What would be said about her eloping with Roy, she wondered and decided it did not matter. While tongues were busily wagging, trying to determine whether or not she had been seduced or kidnapped or merely lost her wits, she would be blissfully happy in her husband's arms in the isolated lodge in Strathconon Forest. Later, they would face the gossip and unpleasantness together. Anne did not want to dwell on that aspect of it now, nor on her brother's reaction or that of Roy's father. Today was their wedding day, and that was all that mattered.

Anne had chosen a gown of pale blue silk, the sleeves and neckline trimmed with an abundance of pure white Brussels lace. About her throat she wore the same string of flawless pearls as her beloved mother had worn on her wedding day and since bequeathed to her daughter.

There was a flush to her cheeks, a sparkle in her eyes that Agnes had never seen before. She loved the man right enough . . . but to marry in secret! Not a word to a soul! It was neither right nor proper and he should not have demanded it. A bride should have all her family about her to wish her well on such a great day, the most important of her whole life. Agnes had said so in no uncertain manner, but her mistress had simply shrugged and said that was not the way Roy Mackenzie wanted it—for obvious reasons which they both knew.

The man had bewitched her, Agnes thought, as she made a last minute adjustment to a stray curl which refused to stay in place. She had brushed the red hair until it gleamed and swept it over one shoulder in a profusion of curls, securing it with tortoiseshell combs. God help them when Ewen Fraser discovered that he was saddled with another MacKenzie by marriage! The heather would run red with blood.

'By God, but you're a cool one!' Coll declared, catching the eye of a buxom waitress at the next table, and indicating he wanted the two tankards replenished. He grinned at her wickedly as she brought his order and slapped her playfully on the buttocks as she moved laughingly away. 'I think I shall come back here after you have tied the knot. Or should I say, tightened the noose about your neck?' He stared at his brother with continued disbelief, as Roy proceeded to consume the ale. 'Man, she'll think it a poor start to the idyllic bliss you have promised her if you breathe ale fumes all over the poor girl.'

'It's time you knew who my bride is to be, brother,' Roy replied, and his voice was harsh with the strain he was feeling. 'Anne Fraser herself!' Roy waited for the announcement to sink in. 'Don't look at me as if I have taken leave of my senses! I haven't. I'm in love with her. It's that simple. I'm going to marry her—and keep her—even if I have to fight off the whole Fraser clan.'

'You'll have to take on Father before the Frasers,' Coll spat. 'You—and Ewen Fraser's sister! You've had too much—or not enough. Is she the one you've been seeing these past weeks?'

'We met by chance at a theatre in Inverness.' Roy threw him an odd smile. 'Nothing seems real since that day. I saw her, Coll, and I wanted her. At first that's all it was . . . that and the fact that through her I knew I would have access to Ewen. And then, somehow, it all changed. I fell in love with her and she with me. I'll do anything to have her, I mean it. Even if I have to leave Tigh an Lóin, I will.'

'Ewen will call you out, you realise that, don't you. Confide in me, that's what you are really after, isn't it?' Coll insisted, still not convinced.

Roy put down the tankard and stared across the table at him—and Coll needed only one look into those glittering black eyes to know every word he said was the truth.

'How can you marry her—and deep in your heart still hope to kill her brother—and expect her to go on loving you, you great fool?'

'I don't know. I'm gambling with her happiness as well as my own. And Mairi's. Fraser can't be allowed to get away with what he has done to Mairi and I'm the only one still willing to fight for her.

She's our sister, Coll. She has been abused, smeared with the dirtiest of lies, sent packing from first her own home, then her husband's. She has no one. Somehow—I don't know how—I have to keep my love for Anne and my hatred for Ewen Fraser, separated. I won't let one destroy the other,' Roy said fiercely. 'For God's sake, help me!'

'You've never asked help from anyone before,' Coll said slowly, almost in awe of the words which had just been spoken.

'I've never been in love before. I'm being torn apart. Please stand by me. Whatever happens—even if one day she thinks the worst of me—stand by me. It's a lot to ask . . . ' his brother pleaded hoarsely.

'What else is a brother for?' They clasped hands across the table and Coll felt his brother slowly relax. A smile touched his mouth as he reached once more for the last of his ale.

'Well, drink up, man. We have a wedding to get to.'

Even as they rode to the house, Coll still found himself unable to grasp the situation fully. Not until they were shown into a warm, pleasantly furnished sitting-room and found the minister awaiting them, did he accept his brother was actually to be married.

Roy had asked Coll to be his best man and had given him a plain gold wedding band to keep until it was needed. He recognised it immediately as belonging to their mother. Coll had not believed him then, but he believed him now and stood quite thunderstruck at the enormity of his brother's actions.

Coll thought he knew his brother well, but now he found himself beginning to wonder if he had ever known him at all. To love the girl and marry her knowing their father's reaction—and that of the

clansmen who adored the Laird's eldest son. To be
prepared to lose all to have her . . . and yet deep
in the recesses of his heart, to harbour a death wish
against her brother. Coll envied him such a love,
but at the same time feared for him and for Anne
and the unsuspecting Mairi, safely hidden away in
the house in Inverness . . .

Coll had no love for Ewen Fraser either, but on
the subject of Mairi's marriage, he had found himself
with no option but to side with his father against
Roy. Mairi had chosen to ignore all advice given
her, she had disregarded all warnings—and in the
very end, the threats which came her way—and had
wed the man of her choice. So if he turned out to
be short of what she had expected—and with a
Fraser, what else could she have expected but disappointment—she had no one to blame but herself.
She should have discreetly dealt with the situation
herself instead of involving Roy. She had ruined her
own life, was she now to ruin his—and perhaps
Anne Fraser's too?

The ceremony was brief and simple. As Roy
slipped the wedding ring on to Anne's finger and
Coll saw the look she gave him, he knew without a
doubt that the poor creature was hopelessly in love.
Even though she bore a name he abhorred, he felt
sorry for her . . . for them both. If it was in his
power to protect them from the wrath of their father
and the hatred of Ewen Fraser, then he would do
so.

'Thank you for being Roy's best man at so short
a notice.' Anne sought Coll out at the first opportunity. He realised that his smile was only half-
hearted and that his brother was frowning at him
across the room. She was lovely, he thought as he
stared into her shining eyes. Would that he had been

lucky enough to find such a woman. But if he had, would *he* have had the courage to stand against all to have her?

He could see how easy it had been for his brother to fall in love with her . . . the only thing that troubled him was how long would it last before doubts and disillusionment invaded their lives—as it had done with Mairi. If Roy called out her brother, would her love withstand the shock—the terrible realisation his love might take second place to his desire for revenge? Coll made an excuse to move away from her, suddenly afraid to stay longer in her presence lest he betrayed himself.

'I do not think your brother likes me,' Anne whispered as she rejoined her husband. 'Oh, Roy, will your father turn away from me also?'

'Hush, lass. Coll meant no insult. He finds it very strange—very strange indeed that I have suddenly taken a wife. I think he is a little envious too. Who could not be when they see how lucky I am. When are we going to slip away?'

It is too soon,' she protested, although secretly pleased that he was as eager to be alone with her.

She was married to the most handsome man in Scotland, Anne decided, contemplating the elegantly-clad figure at her side. He wore his best plaid in the MacKenzie colours of blue and green, striped with red, and a velvet jacket of dark blue, which complemented her own attire. From his ornamented leather belt hung a basket-hilted claymore. Tucked in the top of his stocking was a sgean dubh with a fine cairngorm stone gracing the hilt. She suspected too, that he carried another beneath his armpit where a real Highlander always secreted a weapon, for she had felt something hard against her breast when he had kissed her earlier. He had come prepared for trouble, to defend her and himself against anyone from outside who had intended to disrupt the proceedings. Soon, they would take their leave and be alone.

Apart from Agnes, two servants who had acted as witnesses, and Coll, the minister who had officiated at the ceremony was the only other person present. Anne felt a pang of envy, remembering the splendour of her brother James's wedding to Frances at their house near Eskadale, the many guests who had attended and the splendid food and the pipers to pipe the married couple on their way. Even Ewen's day, though somewhat less of an occasion, for, like Anne, he and Mairi had married quietly, had still been held at the family home with his friends about him.

'What is it?' Roy was quick to notice the quiet mood that descended on her a little while after the sparkling wine had been opened and toasts drunk. She stood with a full glass in her hand, staring at the single table which held the refreshments. He knew she regretted the swiftness of their marriage and, like all women, naturally wished for much more on this day. How he wished he could have filled the room with sweet-smelling, deep red roses to pledge his undying love for all to see. 'Are you regretting it already?' he teased gently.

Never marry in haste, his father had always told him. Select a bride with care, study her, grow to know her and judge whether she is worthy to become the next mistress of Tigh an Lóin. He had no doubts about that. Anne *was* the next lady of the house, whatever his father decided. She had been courageous enough to do as he asked and marry him in secret, risk the anger of her own brother as well as his own stubborn father. She would dwell beneath his father's roof and take her rightful place in the house. He owed it to her! There were so many ways he could show to her—and everyone—how much he loved her. A twinge of conscience touched his heart. The more he could do for her now, the stronger their bond of love became, the less pain she would feel when he killed her brother. That day would come, he knew it. The only thing he could do was to prolong it for as long as possible, and pray she forgave him—when it arrived.

'No. Oh, no! How can you think such a thing? I am being silly and sentimental.' Anne smiled and a brilliance came into her eyes that stirred him, making it necessary to fight the urge to bend and kiss her full lips. 'Forgive me. A white wedding is not important. I have you.'

'When we reach Tighn an Lóin, I shall hold a ball and invite the whole glen,' he promised, and he meant it. 'I shall invite your brother if you ask it of me—and make my peace with him.'

The glow in her eyes deepened. Looking into them, he thought how easy it would be to drown in those blue shimmering pools.

'Will you really do that for me? It would make me so happy to see the two of you together—trying to be friends.'

'You shall see us together, I promise,' Roy assured her, lightly kissing her on the mouth. As he felt an instant response, he quickly drew back. 'Come, let us make some excuse to the minister and then leave.'

While Anne said her farewells, Roy sought out his brother and drew him to one side.

'You will ensure Mairi is well protected before you return home?' he said in a low tone.

'What is there to do that you have not already done?' Coll asked, raising one eyebrow quizzically.

'You have hired men to watch the house and accompany her if and when she goes out. She has money, clothes, security. What else does she need?'

Roy threw him an angry glance.

'I know you never wanted her to marry Ewen Fraser, but when she did, you washed your hands of her like Father. Must I remind you she is still our sister . . .'

'Somewhat changed if we are to believe what we hear.'

'Changed?' Roy could have hit him for his indifference. Would Coll never care for anyone other than himself? Since their mother had died he had withdrawn into a shell of cynicism and sharp rhetoric which earned him many enemies. Only his own brother could drag him from the pit of depression, often with words far sharper and more cutting than any he could think of. 'Did we find her living in luxury, brother, with her child? If she was the whore many say she is, don't you think she would have found some fool to support them both by now? She is innocent of the crimes of which she has been accused, I shall somehow prove it.'

'At the expense of your own happiness,' Coll flung back. 'You are a fool. Take your woman and go. Enjoy her for as long as you can. I don't think you will have much time together. I think your hatred of Ewen Fraser will destroy you both.'

'You are no expert on love, Coll. No more am I. But I do know what I have found is so precious I will do anything to preserve it. Yes, I shall kill Fraser. I have sworn it, but I will not lose Anne in the process. Never! You—will care for Mairi?'

'She shall have my full attention until I return home. I shall see you at Tigh and Lóin, and heaven help us all when you face Father.'

It was snowing as they left the house, and by the
time their journey had taken them far from Inverness, a white blanket covered most of the ground.
In the carriage, Anne snuggled close to Roy, shivering slightly even though she was enveloped in a
heavy cloak, the fur-trimmed hood pulled well over
her face. Now she was alone with her husband, the
enormity of what she had undertaken gradually
dawned on her. She was married. Bound to this man
for life. She leaned her head back against his solid
shoulder and stared up at the profile outlined above
her in the semi-darkness. She was never able to tell
what he might be thinking. He had a way of with-
drawing from everything and everyone she had
discovered. The mood could last a few minutes or
hours, and during that time, he was lost to her.

She had so much to learn about him. The little
that she did know had come from Mairi, before
circumstances forced their friendship to wane and
die. Poor Mairi; even though she had betrayed Ewen
at every conceivable opportunity, Anne wished her
well. She had come to like the girl during the months
they had been together under the same roof. She
had an appealing shyness about her, so unlike
Frances, who was not only strikingly lovely, but
oozing with self-confidence. In Mairi, Anne had
found a soul-mate, someone who suffered from the
agonies of being unsure of herself, of dreading being
in a crowded room, or of meeting new people.

Anne had left home after the death of her brother
James, and had travelled to France where she stayed
for six months with a childhood friend who had
married a French Minister of the Interior in the
government of Louis XV. She had sought to forget
the intrigues being conducted under her brother's
roof, the breakdown of his marriage and the bitter-

ness between husband and wife which affected everyone. Yet at the court of the French King, she had found life indolent and sensual, the monarch himself ruled by his mistresses, in the main, Madame de Pompadour, and had returned to England to stay, not at Eskadale, but at their town house in Inverness, where she maintained her own circle of friends, entertained when it suited her and was alone when she wished to be. She had seen her brother only twice since returning home and then he had been in the company of James's widow, which had immediately made Anne bristle. She could not help but feel that Frances had been instrumental in the failure of Ewen's marriage. From the day of Mairi's arrival Frances had never accepted her and had gone out of her way to emphasise the vast differences between them. Mairi, both quiet and shy, found herself co-mistress of an imposing mansion. Frances, contrastingly confident, attractive, and a gifted hostess, was always at ease with the cream of society.

Now she, Anne, was the wife of Roy MacKenzie. Her marriage would not fail, for she would give him no cause for complaint. Her eyes would never stray to another man while he lived. He was all she had ever dreamed of wanting in a man—more. Growing to know him would be a wonderful experience, she thought wistfully. To anticipate his needs, know his moods and understand what made him withdraw so deeply into his inner self—to learn to live with this man who was at this moment, anyway, almost a stranger.

'You are very quiet,' Roy murmured. She started, for he had been so silent and still himself she had thought him dozing. 'Are you cold?'

'A little,' she admitted, hoping he would take her in his arms and warm her. Instead, he produced a silver flask from inside his plaid and unscrewed the top. 'Take a wee dram; it will set fire to those cold bones. You don't want to spend your honeymoon in bed with a cold, do you?'

Anne allowed him to trickle a little of the whisky between her lips. She had never taken spirits before, and as the whisky went down her throat she coughed and spluttered until he slapped her heartily on the back, chuckling as she pulled out a handkerchief and dabbed at her streaming eyes.

'What is that?' she gasped, barely able to speak.

'Usquebaugh. Good Highland whisky. We distil it at Tigh an Lóin. *Slante.*'

She watched in amazement as he put the flask to his lips and drank enthusiastically. She knew he had been drinking quite heavily before they left Inverness with his brother Coll, but he had shown no effects from it. She could not make the same observation concerning Coll, for he had grabbed her in his arms as she was about to leave and kissed her soundly on the mouth, muttering something about a poor lamb to the slaughter. One brother had a head like a rock, but the other!

'Don't worry,' he added, as he saw her gaze still on him. 'I won't disappoint you tonight.'

'Roy! There are times when I wonder what kind of women you associated with before we met,' she gasped, glad of the dark interior of the carriage so that he could not see the embarrassed colour in her cheeks. She knew nothing of life—of men, apart from what she had seen of her own two brothers and their differing treatments of their respective wives. Was it different when they were alone together, she had often wondered. Did the bitterness and suspicions disappear when they lay side by side in bed and made love? When Roy came to her, demanding his rights as her husband—he would demand, she suspected, not ask, he was that kind of a man—how would it be? She shivered involuntarily and immediately Roy's hands went around her body beneath the cloak, caressing her possessively as he drew her closer against him.

'Of all the women I have known, I can honestly tell you none of them were anything like you. Nor have I considered marriage before,' he said, knowing instinctively it was what she wanted to hear. She sighed and relaxed against him, lifting her face to his to be kissed. He found her mouth in the darkness and for a while forgot the storm that lay ahead for them both.

The hunting-lodge was some ten miles from Tigh an Lóin, set back in a half-circle of trees, with stables on one side and a small croft for servants on the other. Roy used it often when he was riding. He enjoyed the solitude out of sight of his father's eagle eye, the reproach in them he so often saw which condemned him for not taking a wife and giving him grandchildren to carry on the name of MacKenzie. He had his wish now, Roy thought, as he helped Anne to alight from the carriage into swirling, wind-driven snow. She laughed as he swung her up into his arms and carried her over the threshold into the lodge. She gave a cry of surprise as she was set down, filled with sudden joy as she saw the reception he had prepared for her.

They stood in a large room, where a fire piled high with oak logs burned fiercely in the huge stone hearth. Shaking the snow from her cloak, she ran to it and stretched out her cold hands towards the welcoming flames. After a moment she turned to look around her and what she saw brought tears of happiness to her eyes. He had gone to so much trouble to make the place habitable and welcoming.

A table was drawn up in front of the fire with two comfortable chairs, one on either side of it. It was laid with the most mouth-watering array of food. Fresh salmon, sliced breast of chicken accompanied by aromatic sauces and smoked ham. An enormous wedding cake sat resplendent in the centre of the white cloth, together with a bottle of wine, a decanter of port and one of whisky. As if that was not enough of a feast, there were plates of cakes and sweetmeats, pickled fruits and thick wedges of fresh bread and cheese.

A man came from one of the other rooms and greeted Roy with a polite nod.

'Everything is to your liking, sir?'

'Is it?' Roy looked enquiringly at Anne, and she nodded and smiled, breathlessly.

'It is a feast fit for royalty.'

'This is Andrew MacKinney. If you ever need anything when you are at Tigh and Lóin, and I am not about, ask him. He is a good and loyal man. Since I deprived you of a proper wedding, I did not think it fair you should also miss the wedding breakfast as well. Take her cloak, Andrew, and then pour us some wine—we are near frozen.'

He pulled one of the chairs closer to the fire and Anne sat and warmed herself, her eyes shining as she stared up at the tall figure beside her. Since James had died she had rarely been afforded such loving consideration. Roy watched as she drank, aware of the happiness radiating from her like sunshine on a summer's day and slowly he, himself began to relax. The ceremony had been somewhat of an ordeal, although he had not shown it. At any moment he had expected the front door to burst

open and either his father burst in to try and prevent
his marriage to a Fraser woman, or Anne's brother
and his men, bent on killing the man who dared to
wed his sister.

He needed this week to be alone with her in order
to prepare himself for what lay ahead. By the time
they continued on to Tigh an Lóin, he would be
fully prepared for his father's wrath and how best
to combat it. He intended to stand fast—he was,
after all, the eldest son. When his father considered
the possibilities of grandchildren to carry on his
precious name, he would relent and accept Anne as
one of the family. He had to believe it would happen.
Had to believe his hatred of Ewen Fraser would not
force him into a bloody and unnecessary clash.
Whatever happened, he had to keep his temper and
his enmity well under restraint—and await a challenge from his enemy. It would happen when the
Fraser discovered what had taken place. He had
promised Anne he would not be the one to draw his
sword in anger—but once out of its sheath, it would
not be replaced until Ewen Fraser was dead.

'I—I have written to my brother,' Anne said
quietly. He realised she had been looking at him for
some time and quickly forced a smile to his stiff
features. 'You are thinking of him, are you not?
You look—so—so determined.'

'To keep you, my love, that is all. In this bad
weather he may not hear your good news for some
time. More time for us before the storm breaks.'

'I have told him I love you and have married you
quite willingly. I have begged him not to intervene
or try to part us.'

'You should not have begged from him,' Roy
interrupted, and Anne's smile faded at his tone.

'I am not of a mind to have him and a dozen

armed clansmen riding up to Tigh an Lóin the day after we arrive there. Your father would enjoy an excuse to fight with him over the slightest thing. Do you think I don't know for all his protesting, that he has never forgiven Ewen for marrying Mairi?'

The name fell reluctantly from her lips. To bring up the past and all its implications was the last thing she had intended. She caught her breath as Roy's eyes narrowed sharply and looking past him, she caught sight of Andrew MacKinney staring at her with daggered gaze. 'Forgive me, but can you not understand how I feel? Here, I am safe, protected—loved. Once I am at Tigh an Lóin I shall have to endure your father's resentment, even hatred. Even your servant is looking at me as if he would like to cut my throat. I can see he thinks you are mad to have married a Fraser.'

'He can think what he damned well pleases, as can my father,' Roy growled. 'Yes, you are safe here, with me. It is a world far removed from reality, but reality is what we shall have to face in one short week. I believe our love is strong enough to withstand my father and your brother.'

Anne's smile returned slowly, reassured by his confidence.

'I am a foolish—nervous bride,' she confessed softly.

As he looked down at her, Roy found all thoughts of revenge against Ewen Fraser receding from his mind. The flickering light from the flames turned her hair into a halo of fire, throwing soft shadows across her glowing cheeks. She was by far the most beautiful woman he had ever met, although she possessed none of the self-assurance which often accompanied striking looks. If anything, he surmised, she was rather shy, rather like Mairi . . . and then in his mind's eye rose the memory of the heated encounter he had had with his father before leaving for Inverness. The cruel words flung back and forth between them, the slur which still clung to Mairi's name and kept her barred from her home. Anne had seen Mairi and James embracing in his room and thought the worst of them. But was she blind? Had she not seen Mairi's distress? Was she not able to separate a lover's embrace from that of an attempt to console an unhappy woman? So many times he had tried to find the words to question her about it, but had failed. One day he knew he would have to. It was the one thing that lurked daily in his mind. Had she lied to defend her brother's name or had she really believed she had seen Mairi and James acting as lovers might?

'We shall serve ourselves, Andrew. You can go to bed,' Roy said, refilling their glasses despite her protest. When they were alone, he discarded his coat and unfastened the lace jabot at his throat. He was aware of Anne following his every move as he undid his shirt almost to the waist to reveal a muscular chest, dark with hair. 'We can be ourselves now, we are quite alone,' he told her with a wicked grin. 'Why don't you change into something more befitting a bride?'

At the suggestion Anne swallowed her wine more quickly than she had intended, suddenly feeling as if she had wandered into quicksand. She felt tongue-tied and knew she was blushing furiously. Roy chuckled as he came behind her chair and laid his hands on her shoulders, bending to trail kisses down over her ear.

'Why Anne MacKenzie, you are not feart of me, are you?'

'A little . . . ' She could not deny it. She felt her

fingers touch her hair, loosening the tightly pinned
curls until they fell in profusion about her shoulders.
'Am I not an idiot?'

'You are indeed. I'll not hurt you, lass.' Roy
turned her face up to his and kissed her lingeringly.
'I am the idiot to try and rush things. We must
savour every moment we share here and make them
last as long as possible.'

'Do you use this lodge very often?' Anne asked as
he piled chicken slices on a plate, bordered them
with vegetables and set it down before her. 'I like it
very much. In summer it must be heavenly. We
could have picnics here, just the two of us . . . '
She broke off with a shaky laugh. 'Now I am rushing
things.'

'I often stay here overnight on my way home from
Inverness or Edinburgh, especially if I have been
celebrating too much. Father gave it to me years
ago—he had no further use for it. Besides it has
painful memories for him. My mother used to meet
her lover here.' He heard her gasp at his unexpected
frankness, and smiled. 'You are my wife now and I
shall keep no secrets from you. It is best you know
the kind of man you are going to meet when you
arrive at Tigh an Lóin. Coll is obviously taken with
you and will give me no trouble, but my father is a
proud, stubborn old man who will never forget that
Mairi ran away to marry a man of whom he disapproved. Now *I* shall be presenting him with a bride
of whom he does not approve. At least, not at first.
I shall give him a week before he is eating out of
your hand.'

'Will he not be pleased you are married?'

'He has despaired of me ever being wed. I have
always liked my freedom too much.'

'I shall not try to tie you down,' Anne promised.

'No, you cannot. There is a wildness in me that cannot be tamed, so I advise you not to try and mould me to your ways. You must accept me as I am,' Roy warned, a shadow crossing his features.

'Have I not already done so by becoming your wife?' she asked softly. 'I do not want to change you, Roy. But I want to know you. Four weeks is so little time.'

'I have already told you of the family skeleton—my mother's lover. Father has always maintained that Mairi was a product of that liaison, but I don't believe it. She is a true MacKenzie, and I'll kill anyone who says otherwise in my hearing. If you like this place, I shall give it to you. From this night on, consider it as your own. But take heed; if you ever use it as my mother did, I will put my hands about that lovely throat and squeeze the life out of you.'

'How can you even think such a thing?' Anne asked in horror. 'I shall not even betray you in my thoughts. I love you, and I shall remain faithful to you always. You are an unfeeling brute to speak to me so—on our wedding night, too.'

As bright tears sprang to her eyes, he spoke a vehement oath, jumped from his chair and drew her up against him, running his fingers through the mass of tangled curls, smothering her face and mouth with kisses until she sank breathless in his arms.

'I am an unfeeling brute—you are right,' Roy whispered, cursing himself for his thoughtlessness. The softness of her body against his reminded him of his own vulnerability, and he released her and sat her down again. 'Finish your food and we shall talk no more of me.'

'Tell me of Tigh an Lóin then,' Anne begged. 'Will I like it?' Mairi had already told her much of the great house, but she dared not mention it, aware that her name would cause pain and bitterness between them. One day, perhaps, they would be able to speak of her and try to understand her, but not tonight. This was her night, and she wanted nothing to spoil the magical atmosphere surrounding them.

'It has been standing for nigh on three hundred years—at least part of it has. The original fortifications remain, but there have been modifications to the house itself over the years. It was set on fire on one occasion by the King's men, when the clan came out for Montrose. When it was rebuilt it was larger, more splendid and designed to last for a thousand years. You will like it, I know. You shall have the rooms which overlook the loch; the view from them is beautiful all year round. My own are next door and we shall share the master bedroom. You can alter them, if they are not to your liking. It is your home too now.'

'I know I shall like them,' Anne breathed.

'My father rules Tigh an Lóin with an iron hand, but as the the only woman in the house, you will now become mistress. It will do the old place good to have a woman's touch about the place. We have been three men alone for too long. The servants will adore you . . . ' 'As they once adored Mairi,' he almost said, and stopped himself in time. Anne would brighten the house with her presence.

Leaning across the table, he broke the seal on the bottle of port and poured some, the colour of blood-red rubies, into fresh glasses.

'Twenty years old, from the cellars at Tigh an Lóin,' he said as she sipped it hesitantly. 'Is it not nectar?'

'It is, but I think I have had more than enough to drink.' Anne put the glass aside. 'The fire has warmed me, and the wine has made me quite light-headed.'

'Then perhaps it is time we went to bed, my wife,' Roy murmured quietly. He rose to his feet and gave her his arm. She was beginning to tremble inwardly at the look in his dark eyes.

'Give me a moment,' she said, but he, with a laugh, swung her up into his arms and carried her towards the heavy door which stood slightly ajar.

'Your modesty is most becoming, my sweet, but I am impatient to claim my bride.'

He kicked open the door and slammed it shut behind them with his booted foot before setting her down beside a massive four-poster bed with curtains and a canopy of plush burgundy velvet. The only other items of furniture were a table with a lamp on it and a heavy carved oak wardrobe set into one of the thick walls. The single small window was closed and shuttered against the snow which continued to fall ceaselessly. Built into the furthest corner of the room was a small hearth where another fire burned filling the bedroom with a soft, comfortable glow.

Ignoring her startled protests, he began to unfasten her gown, planting kisses on her neck and bare shoulders as he pushed away the material and tugged it down about her waist so that it slipped over her hips and fell in a huddle about her feet. From the way she trembled beneath his hands he knew that no man had previously been so bold with her—knew he would be the first to lay claim to the exquisitely moulded body being uncovered before his searching gaze.

Cupping her face in both hands, he began to kiss her. Gently at first, then her lips sought his, with a fierce passion until she moaned and clung to him, trembling now not from fear but from what he was awakening in her. He had made love to many women, without love. Anne was an inexperienced child compared with the majority of them, despite her twenty-two years.

Unfastening the bodice of her shift, he parted it, baring her breasts to the skilful caresses of his hands until she pressed herself against him in a silent plea for him to take her. Lifting her back on to the bed, he removed the last of her clothing and made love to her very slowly and carefully—and in doing so, lost himself in the wonder that he discovered as he finally took her and ascended on the crest of a huge wave to heights he had never before experienced. Afterwards as he held her against him, listening to the howl of the wind as she slept contentedly against his chest, he studied the composed face, so serene and innocent beneath his troubled gaze. Her response to his lovemaking proved to him the powerful weapon he possessed over her. If—if she had deliberately lied . . . No, he must not allow himself to dwell on it. For one whole week no one existed but her. There was no other world save the one they would make for themselves within the lodge. Safe——together—trusting—loving.

CHAPTER THREE

Anne opened her eyes on to the dark features lying next to her own and momentarily felt quite shocked to find herself beside a naked man. Then it all came back to her and she stretched lazily, moving a little closer to her husband. How gentle and considerate he had been with her, dispelling all her fears with his kisses and caresses, the sweet endearments he whispered against her hair as he brought her to womanhood.

Her body still throbbed with pleasure. Raising her head, she laid her lips against his cheek—and was immediately seized in strong arms.

'You were awake,' she accused as he pulled her beneath him and his searching hands devastated her body yet again. There was no part of her that was sacred to him, and while at first it had somewhat alarmed her, she now accepted she could not give him less, as his wife, then other women had.

'I have been for the past hour. I didn't have the heart to wake you, my little innocent,' he teased, kissing her with rising passion mounting inside him.

'Did—did I not please you?' Anne's mouth quivered as she asked the question. 'Are you laughing at me because I have not had other men before you?'

'God in heaven, no!' Roy declared. 'No woman has given me the pleasure you gave me last night.' Immediately her eyes brightened and she slipped her arms about his neck, her smile still a little shy even after all they had shared. 'I would not have had you come to me otherwise,' he added.

'Are you hungry? There is so much food left over from last night, and we did not even cut that splendid cake. Shall I fetch us something?' But as soon as she tried to move away from him, he refused to relinquish his hold on her.

'I am hungry only for you. We can eat later.' She shivered for the fire had burned low and pressed closer to him as a gust of wind shook the shuttered windows. 'I do not think the snow has stopped. We could be marooned here for days . . . longer than a week, perhaps. You will grow bored of my company.'

'I am sure you will not let that happen, my husband,' Anne murmured, her body already responding to the touch of his hands. Locking her hands behind his head she brought his mouth down on hers, and for a long while, the bad weather outside ceased to concern them.

When he allowed her to leave the bed, she quickly found a robe from among her night things and pulled it on, conscious of him watching her. She brushed the tangles from her hair beneath his watchful gaze and then stirred the embers of the fire with the long, brass poker that stood in the hearth, before throwing on another piece of wood. The last of her fear of him and her inhibitions, had vanished this morning when they had made love for a second time.

He gave a soft chuckle as she gathered up her dress from the floor, where it had been dropped together with the rest of her clothes, and arranged them tidily on the end of the bed.

'We shall have to have more furniture,' she said setting his boots down before the wardrobe. 'I have nowhere to put my clothes.'

'I have told you that this place is yours to do with as you wish, but don't change it too much, I implore you. Its starkness pleases me and I do not want it suddenly filled with a woman's fripperies. Some old pieces of furniture at the house might suit. We'll discuss it when we get home.' Roy raised on one elbow and said sternly, 'What about my food, woman? Am I to lie here and starve? And some whisky.

'So early?' Anne enquired, turning towards the door, but noticing his scowl, she did not argue further.

Andrew MacKinney was nowhere to be seen, but in the large room the fire had recently been rebuilt and the table relaid. The remnants of the meal had been covered with cloths and clean plates and glasses set out. Anne found herself humming quietly as she returned to the bedroom with what she considered sufficient for an army. They sat side by side on the bed and ate the last of the sliced chicken.

She said nothing as Roy consumed several large glasses of whisky with his food. If it was his custom to do so—her brother, James, had always had at least one before an enormous breakfast—she must not try to change it.

'Agnes will not be able to get here if this weather continues,' she said, opening the shutters at last. Snow was piled high against the window, at least several feet thick. The branches of tall trees were bent awkwardly beneath the enormous weight. 'I shall have no other clothes to wear. What a shame! I haven't been for a walk in snow like this for years. I used to love to do so as a child.'

'I am quite content to look at you as you are,' Roy murmured teasingly, and the cloud of red curls swirled about her shoulders as she spun round to

look at him. 'I hope she is delayed until the end of
the week for it will mean that we shall have to spend
most of our time in bed. However, if you are really
determined to have us both go down with frost-bite,
you could borrow some of the clothes I leave here
all the time. They will look outrageous on you—but
if the snow eases, we can go for that walk you so
desire.'

He was as good as his word. Towards the late
afternoon, the weather improved slightly. Anne was
delighted when he opened the wardrobe and
produced several items of clothing. When she
inspected them, however, she could hardly keep a
smile from her face. The tartan trews in the
MacKenzie colours would hang on her like two
sacks, as would the jacket, but she said nothing,
shooed him out of the bedroom—much to his
amusement—and quickly got dressed. By tucking
the shirt into the trews and tightening a leather belt
round them, they seemed sufficiently secure. She
turned the sleeves of the jacket back over her wrists
by several inches before stepping out into the other
room and being greeted by roars of laughter from
Roy and his servant, with whom he was deep in
conversation until the apparition appeared to make
him explode into laughter. He could not remember
such a spontaneous reaction of mirth in many a
long month.

'Do you know this pretty lad, Andrew? Faith, but
that hair reminds me of a wife I once had.'

'I can go alone. You don't have to demean yourself by being seen with me,' Anne retorted, starting
for the door. He had caught up with her before she
reached it, wrapping a spare plaid about her, winding
it over her bare head.

'That's better. I have no desire to have you sniffling and sneezing beside me in bed,' he said, pulling his bonnet well down over his face. 'Come on, then, let's away for this walk. We'll not be long, Andrew. Brew us something hot for when we return—we shall no doubt need it.'

Anne gasped as they stepped out into the crisp air. At her first step she sank at the least a foot into the soft snow, and almost lost her balance as she tried to take another. Roy took her firmly by the hand and led her around the back of the lodge into the shelter of tall pine and spruce trees whose thick branches had allowed only a small amount of snow to penetrate them. He moved purposefully in the direction of a hillock some hundred yards away, and sensing it was in his mind to show her something, she clung tightly to his hand and managed to keep pace with him.

Her cheeks began to glow with the cold, but inside the heavy clothing she wore she was warm and surprisingly comfortable—and content to be at his side, sharing this moment with him, trivial as he might consider it. She felt that he had agreed to walk with her only as a concession, and would rather have remained within the warm confines of the lodge. He had relented because he knew the idea pleased her. She would never cease to wonder at the consideration he had shown her from their very first meeting.

On that first encounter at a theatre in Inverness when she had become aware of the boldness of his gaze, she had been annoyed and then afraid, upon learning his identity. He had followed her from the theatre and watched as she climbed into her carriage. Later he had told her that he followed her home so that he would know where she lived and who she was.

The doubts that crowded into her mind as to his reasons for wanting to get to know her were dispelled in the days and weeks which followed. When she went riding, as she did most mornings when the weather permitted, she would go through the town and out on to Drummossie Moor. She loved the wildness of this place and was never afraid that he rode close behind her, confident that she could outride him and return safely to the town if he tried to detain her against her will. But he did not speak to her that first day, nor the second or third. In desperation, on the fourth, it was she who turned and suggested he either rode at her side, or stopped following her. By the end of the following week, she knew she had fallen helplessly, hopelessly, in love with him.

He never made any attempt to kiss her, or touch her other than to help her to and from her horse. He acted a perfect gentleman at all times, which is what his sister Mairi had always proclaimed him to be. Anne herself had heard tell of Roy MacKenzie and his devil-may-care brother Coll, and of their exploits with the ladies of Inverness. When she was alone with him, she found it hard to believe any of the stories, but once alone, she was plagued by the distressing notion that he might be toying with her too, laughing at her back, discussing her with his friends and his brother.

He never talked about his sister's marriage and after a short reference to it herself, to try and reassure him that she had been Mairi's friend—it was never raised between them again. Gradually she accepted that he sought her out because he liked her company, as much as she craved his—in secret. She was afraid to be too open with him, afraid he would take advantage of her own intense feelings, should he discover them. Not once, in the weeks they spent together, did she ever dream he would ask her to become his wife.

'Look!' Roy said as they halted on a hillock, pointing ahead of them. 'Beyond that line of trees. The house is built of grey stone and it all merges into this confounded white landscape, but if you look carefully you may just see the outline.' His voice was filled with pride as he spoke of the house where he had been born and raised.

'Tigh an Lóin?' she whispered, straining her eyes. Would she ever feel about it as he did. Would she be allowed to? She could just make it out, standing on the far side of the loch that today was looking cold and unfriendly. How it would change when the water became blue in the sunlight and danced with tiny white crested waves in a breeze. 'My home.'

Roy stiffened at her words, but she did not notice. He stared down at her red cheeks for a moment and could not resist the urge to bend and plant a kiss on each of them. His home too, where his father was the master and things might never be the same between any of them again. Such pleasure in her voice as she uttered those two simple words. He turned about and tugged at her hand until she reluctantly followed him, not wanting to dwell on those days when he would not have her all to himself.

'You spoke of a ball at Tigh an Lóin,' Anne began, a trifle hesitantly. He had made it sound so easy. A grand occasion on which to invite all his friends—a time when she would be put on show for their approval. Not an easy time for her, but it would be a demonstration of Roy's love for her, that he accepted her as his wife before the whole world. Had he meant it when he said he would invite

her brother? Would Ewen come if the offer was
extended?

'Ay I did.' He was slow to answer and she halted
and looked up.

'I ask only because—it would be a good time—if
possible—to bring people together . . . healing old
wounds.'

Roy did not answer at once. He had cursed
himself incessantly for making such a rash promise.
At the time he had meant it. He would have said
anything to make her happy. Afterwards, considering the implications of his words, he realised he
might have inadvertently hastened his reckoning
with Ewen Frazer. There was the possibility he
would refuse to come. But if he did . . . would
either of them be able to contain their hatred? He
had made Anne a promise, he would not be the first
to unsheath his sword. But would he be successful
in restraining the provocative words which might
leap to his lips and cause the other to draw his
weapon? He could not give up his revenge, but only
now did he fully comprehend how deeply it was
going to affect his life with his new bride and tear
him apart. Silent agony he must endure alone. He
could confide in no one. Even Coll would never
understand the conflict of having to choose between
those he loved the most—his sister and his wife!

'If that is what you really would like, then it shall
be arranged. Subject to my father's permission,' he
added, forcing a smile to his lips. The lies and deceit
had begun. Why had he not refused her outright?
Made some excuse that his father would never allow
it. As it was he had no way of knowing how his
unpredictable father would act. He suspected Anne's
innocent charm would completely disarm him within
a very short time. He was an old, disillusioned man

who dearly wanted a grandson. Roy was hoping to make that dream a reality.

'And if it is possible—did you mean it when you said you would invite—Ewen?' He nodded slowly and felt her fingers tighten about his. 'I suppose we should also ask Frances. She is kin, but I like her not. She is an adventuress.'

'Then by all accounts Mairi was in good company.' The words slipped out before he could contain them and she stiffened in shock. Even to mention her name brought him sorrow and heartache, Anne thought.

'Hush, no more talk of it until we are at Tigh an Lóin. As you say, your father may not approve of the idea.'

They walked back to the lodge in silence.

Andrew brought them mugs of steaming hot chocolate as they emerged from the bedroom to warm themselves before the roaring fire which welcomed their return. With only her wedding gown to wear, Anne had donned the velvet robe again and slipped her cold feet into leather slippers. She curled up on the low sofa beside the hearth to savour her drink. Her skin began to tingle as the hot liquid spread through her body, warming her and making her unexpectedly drowsy. She had tied her hair back with a bright red ribbon. As Roy sat beside her, he was aware of how young she looked—and again, how vulnerable. Had he been more of a devious nature, more ruthless of character, he would have welcomed the way events were speeding to a successful conclusion of his intentions. As it was, he felt himself sinking into a deep abyss of gloom and was glad she was too tired to turn her thoughts back to Tigh an Lóin and the ball.

He had accepted long ago Ewen Fraser would die

by his hand for his ill-treatment of Mairi, but until this shattering moment, he had never considered losing Anne through his action. He loved her—and she him. Surely their love could survive? He was appalled at the notion her love might turn to hatred, his touch repulse her and Tigh an Lóin become a prison from which she sought to escape. He had not bargained for anything like this!

She turned and smiled at him as she put aside her empty mug and snuggled against him with a contented sigh. She fell asleep within minutes, ignorant of the torment raging inside him. He could not go back on his word to Mairi, not after all she had suffered. The slur cast on her name together with the insults and shame. All those months alone in that filthy room in Inverness.

Gently, so as not to awaken her, he bent his head and laid his cheek against hers.

'Forgive me, lass, what have I done to you? To us both?'

As the carriage rolled and jolted over the uneven ground, the grey stone house loomed nearer with each passing minute. Anxiously Anne looked down at the hands clasped tightly together in her lap. How nervous she was. She could not control it. In less than one hour she would be face to face with Ranald Mackenzie himself, Roy's father. Mairi's father! How would he receive her? She dreaded the encounter and wished she could have stayed at the lodge for another week—and another after that. Why had the wonderful time with her husband ended so soon?

'You have nothing to worry about,' Roy said, seeking to reassure her. By now, if Coll had followed his instructions, their father would have known of his marriage for the past four days. Time enough to get over his anger—and his disappointment that his eldest son had not chosen some local girl of good background and breeding to be the next mistress of Tigh an Lóin. Apart from her name and her involvement in his sister's disastrous marriage, Anne possessed all the qualities Roy deemed important for the woman with whom he would share the rest of his life. He fervently wished she had not. She had been the perfection he had always sought and yet never found before in a woman. He regretted nothing. She was his and his love for her was the most precious thing he could ever possess in this world.

The last day at the lodge he knew he had been curt with her as his thoughts began to turn homewards. Although she had tried to ignore it, he had seen the hurt in her eyes. But she had said nothing and borne his ill-manner without comment.

Agnes had arrived with Anne's clothes and the trivialities carefully packed away in four enormous trunks, so that she was able to find something presentable to wear to meet her new father-in-law. She had chosen a dress of emerald-green velvet, which enhanced the rich colour of her hair. A ribbon of a darker green secured the mass of bright curls at the nape of her neck. As the carriage turned into the long avenue of trees leading up to Tigh Lóin, he saw her touch the wedding band on her finger. His hand covered hers for a moment and felt it tremble. She looked calm and composed, but inwardly he sensed she was quaking. No more was he. He did not fear his father's wrath, but he did care how Anne was received in his home. The first few minutes would tell him exactly how her father planned to treat her.

'Courage! I will protect you,' he murmured. As

servants came running out to meet them, he saw the figure of his father appear on the steps, Coll standing beside him. Taking a deep breath, Roy put behind him all memories of time spent at the lodge. They were back in his domain now and he was prepared for opposition in whatever shape or form it came.

Roy felt Anne's hesitation as he took her firmly by the arm and propelled her towards the waiting reception saying in a low, fierce whisper, 'Has your Fraser courage deserted you already? He will eat you for breakfast and spit out the bones if you let him. You are my wife—and I am proud of that fact. Remember it!'

Anne shot him a sharp glance, aware of a subtle difference in his manner. She knew that he was uneasy about this meeting too, but he sounded strange—yet she could not define in what way.

Uttering a silent prayer she allowed him to lead her to where his father and brother stood. Brother embraced brother with genuine warmth. Father and son measured each other in silence, and then Ranald's eyes turned on the slender creature Roy had dared to bring to Tigh an Lóin. A pair of blue eyes met and challenged his, disturbing in their intensity as they dared him to refuse her entry beneath his roof. Not a word was spoken for a full minute. Servants hovering in the backround exchanged anxious glances, then, as Anne shivered suddenly in the chill air, Ranald stepped to one side and said curtly,

'Bring the lass inside before she catches cold, Roy. Where are your manners?'

Was this acceptance, Anne wondered as she was ushered into a huge hall where the walls were covered in ancient targets and claymores and paintings of the MacKenzie ancestors.

Roy gave her no time to inspect her new home, propelling her into the library, the only room in which a fire was ever burning these days. When Mairi had been at home, it had been different, he remembered.

'My God, Father. You call this a welcome for my bride?' he thundered, his hands on his hips. 'Could you not have a fire lit in the drawing-room, or do you not consider this a special occasion?'

'We have no need to warm every room in the house. This is the only one used during the day. You have not been here, have you? And your brother is mostly out drinking with his friends. With the whisky he consumes he has little need of a fire to warm him.'

'Things will be different now that Anne is here. She will see we have comfort when we need it,' Roy announced with confidence. To the manservant at his father's side, he ordered, 'Bring something warm for the lady Anne and whisky for the rest of us.'

'This is still my house. Neither you—nor she—will give orders here,' Ranald snapped, his lips tightening at his son's arrogant tone.

'I was only remembering *my* manners, Father, and offering my bride refreshment—as you should have done,' he was reminded.

'I didn't ask you to bring her here—another Fraser! Was one in the family not enough for you?'

'Will you judge me by what you believe my brother to be?' Anne asked quietly. She knew to increase the anger she herself felt at this ungracious welcome would only intensify the antagonism raging inside her. 'I know you all consider him to be the cause of Mairi's unhappiness—that has been made clear to me many times and there is nothing I can do about that. I do not intend to begin my wedded life by dwelling on the misery of another and I have agreed with Roy, that it is best we do not speak of her . . . at least not until we can do so sensibly, without rancour. Will you not accept me for what I am—your son's wife? I love him with all my heart and I shall strive to make him happy and I shall never give him cause to doubt my faithfulness. Please—do not turn from me as you did from her,' she pleaded.

For a moment she thought she had gone too far as Ranald's eyes blazed with anger. Then, slowly it subsided. She felt anger still in him, but knew it was not about to be directed at her. She felt Roy's hands slide over her shoulders and gained great comfort from his touch. What a terrible position he was in. She was thinking only of herself, of the reception she had been given. Yet this was Roy's home and his father was scarcely civil.

'Have I not brought a real woman to grace your home, Father? Think of the bonny grandchildren you will soon be bouncing on your knees! I ask your forgiveness for the secrecy in which we were wed, but I thought it best at the time. I wanted no one to try and dissuade me against this marriage for I knew they could not and I cared not for more arguments. Anne means too much to me.'

'Ay, she must,' his father returned drily. 'I've never known you to act like a damned fool before. Your brother Coll does enough for the pair of you. Come here, child—Anne, isn't it? Give this other fool a kiss and let us forget the harsh words. I forget not that you are a Fraser, but that takes second place now. You are my son's wife and so long as you remember that, you are welcome beneath my roof.'

Anne needed no second bidding to run into the

outstretched arms and kiss his leathered cheek. Coll's gaze fastened on his brother's face and wondered at the conflict of emotions mirrored there before Roy realised his scrutiny and turned away to attend to the refreshments that had been brought them.

When a servant took Anne upstairs to show her to her rooms, Roy sat down in a chair with a glass of whisky, able to relax again for the first time since stepping over the threshold. Ranald watched him from beneath hooded lids, surprised at the quiet mood. Where was the fire he had shown before he rode away from Tigh an Lóin, when they had quarrelled over Mairi? What had happened to his determination to kill Ewen Fraser and avenge the injury he believed had been done to his sister's name? Was this meek-mannered man his son? His right arm?

In silence Roy swallowed his drink and then looked up at his father and the eyes which considered the older man challenged the very essence of his thoughts.

'I'll make a bargain with you, Father. Accept Anne as my wife, make her welcome here and believe that I love her—and I give you my solemn oath not to call out Ewen Fraser. That's what you want, isn't it?'

'Ay, but I don't believe you'll leave him alone.'

'You have my word. I have never broken it before, have I? One thing we MacKenzies have in common, we are not liars and our word is our bond. You seem to have forgotten that in Mairi's case.'

'Hold your tongue. You return here, acting the master as if I am already in my grave, bringing a Fraser woman back with you as your wife and expecting me to take her in like a lamb,' Ranald snapped.

'And why not, Father?' Coll murmured from an adjoining chair. 'From all I've heard of Anne Fraser, she has been ogled by half the men in Inverness since her return from France—and been inaccessible to all. Roy has won himself a fair prize. She has bonny hips—she will breed well.' He laughed as Roy threw him an angry scowl, but the remark had turned the conversation away from the argument which could be provoked all too easily.

'You'll be more respectful to the lass, Coll,' Ranald interrupted. 'And I expect to see you at the table this evening. I shall make her welcome—until the mists clear from your brother's eyes and he realises one Fraser is much like another—and so will you.'

'Well done, brother,' Coll murmured as their father quitted the room. 'You promised not to call him out—but if he challenges you . . . '

'From the first day he upset our little sister, he was a dead man,' Roy said quietly. 'You promised to stand by me in this.'

'And I shall. Someone has to be around to pick up the pieces.'

'You have talked with Mairi,' Roy said fiercely. 'Are you telling me you still believe Fraser's version of what happened?'

'No. Fool that I am, she has persuaded me as to the truth of her words. I may get to him first and save you the trouble. When I think of the surroundings in which we found her. My God, Roy! She could have died in that stinking place!'

'He is mine, Coll.'

'And Anne? You want her, too. Somehow I do not think you will be able to have both, brother.'

'Are these rooms not lovely, Agnes?' Anne asked, as she inspected the large sitting-room and dressing-room. 'You can sleep here close to me if you wish. Not that I need a chaperon any longer. I am a married woman now.'

Happily married?' the maid asked, following her into the master bedroom. It was decorated in pastel shades of blue and grey. The carved bed which could have accommodated half a dozen people at one time, had two feather mattresses on it and dark blue and gold curtains suspended above it matching those at the window. On a cold winter's nights she and Roy could draw them shutting out the world while they made love. She blushed at such bold thoughts. How she had changed in one short week!

'Very. I know you disapprove of Roy, but he is a gentle, considerate husband.'

'Who loves you as deeply as you love him?' the woman persisted.

'Of course. He tells me time and time again of his love. In marrying me he has risked his father's anger—nay, more than that, of being disinherited and barred from this house. That is love, Agnes.' Mairi too had once possessed such a love and had turned her back on her family to marry the man of her choice. What had gone wrong? A hundred times Anne had asked herself the same question since the day she had seen the girl in the arms of her brother, James. He had been looking at her so tenderly, holding her close. Quickly Anne pushed the memory to the back of her mind. This was no time to dwell on those times. They were past and to revive them again in this house would cause pain and more conflict. She would not be the cause of that. 'By now Ewen will have my letter. I pray he accepts what I have done as readily as Ranald Mackenzie.'

'Don't be surprised if he rides straight here when he reads it, with enough men to raze the house to the ground. Then you'll realise what an unpleasant business you've started.'

'Nonsense!' Anne bore Agnes's familiarity because the woman had been her nursemaid and she knew the remarks were well meant for all their bluntness. But there were times when she wished she herself had married, so that she would not be so suspicious of every man who looked at her mistress more than once. Every potential suitor who presented himself at Anne's door was preceded by a report from Agnes before he gained admittance.

It was from her that Anne had learned of the many lady friends of her new husband, of his repute with both claymore and dirk, which went ahead of him wherever he went. Of his love for his sister. He had been the only one to side with Mairi when she wished to marry, but Anne knew she must not mention the subject to him for a long while to come, not until the scars had healed a little more. It was the only thing which marred the perfection of a blissfully happy existence.

'We are going to have a ball, Agnes, much bigger than Tigh an Lóin has ever seen before. And I am going to invite Ewen and the Lady Frances.'

'Heaven forbid!' The maid crossed herself several times. 'You'll have him at your husband's throat within the hour if you do. Do you really think he has forgiven your brother for turning his sister out of his house when she was with child?'

'He has accepted that Mairi was to blame for the breakdown of the marriage,' Anne said with a frown. 'She was, we both know that. Don't forget I saw her with James, with my own eyes. In his room! She caused his quarrel with Ewen. She made him ride off in a rage. If he had not, my brother might be alive today. Oh, I don't know! I wish I knew what had happened that day, but I don't—no one ever will. James is dead, that's all I know and Mairi has taken herself off somewhere, probably living with some man-friend—at least that's what Ewen says. He told me he had sent men to search for her. I asked him to do that, Agnes. Even after the way she betrayed him, he did that for me, and for himself, I think. I still believe he harbours some feeling for her. He had no choice but to turn her out. How could he accept another man's child? It was too much! But she is not to be found. She does not want to be, of course. How ashamed she must be of what she has done. Perhaps now, she is beginning to realise how many lives she had ruined with her wantonness . . .'

'Well, she's paying for it now—somewhere, alone with a babe to take care of. Perhaps she has found someone else—who knows.' Agnes shrugged non-committally and continued with the unpacking.

'At least there is plenty of room here for my things,' Anne said, inspecting the enormous closets and chest of drawers—so unlike the lodge. Yet how she had loved that place—she would keep Roy to his word and find more furniture to make it more comfortable. She planned to spend a great deal of time there with him—just the two of them—a continued honeymoon. 'I shall not alter anything,' she murmured to herself.

'I am glad to hear it,' Roy drawled from the doorway. 'I was afraid you would have begun already.'

'It is all too perfect.' She ran to him and kissed his cheek. 'And your father is a dear. I know we shall get on together. Are you going out?' He had changed out of his best plaid into a homespun shirt of black wool, topped with a leather jerkin.

'Coll tells me our cattle have been raided twice this week. I am taking some men to recover them. Father has reminded me of my duty,' he added with a dry smile.

'Do you know who is responsible?' she asked, suddenly anxious. For years the Frasers and MacKenzies had been at each other's throats over one dispute or another. The original misunderstanding, so she had been told, went back as far as the first Highland uprising in 1715. Surely it was too soon for Ewen to be seeking some revenge?

'Ay, the thieving Campbells in the next glen most likely. We often run across each other. Don't fret, lass. Your brother will come here first if he loves you,' Roy replied aware of her growing pallor. It would have made things simpler all round if Ewen Fraser had been responsible for the stolen cattle. 'I've spoken to my father about the ball. He thinks I have taken leave of whatever senses remained after marrying you, but he has agreed. Begrudgingly—but he has said yes. Write a guest list and we will discuss it when I return. It will be Christmas in a month, so why don't we celebrate on St Stephen's? After all, it is the season for love and forgiveness!'

'What if—if Ewen will not come?' Anne asked, voicing a fear that had been growing inside her for days. Her brother had suffered once at the hands of a MacKenzie and might never forgive her for making him do so a second time.

'Then we shall survive without his blessing,' Roy returned with a shrug of his broad shoulders. 'I shall give you all the love and affection you need, never fear.'

He glared at Agnes as she gave a snort, but she ignored the warning in his eyes and continued to lay out her mistress's gowns.

'You cannot understand how much it would mean to me to have him here, acknowledging you as my husband,' Anne said wistfully. 'I am so happy and I want nothing to spoil it.'

'Nor will it. Nothing and no one will ruin what we have.' Roy took her in his arms and kissed her on the mouth. Of course he understood her feelings. Did he not harbour similar ones about Mairi? He wanted his sister home where she belonged, with her baby son. Wanted to see her laughing with them at the festive time which was coming, no longer afraid, unhappy. That was his dream, but he could say nothing of it, even to Anne. 'I care not whether your brother comes to Tigh an Lóin or not,' he lied, 'but if it makes you happy, then he shall have an invitation and if he deigns to appear, he will be made as welcome as any other guest. If he comes in peace, and not with a sword in his hand prepared for trouble.'

'I am sure he will come. I will write out a list as you suggest,' Anne said quickly. She thought it prudent not to prolong the subject any more.

'I shall see you at dinner, then. Remember, the house is yours and you are welcome to inspect your new domain.'

'Hmm!' Agnes stared after his departing figure, her hands on her hips in disapproval. 'Underneath all that charm, I could feel a caged bear waiting to be unleashed. He's a dangerous one. Did you see the way he looked at me? Different now he's in his own home, isn't he? Or haven't you noticed with those eyes full of love? You've taken on a bad one, my girl. Be warned.'

Eyes full of love! How silly. Love did not cloud her vision or her judgment. She had made her decision to marry Roy in a cool-headed manner, weighing up all the consequences and recriminations which would be heaped on her head by her brother and friends—and decided he was well worth the sacrifice of them all if it came to it. Now, it was not so easy to walk away from the brother she loved and if she could find a way to bring them all together, she would—but not to see the character of her husband clearly! In one short week—seven days and nights, she had grown to know him very well, she told herself confidently.

'Agnes, there are times when you make me want to slap you!' she cried in vexation. 'Don't you realise what a trying time this has been for him? For us both? We did not know his father would receive us. He—he is completely open with me. We have no secrets from each other. It is the way we agreed it should be. And I have his promise that he will never be the one to take up a weapon against my brother. Don't gape at me like that! Do you think me some ignorant country wench, that I don't know my own husband? Find me something nice to wear for this evening. I must make a good impression.'

'Be yourself and keep your eyes open. Watch the MacKenzies,' Agnes retorted dourly.

Anne left her maid muttering under her breath and went into the sitting-room. From the window she watched Roy and his brother, accompanied by a dozen armed clansmen ride away from the house. For a moment, before he swung his huge black stallion round towards the gates, his head jerked up and his eyes scanned the windows above. She lifted a hand in a farewell salute and he doffed his bonnet in her direction with a gallant bow which brought many a smile to the faces of the waiting clansmen.

Tonight she would wear one of her most alluring gowns from France, and perfume her body with the

scented oils she had also brought back with her. She
would show Roy how well she assumed her role as
mistress of Tigh an Lóin. He would be proud of her
and forget all the past unpleasantness with her
brother and Mairi.

A smile lighting her face, she returned to the
bedroom to inspect the gowns Agnes was unpacking.

In the weeks which followed, Anne lost herself in
the wonder of the great old house. The library was
crammed full, rather untidily she found, with books
of every description, including ancient documents of
the clan MacKenzie, relating to their courageous
exploits since they came to settle in the county of
Ross in the early fourteenth century.

She was overawed by the dining-room, which she
was told had at one time seated over three hundred
guests. There was a large sitting-room where the
family now sat after meals, a smaller one where
visitors were received and a sparse-looking study
containing a desk and cabinets, which Roy and his
father used to conduct estate business. Various other
rooms had not been opened for several months, she
realised, as she peered through half open doors at
shuttered windows, noticing the musty smell which
always accompanied damp.

Upstairs, only one set of rooms was barred from
her—those of Mairi. She learned they had been
locked by the Laird himself the day she had run
away and had not been opened since. She dared not
ask Andrew MacKinney for the key, although she
longed to looked inside. She had been given all the
others, for it was her right as the new mistress to
take charge of such things. She suspected Ranald
himself had retained the key to those rooms so that
they were never opened again, without his permis-

sion. Perhaps the answer to the girl's indifference to Ewen, her need to seek other lovers when her own husband adored her lay hidden within those rooms. Anne wondered if she would ever understand why their marriage had not been a success. They had been so much in love on their wedding day. Did Mairi really possess 'bad blood' as Agnes had said, inherited from her mother, who had also taken a lover? Roy vehemently denied this, but then he had idolised his sister and could not bring himself to condemn her—although he did accept her wantonness. How could he deny it when Mairi had brought a bastard child into the world? And yet there were times when Anne found herself wondering at his attitude. Did he really believe the stories of Mairi's many affairs—deep in his heart did he still consider her the pure, innocent girl who had left Tigh an Lóin that last day? No, that could not be so, for that would mean he blamed Ewen and nothing would stop him from calling him out. And how could he have courted her, Anne, and love her as he did if he secretly harboured hatred against the Frasers?

She stood for a long while in her husband's rooms. They were typically a male domain, with heavy furniture, lacking any comforts apart from an old leather chair beneath one window. Ancient maps and weapons covered the walls, as they did in many of the downstairs rooms. On the table was a decanter of whisky and a glass. To her way of thinking he drank too much, but having seen him with his father and brother, she realised it had been a way of life for all three of them for some considerable time. They had not been weaned on goats' milk, she mused, but usquebaugh! The mere smell revolted her, much to their amusement, and she never touched it. Sometimes she drank a little wine at dinner, but apart from that preferred hot chocolate or sherry.

Roy was content to allow her to go her own way during the day. Mostly he was away from the house with Coll or his father. Sometimes she went riding with him, but not as often as she would have liked. When they came together at night, however, and lay side by side in the canopied bed, their love-making was more intense, more satisfying, than it had been at the lodge. The tenderness and sweet endearments whispered in her ear as his hands devastated her willing body. The passionate kisses which took her mouth by storm. Sometimes he took her several times in one night, but he was nearly almost always gone from the bed when she awoke in the morning. As if the power of his feelings embarrassed him—or frightened him—she thought. She would have loved to lie in his arms in the early hours and talk, but he never gave her the chance.

But it did not unduly worry her. Each time was more wonderful than the last. Some nights she felt as if she would die, so great was the love which possessed her, enslaved her mind and body, brought her such exquisite pleasure—and peace.

Christmas loomed closer. The house began to buzz with excited chatter. Acceptances poured in for the ball planned for St Stephen's, which heightened everyone's anticipation. Of the one hundred and thirty invitations sent out all over the Highlands, there had been only four refusals and those through illness or the length of the journey. The weather was still so atrocious she was amazed that so many people were willing to travel. They were coming to inspect her, Roy told her, a strange look in his black eyes. To inspect the new mistress of Tigh an Lóin. She had secretly thrilled to his words, eager for a chance to show all his friends and relatives how well matched they were.

She was having a new ball gown made of white silk. It was the custom to choose a plain colour so that the dresses did not clash with the vivid colours of the plaids worn by the men. The village women surprised her with a shawl woven in the MacKenzie colours, and many gifts of linen and handkerchiefs all embroidered with her initials. The smith had beaten out a large oval brooch in silver, a flawless cairngorm stone set in the middle—a present for the MacKenzie's lady. She had been near to tears as she was handed so many presents and known she was accepted by her husband's tenants.

By way of showing her thanks, Anne made a point of riding through the village at least twice a week to enquire if anyone needed any kind of help. She gained the impression they found it easier to confide in her—a woman, rather than Ranald, their ageing laird, who was not known for his patience these days. Since Mairi had run off, she discovered, the world had turned sour about him!

No word from Ewen. Her heart beat anxiously every time a messenger arrived. He *would* come, she told herself. He *had* to come. Yet there had been no contact from him since her marriage. She had suffered weeks of waiting, half expecting him to arrive at Tigh an Lóin with armed men and when he did not, she presumed that he was too angry with her to show himself. Waiting—waiting for some message, however small to tell her he still acknowledged her as his sister. He might not accept her love for a MacKenzie, but surely they were close enough for him to realise she had married for love, as he had done. If only she could say those words to his face, let him hear the sincerity in her voice—see it in her eyes—and believe, nothing short of death would part her from Roy Mackenzie. Her husband!

Perhaps Frances had persuaded him things were best left as they were. No further contact with the sister who he might consider had betrayed him with her choice of man. The two women had never liked each other. Anne had tolerated her because she had been James's wife. As fickle in her ways as Mairi had turned out to be, Anne was reluctantly forced to admit that Frances had turned away from her husband for a good reason. Had his attentions not already begun to wander in another direction? Two husbands and two wives under the same roof did not make for an easy life, for there could only ever be one mistress in the house. Anne had always considered herself mistress of her brothers' home, but in the end she had relinquished that place to Frances. Then Mairi had arrived to further complicate matters. In the end, the house in which she had once been so happy, became unbearable to live in and after the death of James, she was glad to leave it.

Ewen's acceptance to the ball came as she was in the midst of supervising the table arrangements for the special night, and she ran to find Roy, her eyes shining with joy—and relief. No letter had accompanied the brief card, but that did not matter. He was coming! Coming to make his peace with her—and with her husband! Roy had been right to suggest this way of bringing them together. Why had she ever harboured any doubts as to his sincerity? Even Ranald and Coll had begun to show signs of enthusiasm over the affair. They were all trying very hard to make her feel she was accepted both in their home and in their hearts—and now they were willing to offer hospitality to her brother. She could not have asked for more.

She found her husband engaging in playful swordsmanship with Coll, out by the stables, and for a moment as she stood and watched the encounter, she became increasingly aware of the uncanny ease with which Roy wielded his weapon. He did not seem to be making any real attempt to disarm his brother, yet each move blocked a potentially dangerous thrust or lunge, and she gasped as Coll's sword was sent spinning into the air.

'That makes a fair amount you owe me. I'll settle for the roan mare we saw at our neighbour, Robert Grant's last week,' Roy said good-humouredly as he retrieved the blade with the tip of his sword and send it flying back into Coll's waiting grasp. Both brothers were accomplished swordsmen, Anne realised.

'But that's twice as much as we wagered,' Coll groaned, wiping a hand across his sweating forehead. 'You have the devil's own luck, brother. Do you never make a mistake?'

'If I did it would be likely to result in my death and I have no plans for such an event yet.'

'I am glad to hear it,' Anne intervened, crossing the yard to join them. Roy sheathed his weapon, his eyes fastening on the paper she held in her hand. 'It has arrived. Ewen has accepted our invitation, and I am so pleased. Are you? It means that he has forgiven us for not telling him about our wedding.'

'You, perhaps. We shall have to wait and see as to whether his forgiveness extends to me,' her husband replied somewhat drily. Damn the man, why had he left it so late before accepting? He was almost sure the Fraser was not coming and he was glad, not to say relieved. Suddenly he wanted St

Stephen's Day to be everything Anne wished it to be. The ball a success, the two of them together, proud before his friends and relatives. Accepted by his father. Not one word would be said against the marriage when everyone saw how Ranald had taken Anne to his heart. He was often withdrawn with her at times, not easily prompted into conversation when they were all together, but she had told Roy how they conversed when they were alone. Roy had also noticed the fond glances his father had given her from time to time, and felt assured that Anne was rapidly assuming her rightful place in his eyes.

And now Ewen Fraser had raised his ugly head to spoil everything. It was his own fault for suggesting the stupid ball, Roy decided. But he had wanted her to know how proud he was to have her standing by his side.

'I hope he has forgiven you too,' Coll murmured. 'I would not like to see blood spilt on St Stephen's.' The blood ebbed from Anne's cheeks and she looked from one brother to the other her eyes wide and questioning.

'He jests, my love,' Roy said, slipping an arm about her waist and drawing her close against him. He flashed a warning frown at his brother. 'I've just won a horse off Coll. I shall give it to you by way of an apology for his careless words. Forgive him, he is a bad loser always.'

'Sometimes, when either of you mention Ewen's name . . . ' Anne began, and he frowned in sudden irritation.

'Confound it, I've apologised for him. His words meant nothing, not that you can blame him for his bitternes, can you? Will he stay overnight? If so, you had best make the arrangements and give him a room close to yours—for his safety and your peace of mind. He comes alone?'

'No, with Frances. James's widow.'

'Ah, the adventuress,' Roy chuckled, the moment of ill humour quickly stifled. The news had plunged him into a black mood which he knew she must not see and wonder at—or question. 'Well, there'll be many a man here to catch her eye, so she'll not be bored. Coll, you might take a fancy to her.'

'And risk giving Father a heart attack?' his brother returned with a grimace. 'Thanks, I'll stay with little Maisie at the ale house. She may be a little on the plain side, but she's willing, and her mother's a widow and she has no brothers to call me out.'

'Oh, you men!' Anne declared, outraged by the way the brothers always discussed women as if they were no more than breeding cattle. 'Sometimes I despair of you both. It will be a pleasure to have some real gentlemen here, if only for one night.'

Roy's arm tightened round her waist. He pulled her possessively against his chest with a broad smile. There was an odour of sweat and horses about him and she wrinkled her nose in disgust as he bent his head and kissed her full on the mouth, ignoring her indignant protests.

'Remember you are a married woman, my sweet,' he said teasingly. 'I would not want your eyes to stray in some other direction.'

'There are times when I do believe he thinks I could be interested in another man,' Anne said, disbelievingly as he went into the house. 'He knows how much I love him, Coll. Yet . . . '

'My brother is a very jealous man.' Coll picked up his jacket from the ground where he had tossed it when the fight began and brushed specks of dirt from the faded cloth. 'Would you not feel the same if he smiled at another woman?'

'There were so many before me . . . Don't bother to deny it, I know there were! You both have quite a reputation in Inverness. At first I didn't believe Roy could be interested in me, not after all his other . . . conquests?'

Coll laughed, his boyish face alight with mockery.

'My dear misguided girl—I am the romantic one in the family, not my oafish brother. I used to take him along with me so that he could—broaden his education in that direction,' he teased. 'You are the first woman he has ever loved and that is the truth. The trouble is you have never been in love before, either. It can be frightening, I suppose, realising you have tied yourself to one man—or one woman, for life. It gives me the shudders to consider such a thing.'

'You are right. I have never been in love, I am jealous—and I am being silly. I am nervous over the ball, I suppose. I wanted Ewen to come and I am glad he has accepted, but to see him walk into the Great Hall, with all your friends and relatives there. Coll, I am more than a little apprehensive. One wrong word . . . '

'Do you not think Roy is thinking exactly the same thing?' Coll turned away from her, staring at the stables with fixed gaze for several minutes. He did not want to dwell on what could—and would- —happen on St Stephen's if he had his way. It would not involve his brother, nor his father, only himself and Ewen Fraser. He had nothing to lose if he called the man out. Roy had everything—and the fool was prepared to risk losing it—wife and life—to settle the issue between them. 'I didn't realise how deeply you really loved that idiot brother of mine. Be careful.'

'Of what?'

Be careful you do not become too vulnerable, was what he wanted to say. To try and warn her should anything go wrong with the scheme taking fashion in his head. He looked back at her and shrugged his shoulders.

'Of smothering him . . . ' His eyes considered her for a while and Anne felt the colour rise in her cheeks at his scrutiny. There were times when she found him a pleasant companion, immensely witty and entertaining and fun to be with, then there were times like this, when the strangeness of his words puzzled her and his manner made her feel quite uncomfortable. 'Why don't you ride over to see the mare with me tomorrow? I don't think Roy will find anything too alarming in us spending a little time together, do you?'

'I would like that. The fitting for my dress is not until the afternoon. I want to buy something for him, Coll, but I'm not sure what to get. Can you help me?'

'We'll put our heads together as we ride. We'll think of something suitable.'

CHAPTER FOUR

'WHAT ARE YOU looking so pleased about?' Roy asked, coming into the drawing-room in time to see Anne relax into her chair with a satisfied smile on her face. The moment he entered, Coll had moved away from her and his dark eyes narrowed suspiciously. His brother's lips deepened into a smile at the glower which came his way and Coll said cheerfully,

'My, what a long face! You should spend more time in the company of your wife—she is a ray of bright sunshine on these dull days.'

'If I was not doing the work of two men these days, I might be able to do just that,' came the sarcastic retort. 'However, I am sure you are an excellent replacement.'

'And you can take that bearish mood back where you came from,' Ranald reproved from his chair beside the fire. He too had noticed the way Anne and Coll had been spending a great deal of time together over the past days, but he had put it down to the fact that the former was in need of company other than that of her husband or an ageing old man who lived too much in the past. But what troubled his elder son? For days, ever since Anne had received word from her brother, if his memory served him right, Roy's temper had been quick—his tongue sharp—with family and servants alike. It was not like him at all. Had the love-mist begun to lift from his eyes? Was Anne Fraser no longer the most wonderful woman in the world?

As much as Ranald wanted to—and had tried over the weeks—he could find no fault with her. She was polite, industrious, considerate and gave herself no airs even though she now ran the house almost single-handed. She would be the perfect hostess at the ball and he realised he was eager to see her receiving their guests, to hear their comments, nay—their congratulations on his son's good fortune. He was proud to call her his daughter-in-law. She filled the empty place in his heart left by Mairi and filled it well.

'Forgive me, Father. You too, Anne. Even you, Coll.' Roy threw his brother a half smile. 'I'm tired and irritable. I've been riding the moors these past two days looking for our cattle. We lost another six head the night before last and there's no sign of them. If it snows and they are hidden on high ground, we shall never get them back.'

'They are probably already inside the stomach of some Campbell,' Ranald retorted frowning. 'Thieves, the lot of them. One more head, and you'll take the men across the burn and deal with them properly.'

'Ay, I agree with you.' Roy sank into the nearest chair with a tired sigh. Quickly Anne rose and fetched him some hot chocolate from the tray on the table.

At mid-morning on most days, they gathered to talk. Anne found the time invaluable as the day of the ball loomed closer and the amount of work never lessened. She had often entertained at home, but never to this extent. Due to the uncertainty of the weather, some guests had advised that they would be arriving at least two days ahead of schedule, but no one seemed to mind. Rooms were made ready, beds aired, warming-pans cleaned, more food prepared for those additional days. She thought the servants very capable to manage as they did. Not once had they shown any signs of being ruffled at the prospect of having to feed a very full household, or to pander to the whims of awkward visitors. She could hardly contain her excitement now that the actual ball was only three days away.

She felt as nervous as she had at her first function at the age of sixteen, tripping clumsily over the feet of her dancing partner. She had not taken to the floor for the rest of that night. She had never forgotten her embarrassment, the chagrin of being laughed at by both James and Ewen, when she had considered herself grown up and confident. She had yet to dance with Roy, but instinctively she knew while she was held in his arms, she would be neither nervous nor clumsy.

'As you have been away all night, you won't have been told the Cameron brothers arrived early this morning,' Ranald said. 'They have a mind to go hunting with you and Coll on Christmas morning—as you did last year. Will you arrange it?'

'A good idea,' Roy agreed. 'We haven't had a good hunt now in—how long is it, Coll? Six or seven months. I'm sure we shall get others willing to join us.'

'And if we haven't found our cattle, I know what I shall be hunting,' Coll murmured.

'I would like to ride with you,' Anne said, and saw Ranald's mouth curve into a quiet smile. At least he did not disapprove of the suggestion. 'I shall keep up with you, never fear. I am an excellent horsewoman.'

'Of that I am well aware. We have ridden together, remember?' Roy answered and for a moment as their eyes met, memories of those rides across Drum-

mossie Moor came into both their minds. It was a
silent moment of sharing something they both wished
to experience again. 'Why not.'

'If she gets lost, she will have to find her own way
home,' Coll snorted. 'Ach! The hunt is no place for
a woman.'

'I shall see she does not get lost,' Roy chuckled,
aware how the thought of riding with Anne, sharing
something with her, was lessening his sombre mood.
'Will you be joining us, Father?'

'Nay, lad, much as I would like to see your
woman riding like the wind with you, I shall stay
here and entertain our not-so-adventurous guests.
This leg is too uncomfortable for me to sit astride a
horse.' Ranald was referring to an injury he had
sustained in an accident some years ago. Although
it had not left him with a limp, his left leg was at
times, extremely painful, especially in cold weather
when it swelled up and had to be rested frequently.

'Let me pour you some more chocolate,' Anne
said, reaching for his empty cup, but he shook his
head. 'Some brandy then—medicinal, of course.'

'Your wife is a very understanding woman,'
Ranald said, smiling at her warmly.

Roy watched her cross to the decanters. During
the weeks she had been at Tigh an Lóin, the relationship which had developed between her and his
father had grown beyond his hopes. He had expected
a prolonged antagonism between them, mainly on
his father's side, but it had not been so. After the
initial strain of their meeting, they had become at
ease with each other almost at once. He had never
known the old man to take to anyone so quickly.
Proof that he missed Mairi more than he would
admit—more than he realised himself perhaps. He
was substituting Anne for his daughter. The knowl-

edge not only angered, but also saddened Roy. Mairi
had her own place in the house and he intended one
day she should return and take it.

Christmastide could not be over soon enough for
Roy. Even the ball was beginning to grate on his
nerves. If Ewen Fraser came in peace, then he would
depart from Tigh an Lóin without one hair on his
head being touched. No man, including Roy, would
draw a weapon against him. He would find some
other way—another place and time to deal with him.
Somehow, it did not seem the most important thing
in his life just now. But if he was coming to issue a
challenge—then he would die. And with his death
would die the marriage he so dearly wanted to
preserve. He had come to accept Anne was incapable
of choosing between husband and brother. He did
not want to put her to that terrible test and make it
necessary.

'I have displeased you,' Anne said when they were
alone together. Ranald had gone upstairs to rest and
Coll had ridden away to visit his latest lady-friend,
of whom he was most reluctant to speak. No one
expected to see him again before morning. Anne
walked into her husband's bedroom as he was stripping off his shirt. 'I shall not come hunting with
you. I should not have suggested it. I—just wanted
to be with you a little more . . . '

'You will come. I insist. I'm tired, my sweet, and
my temper doesn't improve when I have to stay out
all night on some freezing hillock and leave you
alone in a very warm bed. That's not all I miss,' he
added wickedly and she blushed. She watched as he
searched for a clean shirt and asked quickly,

'Are you going out again—so soon?'

'Down to the village only. I shall be back before

dark, I promise.' As he saw the crestfallen look on her face he caught her hand and drew her down beside him on the bed. 'I don't have to go yet. I have been neglecting you lately, I know, but with Father incapacitated, or nearly so, there is much to be done. The estate does not run itself, especially at a time like this. You must not resent the time I give to other things, there will always be more than enough for us—and this . . . ' His lips began to trail kisses down over her cheek and shoulder.

'But I do,' she admitted. 'I cannot help myself. When you are not with me I hate every moment of being alone. Please don't misunderstand me; your father and brother could not have made me feel more welcome, but it is you I love. You I want to be with all the time.'

'Hush, you are wasting valuable time now,' Roy whispered, quickly covering her mouth with his. Moments snatched like this made it possible for him to shut out the other side of him: the black beast that desired revenge and hungered for the sight of Ewen Fraser dead at his feet: the longing for his sister to be brought back to Tigh an Lóin where she belonged. That time would come, and soon, but he did not want to consider what had to be done to make it possible. Not when Anne's lips were so responsive beneath his own, not when she was loosening the bodice of her gown and drawing his hands against her breasts, sighing softly as he cupped them, explored them . . .

Later she lay contentedly watching him as he pulled on his clothes, no longer embarrassed by the sight of his bronzed torso, the muscles which rippled across his broad back as he slipped his arms into a shirt. She drew herself up on to the pillows, brushing back a tangled mass of red curls from her face.

'Are you anxious about my brother coming to the ball?' she asked.

'I would be a fool if I was not, but I have promised I shall not be the one to start any trouble.' The gentle side of him that had lain with her and made love, abhorred such a thought, but the devil in him wished for it and chided him for the weakness love had brought to his life. He wanted the love of his wife to remain as true as it was now and he also wanted the return of his sister to Tigh an Lóin. Coll had said he could not have both. Anne or Mairi? How could he choose between them any more then she could choose between him and her brother. They were both caught in a vicious web. He loved them both . . . yet he was beginning to fear he might lose one of them.

'I shall speak with him the moment he arrives and tell him to behave himself,' Anne said firmly. 'Why else should he come but to be friendly and to show us that he accepts our marriage?'

'I think friendship between us is asking too much,' Roy replied. 'But I shall receive him in this house with all the civility due him as your brother. I shall never call him friend, however, and you must accept that.'

'I do.' It was more than she had ever expected.

Christmas Day was normally a quiet day, a family occasion, and as it progressed, Anne thought she was growing closer to each of the family than she had ever dreamed possible. Early in the morning she attended a service in the small chapel which adjoined the house, escorted into the single stone room on the arm of Ranald himself. Here, only the four of them were present, the service officiated by the minister from the village.

Afterwards, there was spiced ale and whisky served in the drawing-room where a huge fire blazed, dispelling the winter gloom which prevailed outside. She left the men deep in conversation to go and change and brought broad smiles to the faces of them all—even that of the dour old minister—when she reappeared clad in a pair of plaid trews and a heavy fur-lined coat, complete with a bonnet set at a saucy angle on her red curls.

'You are a wicked minx,' Roy whispered in her ear as he handed her a hot toddy before they left for the hunt. 'The poor man almost had apoplexy.'

'Would you have me ride about the countryside in my best gown, Roy MacKenzie?' she returned demurely. 'I am saving that for the ball. I intend to dazzle you.'

'There has not been a day when you do not. Even dressed as some village urchin who looks as if he is about to steal the cook's best pie, I am still awed by your beauty.'

'Wretch! I shall make you pay for mocking me.' She almost choked over her drink.

'I look forward to it . . . later.'

Heavy snow brought what had promised to be a pleasant hunting session, together with the Camerons, Coll and four other men from the village to an abrupt end. They all struggled against driving snow on the ride back to the house and Anne went directly to her room to rest. Brief though the outing had been, it had been another part of Roy's life that he had allowed her to share and she was well satisfied. But how she ached from trying to stay in the saddle on the way back. The snow had smacked against her cheeks until they felt raw. Not until she had soaked herself in a hot bath did she feel as if her frozen limbs were thawing out and returning to normal.

In the evening, everyone went to the village, the servants following by cart or horse, to the carol service held in the kirk. By the time they returned for a late supper, she was exhausted. The morrow would be taken up with the entertaining of the guests who had already arrived for the ball and final preparations for those who descended on them that day and in the days to come. She was excited as she had never been before and with Roy's promise that he would not provoke any trouble with her brother, she fell asleep, blissfully dreaming of Ewen holding out his hand to her husband and offering an olive-branch. She had successfully achieved the impossible with her marriage to a MacKenzie, now she was praying for a miracle!'

'Are you ready to come downstairs, Anne? Father will be waiting for us.'

Roy looked at his wife, who was sitting in front of her mirror, pinning her hair back from her face. He had observed her for a full five minutes without her knowledge before he came out of the bedroom and announced his presence. He liked to watch her. She always seemed so unaware of the effect she had on him.

'I won't be a moment. This ribbon keeps slipping. Can you fasten it for me?'

She could have tied it well enough herself, but she wanted him to hold her for a moment before they went downstairs. She expected they they would have little time to themselves in the hours to come. How she was looking forward to seeing his face when he discovered what she had bought him!

As she felt his fingers brush the nape of her neck

as he tied the pale yellow ribbon in a bow about her hair, she leaned back slightly so that she could rest against the solidness of his body. In answer to her silent plea, he bent and kissed her cheek, then turned her so that he could take her mouth.

While they embraced, Roy knew, whatever happened when Ewen Fraser showed himself, he would never allow Anne to leave Tigh an Lóin—to leave him! She was his wife. For a long moment he buried his face in the cloud of loose hair so that she would not see the torment in his eyes. Only a few hours more before he knew what fate had in store for him.

Anne wore one of the gowns she had brought back with her from Paris, a pale grey watered silk—and very décolletée. She rose and allowed his gaze to study her. How long had she been married? Four short weeks. She had known him less than two months yet she felt they had been together for years.

Once downstairs, Ranald rose from his chair to greet her. 'My dear Anne, you are like a breath of spring in this old house.'

A warm look crept into Roy's eyes as he watched them embrace.

'Anne, you are fast persuading me to seek myself a wife, but where shall I find one as perfect as you?' Coll chuckled as he too came forward and took her in his arms, kissing her not on the cheeks, but on the lips.

'You are too bold, sir,' she said in mock indignation. 'I shall indeed have to find some eligible young lady for you.'

'If only you would,' Ranald agreed with a grimace. 'But make sure she's a strong one. She'll need to be to manage this wild young fool. Get him a bride, Anne. I'm fast growing old and I want to see some grandchildren before I die.' His eyes fastened on her robe and his expression grew questioning. 'You have no news for me, I suppose?'

She gasped and coloured profusely, while a chuckle broke from Roy's lips.

'We have been married only four weeks, Father.'

'Time enough to get her with child. You spend enough time together. You want children, don't you?' he challenged.

'With all my heart,' Anne assured him. 'You shall have your grandson, I promise you.'

'The respite is over. Half our guests may not get here at all tonight,' Roy remarked, looking at the heavy snow falling outside the windows.

'Then we can gorge ourselves on an excess of food and good liquor,' Coll remarked with enthusiasm. 'It's been a long time since you and I got drunk together.'

'At least six hours!' Anne reminded him. She had seen Roy ride up in the early hours of the morning and watched him unload his brother's inert form from the horse. 'I shall be very surprised if you can touch even a wee dram tonight.'

'For your information, I have already had two—for breakfast,' Coll retorted, with a cheeky grin.

'I thought you were asleep when I came to bed,' Roy murmured, as his brother turned away to gather up the presents set out on a table. Ranald had decided to give them out a day early lest they became too engrossed with their guests the day after the ball. It would be a day of clearing up, and soothing aching heads, Anne realised. A wise move.

'How could I sleep, not knowing where you were?' she chided softly.

Hot chocolate and oatcakes were brought while

the presents were opened. Roy's present to Anne
had been the horse he won from Coll, but he had
added to it, a beautiful bolt of velvet cloth. From
his brother she received a silver bracelet engraved
with a Celtic design. In return she gave him a silver
drinking flask. Very appropriate under the circumstances, she thought, and knew she was right by the
warm hug Coll promptly gave her. For Ranald, she
had chosen a new sword-belt in Moroccan leather
with an engraved buckle bearing the heraldic design
of the MacKenzies upon it. She was sure the old
man's eyes had filled with tears as he stared at it.
Turning away, he whispered to Andrew, who
immediately left the room.

Now it was Roy's turn. Anne caught her breath
as the ribbons and wrappings she had carefully
folded round the pistols fell away. He did not
move—or speak. She felt anxiety rise inside her, and
asked falteringly,

'You—you do not like them?'

Very slowly, Roy lifted the belt pistols and held
them out for his brother and father to see.

'Will you look at these!' he exclaimed, deep
pleasure rising in his voice. He could not hide it.
What a present! 'Anne, girl, have you second sight?
I was trying to buy these from that skinflint not a
month ago. He'd not sell them to me.'

'Perhaps he was bewitched by your wife's blue
eyes,' Coll laughed. 'Man, this is some wife you
have. If you could have heard the way she bargained
a price with him!'

'You *are* pleased,' Anne said, relieved, and he
lifted his eyes to hers and she saw the depth of his
pleasure glowing in the blackness of them.

'Thank you! You make me feel ashamed that I
have nothing to give you now.'

'I have a new horse. As fleet of foot as any in my . . . '—she was about to say 'my brother's stables', and halted just in time—'as any I have ever ridden. When we next race, you will not win against me. You will see.'

He liked them! She could have flung her arms about his neck with joy and barely contained herself from doing so. She had never seen him so lost for words before.

Andrew returned, carrying a brass-hinged box which he set carefully down into Ranald's hands. Immediately she was aware of not only Coll's face growing grave, but that of Roy too. And then across Roy's features spread something near to rage. The black eyes glittered like pieces of jet as he snapped unsteadily,

'Are those what I think they are?'

'Yes. Your mother's jewels. I intend to give them to Anne. She should have had them the day she set foot in the house. However, I do not think she will hold an old man's reticence to accept her against him. We have grown to know each other well these past weeks. She is a good wife for you, Roy. In time I pray she will temper some of the bitterness and hatred simmering away inside you.'

Bitterness! Hatred! What did he mean, Anne wondered, unable to bear the look on Roy's face. Such torment there—and anger! Hatred and bitterness for whom? Surely not her brother? Ewen was not to blame. Roy had not said that he accepted Ewen in so many words, but surely if he felt hatred for him, he would not have allowed her to invite him to Tigh an Lóin.

'They belonged to my mother. You have no right to give them to anyone.' Somehow he retained a hold on his temper although he could feel it was dangerously close to breaking-point. If he unleashed it now upon his father he would betray himself, and he could not afford to do that.

'They belonged to my *wife*,' Ranald thundered, climbing awkwardly to his feet. Anne moved instinctively to help him, but a warning frown from Coll halted her. She threw him a beseeching look, imploring him to intervene before more sharp words spoiled the pleasantness of the morning, but he shook his head. Either he would not—or could not—pour oil on to these troubled waters. 'Many of them I gave her myself. I can do with them what I please.'

'And those she brought with her when she married you? The family heirlooms? She intended them for someone else, you know that. They belong to Mairi.'

'I know of no one by that name. You young pup, how dare you mention her on this day! If I had my whip . . . '.

'You would what, Father?' Roy challenged, moving forward to face him. They stood not a foot apart, glaring at each other. The friendliness and close family ties they had all shared a moment or two ago had vanished completely. 'You will not touch me. You need me to run the estate, to give you your precious grandchildren. You will do nothing to me!' The words came without thinking. Weeks and weeks of being torn apart by love and hate suddenly erupted like a tidal wave. He could not stop it. For Mairi to inherit the jewels had been his mother's dying wish, and he had promised her it would be so. As much as he loved his wife he could not allow her to have them.

'Very well. I shall take out those belonging to your mother's family. You can have them. Give them to—whoever you wish. Before me and your brother, you have insulted your wife, and for that, I do not think I shall ever forgive you.'

'There is much I cannot forgive you for, old man.' Roy's voice was like tempered steel cutting through the stillness of the room. Suddenly Anne felt inexplicably afraid. This stranger, this black-eyed, black-hearted man was not her husband! He spun round on her, his features bleak and without realising it, she recoiled from the hatred in his expression. 'I hope you are satisfied. You have taken her place. He has substituted you for Mairi!'

'Damn you, apologise for that,' Ranald demanded, but Roy brushed aside the outstretched hand meant to detain him and slammed out of the room. 'Go after him. Fetch him back,' he ordered Andrew MacKinney. 'He'll not come though, I know my own flesh and blood. He is too much like me. Too proud—and when he's wrong, he knows not how to admit it. God help us—how alike we are.'

As Ranald sank back into his chair, Anne ran to him. His face had become so pale with the encounter that Coll poured him a drink and pressed it into his hand.

'Drink it,' she insisted. 'I'll go after him. He'll come back for me.'

'No!' She looked up at Coll in surprise. 'No, Anne, don't. Let him calm down. I know what I'm saying. He'll not come back. Maybe you won't see him again until tonight . . . perhaps it will be better if you don't. There is still a part of my brother you do not know, for all that you share with him. Give him time. That's all he needs.'

'I—I don't understand.' She was shivering now, although the room was quite warm. What part of Roy? She prided herself that she knew him better than anyone. When they were so close—so in love, how could she not know every part of him? Coll took her hand and lifted her to her feet, smiling into her pale features.

'As Father says, they are too alike. He did not mean what he said to either of you, believe me. I know him.'

'Better than I do?' she asked in disbelief and he nodded, grave-faced again.

'Yes, sweet sister-in-law. Better than anyone.'

Anne sat staring at her reflection. Open before her was the jewel-case Ranald had pressed into her hands earlier that morning. The contents were spread out across the velvet top of her dressing-table. In the candlelight, diamonds and emeralds shimmered. Rubies glowed with dull fire. Sapphires, bright like her eyes, begged to be worn, to adorn her fair skin and be admired. Ranald had taken several necklaces and rings from the case with muttered apologies; all the things that had belonged to Roy's mother and were now Mairi's by right. She accepted that without rancour and wished her husband had been less incensed by the whole episode. It was not like him at all! Why such a terrible fuss? Why had he lost his temper and brought his father such pain? When she left the old man he had been sitting like a stone in his chair, staring sightlessly at the jewels in his hands, his shoulders bowed, as if pressed down by some enormous weight.

She had found Ranald was indeed a very tired old man who wanted only to live out the rest of his days in peace. Not until she watched him with his eldest son that morning, had she envisaged the bitterness and enmity which could come between them. The MacKenzies had many dark secrets, she mused.

Perhaps she would never know them all. Perhaps it was best she did not!

Roy had not been in his rooms when she went upstairs. Agnes said she had seen him ride away from the house a few minutes before Anne arrived. He was deliberately avoiding her, she decided, and so he should. She was greatly shocked by what had passed in the library and found it hard to cast off a feeling of apprehension which enveloped her for the duration of the afternoon. Only when it became time to dress and go downstairs again to greet her many guests upon their arrival, did she begin to brighten slightly. She had to. She could not appear with a long face when she was the hostess.

Although she heard Roy moving about in the bedroom later, she did not go to him. Her hand was on the door knob when she turned away and went back into the sitting-room. Let him calm down, Coll had said. It was good advice. He would come to her in his own time and tell her what troubled him. They would solve the problem, whatever it was, together.

Anne dressed with great care, conscious of the enormous undertaking she had accepted in becoming the wife of Roy MacKenzie with so many responsibilities falling upon her young shoulders. Her acceptance into the family had caused her much apprehension—unnecessarily so, as it turned out—for she now considered Ranald and Coll as close as her own kinsmen. She loved them both dearly and knew that her affections were reciprocated. Roy had painted a picture of a hard-hearted father who would not accept her under any terms. A man tired of battles, of fighting, wanting only to live in peace—strictly under his own conditions, which did not include another Fraser in the family. One day, she thought, she would ask him of the blood-feud between the Frasers and the MacKenzies.

'How do I look, Agnes? Do you think I will pass the inspection of all those searching eyes? Will Roy's family and friends see another Fraser infiltrating their domain—or a woman who has fallen in love with a man who should have been denied to her?'

The maid shrugged bony shoulders as she took up her sewing after a cursory glance at the exquisite figure in white.

'You have no need to ask me that! Ask him—or if he does not care to give you an answer, go downstairs and see for yourself.'

'There are times when I could cheerfully cut out your tongue, viper,' Roy declared from the open doorway to his bedroom. Anne had been so intent on inspecting her reflection that she had not seen him. She turned slowly and heard him utter a soft exclamation. So he was not displeased with what he saw!

'Woman, you will have every man's eyes on you tonight,' he declared, advancing towards her. 'Turn round, let me feast my eyes on you some more before everyone else has access to you.'

She spun around before him, her face lighting up with pure delight at his words. There was no trace of antagonism in him now. And if he thought her appearance suitable, she thought his . . . she had no word to describe the love which rose in her as she studied him.

His jacket was of deep green velvet, blending well with the plaid fastened at one shoulder. The white lace jabot at his throat accentuated the swarthiness of his skin, deepened the tan of those strong hands, revealed beneath the frilled cuffs. The harshness of his words that morning were forgotten—had never existed as he came towards her and took her in his arms.

'Did I not warn you I have a devil inside me which will never be tamed? When I saw Father about to give you Mairi's jewels . . . '

'I would have given them to you, had you asked—in a reasonable manner,' she chided. 'You did not have to make me feel so—so awkward about accepting your father's gift. It was meant well. I think you owe him an apology.'

'Do you now?' The brilliant black eyes gleamed down at her, but then he nodded.

'Ay, I do and he shall have it. And you, Anne?'

'You have what you want. He took them from the casket before he gave it to me,' she returned. 'You love your sister, Roy, I accept that. But I am your wife. Am I not to be afforded the same affection?'

'Affection?' Roy drawled, dropping his lips to her face. She turned it quickly away and he frowned in annoyance. 'Never do that, woman. You belong to me and I shall kiss you when I please.'

'This morning you accused me of wanting to take Mairi's place. That was unworthy of you.'

'It was, and I apologise. Now kiss me, damn you, before we go downstairs and I lose you to every handsome man who comes your way.'

She relented and raised her face for his kiss. Agnes gave her usual snort of disapproval as the two figures blended into one—forgetting her presence totally.

Roy held his wife at arm's length, surveyed her with pride in his eyes. He could not hide it. Every man downstairs would be envying him the woman he had tonight! The over-skirt of her white silk gown divided to reveal panels of frothy Brussels lace. The low-cut neckline exposed the firm swell of her breasts, and yet he saw, with surprise, she wore no jewellery, apart from his wedding band and a diamond cluster ring on her right hand. Tiny bows of green velvet matched the plaid sash she also wore fastened at her right shoulder, and, he noticed with satisfaction, she had chosen to wear the cairngorm brooch the smithy had fashioned for her.

The wide, full sleeves of the gown, frilled with an abundance of lace, reached just past her elbows and left bare slender wrists and long, tapered fingers. She held a tiny reticule in MacKenzie tartan, with a Celtic pattern in silver on the cantle.

'My grandmother's,' Anne said as she followed his gaze. 'I had one of the women in the village re-cover it for me. I hope you don't mind.'

'Who else should wear my colours, but my wife,' Roy returned. 'Why are you not wearing something my father gave you? Surely there was enough to choose from?'

'And have you sound as you do now?' she retorted quickly. 'I could not refuse them, but I will not wear any of them while it offends you.'

He gave another expletive, this time not so quiet as he crossed to the vanity where the contents of the jewel-case were still spread and stared down at them.

'Rubies,' he said, as if to himself. 'To match the fire you possess when we are together.' He came back to her, holding a necklace of blood-red rubies, four in all in a barbaric gold setting. 'These belonged to the wife of Douglas MacKenzie, a Spanish woman who accompanied her brother on the armada which sailed to attack England. After its defeat, the ship foundered on the rocks near Mallaig Point. She was the only survivor. Douglas happened to be in that vicinity at the time and saved her from a horde of angry villagers who thought her a Spanish witch. From all the portraits of her, with her flaming red hair—just like yours—she must have seemed one. He brought her back to Tigh an Lóin, nursed her himself when she collapsed with fever, and married her when she was recovered. She never accepted him as her husband. They were wild creatures, both of them . . . impossible to tame, yet between them was a strange kind of affection. She bore him four stalwart sons.'

'As I am expected to do,' Anne said, and he stared at her with mockery in his veiled eyes.

'Is that not the duty of a wife?'

'Is that why you married me? To give your father a grandchild? You could have chosen any one of a dozen women to do that.' His words had deeply hurt her and he came to realise it as he looked into her troubled face.

'Anne—sweet witch, for that is what you are.' He forgot Ewen, forgot his father—forgot Mairi as he drew her to him. His fingers lightly brushing across the exposed part of her breast made her blush with pleasure. 'Of course I want a child. A son. What man does not? But for me, not Father.' It was the truth! A son with her colouring and none of his temperament. If only that was possible. She would hate him soon enough, but a child born from the union now would have been conceived in love—on her part, at least. He fastened the necklace about her throat, stood back and nodded. On to her fingers he placed two rings, both huge cabochon rubies. In her ears, he secured matching stones which caught the lamplight and glowed with rich hues. 'Take me as I am, woman. I can give no more than I do,' Roy declared with sudden fervour and seizing her in his arms, bruised her mouth with a slow, relentless pressure for several minutes, leaving her spent and breathless when he released her. 'Let's away to greet our guests. They will think I have married some hideous monster who is too afraid to face them.'

She placed her hand in his, her mouth trembling at the ferocity of that savage kiss, and allowed him to lead her from the room. But her eyes were alight with happiness. Words did not matter. Each time he held her—kissed her—made love to her—she knew she meant everything to him. No man could feign such deep passion.

CHAPTER FIVE

ANNE CLUTCHED a little more tightly to Roy's hand, seeking reassurance as they descended the stairs to the Great Hall. The look which passed between them, the fierce glow of love and pride in the depth of her husband's eyes, gave her all the additional courage she needed to face the people gathering below.

'You are beautiful and I love you,' he whispered. 'My aunts and uncles no longer think you have two heads now they have met you, and I think at least one of my relatives has fallen madly in love with you.'

Throughout the days leading up to this night, she had borne herself with a quiet dignity which made him ashamed of his own short-tempered bouts. He had done little to ease the strain and misgivings she must be experiencing at this moment. He had wanted this night to be the happiest of her life—the proudest of his. His aim had been achieved—now he had put things right for her.

'I think one MacKenzie is all I can manage just now,' Anne returned, blushing furiously at the remark. 'Behave yourself! I am nervous enough as it is.'

'You have no need. Tonight I shall show them all how proud I am of the woman I have married.' She looked up at him, a silent plea in her eyes and he nodded. 'Even Ewen Fraser himself when he comes. If . . . he comes.'

'The weather has delayed him. He will come,' Anne replied. But whether to tell her he accepted her marriage or to remonstrate with her, she did not know.

Ranald left his companions to come to the foot of the stairs. She saw his eyes alight on the jewels she wore and a sigh went through him at the sight of them against her flawless skin. He lifted his eyes to those of his son and there was hostility in his stare.

'Please,' Anne begged softly, 'make your peace. You are both stubborn men, but I love you both and I cannot bear to see you at each other's throats. Will you do this for me?'

It was Roy who stretched out his hand first, a slow flush stealing beneath his tanned cheeks at the sincerity in her voice. She was part of them—of him—why was he not able to give up his notions of revenge and accept what God had given him? The love of a beautiful woman, her acceptance by his father, the prospect of a family to unite them all still further, bind them with chains of love from which he knew he would never want to be released.

Roy became aware of Coll watching him. His brother knew he had no choice. He could not abandon Mairi to a life of solitude—a life with only a babe to comfort her for all she had lost. Ewen Fraser's child! What comfort would that be? She should have been here tonight, celebrating with the rest of them, infecting the whole household with her laughter, her joy of living. The Frasers had denied her that right.

'I spoke in haste, Father. Forgive my sharp tongue. I love Mairi too much, perhaps. And you not enough.' Even now, with an apology on his lips, his words still proclaimed his deep love for sister, Anne

thought anxiously, but Ranald saw fit to overlook
the remark. He clasped his son's hand in a firm grip.

'When you have children of your own to rear and
they tear your heart apart with their ingratitude and
selfishness—then tell me I love her not.' His tone
was very calm—very controlled. Anne marvelled at
it as she kissed him on the cheek.

'With age also comes wisdom,' she smiled and
saw Roy's lips curve into a smile also. 'If we are as
wise as you at your age, Father, we shall bless our
good fortune.'

There were a few raised eyebrows and a good few
fluttering fans as Ranald took Anne in his arms and
hugged her. She had called him 'Father', and he had
loved it. In that moment she slipped totally into the
place in his heart which had always been reserved
for Mairi. The change-over was complete. *She* was
his daughter now. He had no other. Poor, disillusioned old man! Instead of anger, Roy was surprised
to discover he pitied Ranald. Would that he had
tried to understand his own flesh and blood so well.

'Come, our guests are waiting,' he murmured and
led her on towards the other room, where musicians
brought from Inverness for the occasion, were seated
in the long gallery above them, waiting for the signal
to begin to play. 'We are expected to lead the
dancing.'

The room was decked with holly wreaths and
other colourful decorations which hung from beams
high above. A piper stood to one side of the fiddlers
patiently waiting for the time when he would be
called upon to enthral the guests below with stirring
pipe music while one of the clansmen recalled ancient
battles and sang of past glories of the clan
MacKenzie.

Coll was already making the most of the occasion,

Roy saw, as he discovered his brother standing beside the punch-bowl, his eyes alight with devilment as he considered the fresh-faced young girl in flounces and curls near by. Heaven help them all if he charmed her tonight! He had never considered the possibility before, but now to his amazement, he accepted that Anne could be right and that his brother needed a wife to make him give up his flippant way of life. They had shared a good many times together, but his brother was not like him. He was easily led, drank far too much and, as far as Roy could ascertain, gave no thought for the morrow. A strong-willed woman would change all that . . .

And then he grimaced at the thought of his irresponsible brother being under restraint. Let him enjoy his life while he was able. Roy had chosen the way he wished to live, but that did not necessarily mean that Coll had to follow him. Perhaps he would be lucky in love—Roy hoped so.

Roy glanced continually at the woman beside him as they first led out the dancers and then began to mingle with the guests. He found himself introducing her to kinsmen and women he had not seen for years. They had all come to inspect the bride and some, he knew, were hoping to find something more. A confrontation, perhaps? A look—a word, that denied they were the cosy couple they appeared to be. Damn them! Their suspicions and resentment against the Frasers was what helped to keep his own enmity alive. He had disliked Ewen Fraser and his whole family before he had ever seen them . . . before Mairi had fallen in love with the man who was to marry and then abandon her. Before he saw Anne Fraser and fell under her spell. His love for Anne meant that he had accepted her innocence over the affair—she was ignorant of her brother's atrocities. He had to believe that she was not like him. How could she be? She had risked everything to marry him! As each day passed, he convinced himself that she would side with him against her brother. The love for her husband would prove greater. It had to—or they were lost! But tonight would not be the time to arouse that confrontation, he was decided on that. This was her night and he would allow nothing to spoil it.

How well she conducted herself. A trifle shyly, which endeared her to the womenfolk—at least those past forty who could sensibly assess the attributes she possessed. Anyone younger, jealous of what they saw, could cheerfully have clawed her eyes out, he suspected. The men ogled her, held her hand for far too long in his estimation, and commented too liberally on his good fortune. He could have dunted a dozen jaws without batting an eyelid. Perhaps he would have cause to do so before the evening was over, he thought, his eyes narrowing as a distant cousin from Edinburgh slobbered over her jewelled fingers and she withdrew them in obvious distaste.

'What do you say we have a dram before we continue?' he murmured, drawing her towards the punch-bowl, where Coll was now deep in conversation with the girl he had been admiring. She was no more than seventeen, Roy realised, and tried to signal his disapproval to his brother, but it was ignored.

'This is Eireen Campbell, niece of old Kincarry,' Coll grinned, and Roy almost choked over his whisky, for the man was a close friend of his father's and the girl was the idol of his eye.

'I am glad you could come, Eireen,' Anne smiled at her, aware of her husband's discomfort. A Campbell! She herself had connections with the clan that was hated by the majority of Highlanders. Did Coll realise what he was about? She saw amusement in the brown eyes and tried to hide her smile. He knew! His smile deepened as he handed her a glass of punch, and between them there was a look that stated he would go no further than to enjoy the girl's company. What a wicked rogue he was, but so like Mairi in his ways . . . although far more adventurous. 'Please do not allow your head to be turned by Coll here. He is lovable, but utterly untrustworthy, and we do not wish for another clan war, do we?'

The girl laughed at her frankness, yet when Coll offered her his arm, she went with him out into the Great Hall and joined the dancers. Roy's eyes followed them thoughtfully—a trifle wistfully, Anne thought as she looked up into them.

'Perhaps next year,' she ventured to say.

'I don't understand you.'

'Yes, you do, my love. Mairi will be here again . . . I pray for it every night, for I know you desire it with all your heart, even though you have said nothing to me. I pray for you all to be together again and the bitterness between you forgotten.'

'It can never be forgotten,' Roy returned.

'Put aside then, so that we may live beneath this roof in harmony. If . . . No, you may misunderstand . . . ' He looked at her sharply, questioning her hesitation. 'Do you think it would help if I spoke to your father? If we—the two of us—found her and brought her back.'

'You don't know what you're saying, woman.' She recoiled from the harshness of his voice, grew embarrassed as several people turned to gaze at them curiously, attracted by his loud tone. Bring Mairi home? Was she serious? Then he would have to question her about what she had seen that day at her brother's house and he wanted to forestall that day for as long as possible. She had not lied in what she believed she had seen—he told himself, but had she deliberately come out on the side of her brother because she was of his blood and Mairi was already tainted with her mother's affair?

'Very well, I will not mention it again. I wished to try and make you happy, that's all. You have made it very clear to me this past week, that your thoughts are preoccupied, and who else could do that, but your sister?'

'Mairi is my responsibility, not yours. Nor my father's.' Roy forced a smile to his stiff lips. His words admitted she was right in her suspicions, that although he did not discuss his sister with anyone, she was always in his thoughts. He had not forgotten—nor forgiven—Anne realised. What would happen when Ewen walked into the room? Would he keep his word to her or would Mairi rise up to demand he called out the husband he believed had rejected her so callously?

His responsibility! His words stayed with her long after he had left her to go his own way among his friends and she stood amid a group of chattering women eagerly questioning her about the love-match which had taken them all by surprise. Roy maintained he did not know where his sister was—or the child which must be two or three months old now. Once only, he had hinted he accepted that Mairi was at fault, or had she misunderstood. His manner now seemed to indicate otherwise. She accepted he loved her—but maintained Ewen was not to blame. Anne had seen with her own eyes, Mairi and James embracing, watched them walking and riding together like two lovers. Neither seemed to care about the gossip they caused. James had not been easily led, yet he had fallen under Mairi's spell, as if bewitched. 'Sorely maligned' was how he had once described her to Anne. And Ewen as 'blind' and indifferent. How so? Ewen had been infatuated with the girl from the first moment he met her, had married her knowing how the MacKenzies would react—and then within months had found himself a cuckold—his role as husband taken by a mere stable-lad.

And this was the woman Roy still adored with every breath in his body and longed to bring back to Tigh an Lóin. Was he driven by pity for her, or true love for the sister he had never really abandoned? If the latter, it was becoming apparent that he had deliberately deceived her in allowing her to think otherwise. No, they had no secrets from each other. She knew him! Or did she? She loved him so passionately that she had been willing to risk her brother's anger to marry him and live the rest of her life with him. Yet, did she know what went on inside his mind? Had he not reacted strangely, even violently, when Ranald had wanted to give her his wife's jewels? The matter, she was sure, could have been resolved quite peaceably, without making a scene. He could merely have asked her for what he considered to belong to Mairi when they were alone together, and she would gladly have given them to him.

She had seen a side of him which alarmed, nay, frightened, her. Passion, other than for her, had surfaced, showing itself before his father and brother—and herself! Passion for his sister!

'Has your young lady deserted you already?' Roy

asked amusedly as he stood beside Coll while watching his wife dancing in the arms of another man.

'I am as desolate by her absence as you are for Anne by the black look on your face. Something wrong?'

'No. She—She is quick to notice things, that's all.'

'Your filthy temper of late? The way you have grown increasingly preoccupied as this night drew nearer? She isn't blind, my dear brother.She's an extremely astute young woman—and you are going to have trouble with her.'

'Nothing I cannot handle,' Roy returned quickly.

'Don't be too sure. By the way—as a mere precaution, you understand, not wanting anything to spoil this enjoyable evening—and not trusting the Frasers one iota—I have posted men at the main gate and around the house. If he does not come alone, we shall be warned.'

'I know.' Roy looked at his brother in appreciation. 'You're not as drunk as you look, are you? I, too, had the same idea until I saw how well we are guarded.'

'I do my best—in a small way.' Coll gave him a crooked grin, helping himself to two glasses of whisky from the tray of a passing servant. 'Here, get this down you. For medicinal purposes only, of course. Leave Ewen Fraser to me. Will you do that? Let me go after him when he leaves here tonight, and settle with him. For Anne's sake, if not your own.'

'And have Father turn you out of the house?'

'I'm not likely to leave a calling card. I can handle him . . . '

'No. He is mine.'

'So you are still determined to destroy your marriage. You are a fool!'

'I promised Mairi he would pay.'

'And what did you promise Anne when you stood by her side and took your marriage vows? Can you remember? I suggest you do—and soon. He must arrive within the hour if he's coming at all.' Coll turned on his heel to greet the reappearance of his companion.

Anne searched the room for Coll and finding him, quickly made her way to his side as soon as he was alone again.

'I gave heed to your warning,' he said as she came to his side. 'I am allowing the love of my life to seek the company of others, less worthy than me.'

'She is infatuated with you—I suspect this is not the first time you have met,' she said lightly. Despite his red cheeks which gave cause for many frowns about him, the eyes which considered her were quite serious. She had seen him talking with Roy and she was curious about their conversation. 'Where is your sister, Mairi?'

His eyes widened a fraction before he shrugged his shoulders.

'God knows.'

'And Roy? Does he know?' Anne insisted. 'I think he does. I want to know too.'

'Why—what can you do for her that he cannot? Bring her home? Leave well alone, Anne, you will only be hurt, and I do not want to see that happen.'

'You do know something. I knew it. Tell me, please.'

He hardened his heart against the entreaty in her voice, the pleading look in her blue eyes.

'I know nothing. I have not seen or heard from Mairi since your brother turned her out of his house to fend for herself,' he lied.

'I don't believe you. You both know where she

is . . . I can feel it. Roy has been acting so strangely lately. I thought he was anxious about tonight, but now I am certain he has another reason.'

'Accept what I say for your own sake. Lass, why do you torture yourself? Is he not enough for you that you want to take Mairi's place in his heart as well as in Father's?'

'Roy accused me of that. It's not fair—and not true,' Anne whispered indignantly. 'You are looking at me as if you pity me. Why should you, Coll? Am I blind? What is happening that I do not know about? He has found her, hasn't he? Why did he not tell me? This is her home, where she should be. No matter what has gone before, her family love her.'

'Some women would be averse to sharing their home with another. Especially as things between you and Mairi must have been awkward, to say the least, before you went to France.'

'I was mistress of James's house until he married, and then I shared it with Frances. I tell you I liked it not, but what other choice did I have? James and I were too close for me to leave because of her . . . '

'And Ewen? Are you close to him?' Coll asked slowly. He prayed that she was not, and inwardly shuddered when she nodded, a slight frown masking her features.

'Of course I am. He is my brother. Our behaviour at times is quite contrasting, and I cannot say truly that we are as devoted as I was to James—but yes, we have great affection for each other. Before I met and married Roy, he was all I had. He has been maligned, Coll.'

'Maligned? He! Not from all I've heard.'

'Give me proof! I saw Mairi and James together in his room, kissing. I saw the way he kissed her—I heard him say to her . . . " if only I had met you first." '

The colour receded from Coll's cheeks. The sincerity in her tone told him she believed the scene that had been enacted before her eyes. She believed her brother and ·Mairi had been lovers! She was innocent of the crime of deliberately lying to protect Ewen Fraser as he had at first thought—as Roy feared and refused to consider, because to accept that fact would mean she had deceived him. Coll did not think her capable of such guile

'As always Coll succeeds in commanding the attention of the prettiest woman in the room.' Roy's amused tones behind her made Anne swing round with a gasp. How long had he been standing there? Had he overheard their conversation?

'And as I am about to be deprived of her very special company, I must turn my attention elsewhere,' Coll said with a grin. 'Difficult though the choice will be after you, my dear Anne, I shall console myself as best possible.' Turning quickly away, Coll left them.

'What were the two of you so deep in conversation about?' Roy asked as he led her towards the dance floor again. 'And looking so serious,too.'

'Am I not allowed to converse with your brother without you thinking . . . ' She broke off as a gleam sprang to his eyes.

'You are even more beautiful when you are angry, do you know that,' Roy laughed as he swung her into the midst of the dance floor. 'I must do it more often. Your eyes flash with blue fire and there is a touch of green in them, like the sea on a stormy day . . . and your cheeks flush with bright colour, like an innocent maid who has had a first kiss stolen from unwilling lips.'

'Oh, you are impossible,' Anne gasped, unable to remain angry with him when he held her more tightly against him than propriety demanded. A blush began to stain her cheeks as he laid his lips against her hair and whispered audacious suggestions as to how they should occupy themselves when everyone had retired. He was incorrigible!

'I am,' he admitted modestly. 'And you rouse the very devil in me when I see you closeted with Coll like—like . . . '

'Brother-in-law?' she suggested sweetly, and his eyes glittered with wicked lights as he stared down into her upturned face. 'I will never think of him in any other light. Why can you not accept that we are friends?'

'He is a man, isn't he? And he likes looking at you. I know my brother.'

'He says the same about you.' He was jealous! The knowledge swelled her with sudden joy. Jealous of her spending time with his own brother. Why was he not more honest with her all the time? She did not understand why he chose to be so casual about his feelings for her whenever anyone else was about. How different he was in bed! Then he was his own master, and hers too, and she revelled in his mastery of her body, his acceptance of the love she offered and which he took and returned with an eagerness and passion never allowed to be shown before the rest of his family.

'Does he, now! Do you presume to know me also?'

She looked up into the handsome face and shook her head, longing for the ball to be over so that she could be alone with him. Would she never cease to want him so ardently?

'I am content with what you give me now. If you

wish me to know more—share more with me, then you know I shall be willing to do so,' she answered quietly. There was a momentary lull in conversation, a slight fluttering of fans, together with hushed whispers as he bent his head, found her lips and soundly kissed her in the midst of the dancing.

'You—You have shocked everyone,' she gasped as he led her from the floor, cheeks flaming.

'I have indeed. Most of the men here tonight would prefer to kiss their mistresses than their wives. Perhaps I have set a precedent.' His amused gaze considered the faces in front of them before Anne saw his mouth tighten as his eyes wandered across the room. As she, too, saw the two figures standing beside his father in the doorway, her fingers immediately tightened over his arm.

'Ewen! He has come,' she breathed, and Roy quelled the momentary surge of anger which had possessed him at the sight of her brother standing in Tigh an Lóin. This was for Anne because he loved her, but he did not like it, and he knew from the looks on the faces of the men around him that Ewen's presence had brought disharmony to what had been a gay gathering.

The musicians stopped playing, dancers retired from the floor and stood at the sides of the room, their attention centred equally on Ewen Fraser and the woman at his side and Roy.

Waiting for a sign to fall upon them, he realised. If he so much as flickered an eyelid in displeasure, his enemy would be dead within minutes. Coll came pushing his way to the front of the onlookers to face his brother. Coll too, Roy thought, praying for a fight. How easy it would be to whisper a few words into the right ears when the Fraser left later on. Roy would never have to touch one hair of his head, he

would be blameless of his death—yet he could not
bring himself to delegate the matter to anyone else,
not even his own brother. It was a personal thing
and he must deal with it regardless of the consequences to himself and his marriage. If Anne loved
him, she *must* understand.

'We must greet him,' Roy stated.

'Yes, quickly, before your kinsmen fall upon him
like a pack of wolves. See how they look at
him—with such hatred.'

'Can you blame them? The Frasers and
MacKenzies have been at each other's throats for
years. It has become a way of life for all of us. Have
no fear, my love.' He gently patted her hand as he
led her towards the door. 'Your brother is under my
father's roof and will be protected.'

'I did not realise what I was asking when I invited
him. I should have gone to him . . . ' Anne had
become deathly pale and he could feel her hand
trembling beneath his own.

'Nay, this way is right. He will see you as mistress
of this house and my wife. Is that not what we both
want?'

She looked at him, her eyes questioning. 'Of late,
I am not sure what you really want. You have me,
and I thought that was all you wanted, or needed.
Now, I am not so sure. These past few weeks I feel
as if there is a part of you I do not know and which
you do not wish me to see . . . '

'You are still angry over Mairi's jewels. I was
tired, love—irritable . . . '

'And you resent the fact your father has placed
me in the position that rightfully belongs to your
sister. I am not a fool, Roy. I not only saw your
disapproval—I felt it and I was hurt. I have not
deliberately pushed my way into his affections. He

is lonely . . . and he misses his true daughter. If you know where she is, bring her home. I never want to see that reproachful look in your eyes again. I do not deserve it.'

'Ewen—welcome.' Disengaging herself from his grasp, she hurried to her brother, her hands outstretched to greet him. He looked older, somehow, she thought, noting with some concern the hard line which now deepened the thin mouth. She saw that he wore his sword, and a sgean dubh showed above the top of his stocking. He had come prepared for trouble! She slipped her arms round his neck and kissed him and felt an involuntary response. He was embarrassed and angry at her for her elopement. She had been thoughtless not to realise he had probably compared it to his own runaway marriage to Mairi. That had ended in disaster. Hers would not, she silently vowed. 'I am so happy you have come.'

'Are you?' Ewen eyed her, not without some surprise flickering in the depths of the pale blue eyes. They were alike in looks, Roy saw as he watched them together. But what else? 'Once we were close as brother and sister should be, yet when you find yourself a man to wed, do you tell me? Ask my permission to wed him?'

'I am of age, I need no permission,' Anne replied quickly. 'Besides, what would you have said had I told you I wished to marry Mairi's brother?'

Only she could have uttered that name so innocently, Ranald thought, pride swelling inside him at her stand. What a woman his son had chosen! What grandchildren they would give him. The MacKenzies of Tigh an Lóin would live for ever with such a stalwart bloodline!

'I would have shut you away until you came to your senses.'

'Then you have your answer as to why I said nothing. Besides—it all happened rather quickly.'

'And had you attempted to keep Anne from me, I would have had to come and fetch her,' Roy murmured and Ewen Fraser lifted his eyes to the face of the man who stood beside his sister and hatred burned there for all to see. He cared not! This man had bedded his sister! Mairi's brother! He was well aware of the man's feelings for him and those of his kin. He adored his baby sister with every breath in that huge frame . . . and now Anne was his wife . . . he could not accept it even now, standing before them and hearing her say so calmly how pleased she was to see him. Anne in the MacKenzie stronghold of Tigh an Lóin . . . Anne, the wife of the man whose narrowed black eyes told him he would pay for his ill-treatment of Mairi.

'By heaven, if he has seduced you . . . ' he began, and Anne interrupted him with an angry toss of her head that almost dislodged the carefully arranged curls.

'Ewen, you presume too much! Have you ever known me to allow a man to touch me? I am the wife of Roy MacKenzie because I wish to be. I love him and he loves me. His family have accepted me . . . Look around you, see for yourself. What—What happened between you and Mairi is your own affair, not ours. We wish only to seek our own happiness. Will you deny me that?' She took his hand and lifted it towards Roy. He stood like a statue, his eyes glittering at her words. God, how proud she was! She would defy Dhommil Dhu himself to get what she wanted. 'Roy, your hand——please. For me.'

He thrust it out, unthinking. The hand which clasped his was limp, like that of a child, with no manliness about it, and he quickly withdrew his own with a look of distaste.

'There, now . . . you are friends. Family,' Anne said.

'Am I not also family?' The woman at Ewen's side regarded her with a slow smile. She was exceedingly beautiful with raven black hair coiled into a tight knot at the nape of her neck and covered with a jewelled net. Diamonds shimmered at her throat and on the fingers she extended towards Roy. 'As no one else seems in a hurry to introduce me, I will do it myself,' she purred, her voice all velvety softness as she gazed into the handsome face before her and liked what she saw. 'I am Frances Fraser, the widow of James.'

'I know who you are well enough,' Roy said, touching her fingertips to his mouth. As he released her, his gaze considered her in a way that Anne thought almost insulting, although she sensed Frances adored the boldness of his eyes. 'Had I known what I was missing in not paying my respects to you—both—earlier, I would not have been so remiss in my manners.'

'You are forgiven. Ewen and I both understand Anne's desperation to keep you to herself. She never did have very much luck in holding a man—and you, Roy MacKenzie, are a man indeed. Anne, my dear, you are to be congratulated. Keep a tight rein on him, or he might escape.'

'I have no need of reins to hold a man,' Anne returned with icy sweetness in her tone. 'When you know love as we do, you will discover the ties are far more binding—and they outlast all manner of inducements—temptations, shall we say?—to stray?'

The rouged cheeks deepened into a scornful smile as Frances linked her arm through Ewen's. They had never liked each other. Frances had not only gone straight from James's bed to that of his younger brother, but to those of many men who took her fancy. Anne had never understood why they had not sent Frances packing months ago. She disrupted lives wherever she went with her sheer contempt of rules and morality. Poor Mairi, already under a cloud from her birth, had no doubt learned a great deal beneath her guidance. At least, that was what Anne suspected had led to Mairi seeking her pleasures elsewhere. Perhaps Ewen, sometimes too boisterous and egotistical for his own good, was remiss in his treatment of his wife, preferring his horses and his friends to the creature who had left her family to be with him. But he had loved her. He had sworn it on the Holy Bible. Only Frances had emerged unscathed from the unpleasantness. And now Ewen was still her target. Anne had expected him to be cast aside long ago, but still she clung to him—or he to her. She had a strong will, she would seek to dominate him with the force of her personality, in place of love—affection.

With pride blazing out of her lovely face, Anne took her husband's arm, saying coolly, 'Roy and I both wish you well at this festive time of the year and hope you will enjoy yourselves while you are beneath our roof.'

Roy could feel her quivering as she held his arm, yet marvelled at the calm front she presented. No one would have guessed the anger she felt towards this other woman. An adventuress was what she had called her. A whore would have been his description. Brazen, unfeeling, ambitious, and a whore!

'The MacKenzies of Tigh an Lóin have bid you

welcome, Ewen Fraser, have you no words in return?
Take out your spleen on me, man, when we are
alone, but not on the sister who loves you,' Roy
drawled, a dangerous note in his voice. He felt
Anne's fingers tighten on his sleeve, but did not look
at her. He had meant to say these words, but with
a different interpretation upon them. They had been
meant to goad. But he said them now in all sincerity
because he could not bear the anguish on his wife's
face. And in this moment, strange as it was to
him—so hard to accept—she mattered over all. 'I
have shaken your hand in friendship. Does that
mean nothing to you?'

'You are sure?' Ewen's words were for Anne
alone. She smiled into his anxious eyes, ignoring the
sharp look Frances directed at him. She was jealous
of what Anne shared with her own brother? How
could she be? With an annoyed protest as brother
and sister drew close together, she withdrew her
hand from Ewen's arm, offered it instead to Roy
who accepted it without a word. He led her into the
other room under Ranald's angry gaze, but Anne
was prepared to accept that her husband was merely
trying to keep the peace she so desired, and took no
notice.

'Come, let us talk,' she said, drawing him away
to a quiet corner of the room. They found themselves seats and sat down. 'I am happy, Ewen, you
can see that. Do you not wish me well?'

'He is *her* brother!'

'Am I to lose the man I love because your marriage
turned sour on you?' she whispered, only too aware
of the eyes turned in their direction. 'Look at them!
Like hungry wolves awaiting a kill. They want to
see you and Roy at each other's throats.'

'I came here for you,' Ewen muttered, not liking

the strength of her argument. Love! He had never known it. He had married simply to try and avoid the snare looming up before him in the shape of his brother's wife—and failed. Within a week of his marriage to Mairi, Frances had come to his bed again. Even when Ewen tried desperately, hopelessly, to try and end the web of entrapment, she had crawled into his bed and pleaded for his love. He—fool that he was, idiot to believe her—had allowed her to stay. He had never loved the pale-faced girl who had given up everything to marry him. She had been his means to respectability while his brother lived. Now, with James dead, he still sought to condone his actions by blatantly lying about her adultery.

Mairi, an adulteress! The little fool worshipped him, and for a while he had been able to lose himself in her blind adoration. And then Frances had become impatient with the new woman in his life, sought to revive his attentions, and succeeded. The whore! He wished her dead a thousand times—yet could never bring himself to end her life. So long as she came to him, wove her spell about him, he would want for nothing else! He had rid himself of an unwanted wife to have her—to keep her—even knowing she would still look elsewhere for her satisfaction and no doubt receive it from fools like himself who grovelled beneath her feet for want of a look, a kiss, a caress. He had lied and debased himself for want of a woman! God forgive him! And the child he had disowned for love of her! His seed and that of Mairi. Shy little creature that she was, she had given him a few moments of pleasure, made him forget the vixen who clawed at his back demanding satisfaction, demanding the world from him. If he had it, he would give it to her . . . Frances owned him—body and soul—and conscience!

Now, just when he thought he could hold her—bind her to him with a common bond of the blood he had spilt for her—his sister had taken it upon herself to marry not just any man, but a MacKenzie! The brother of his wife. Of all men to choose from, she had found him. Or had he found her? He had made no secret of his suspicions regarding the ill-fated liaison, and when Mairi had been turned out of the house, Roy MacKenzie had sought him out in Inverness, and uttered dire threats against his life if anything happened to her. And now he was Anne's husband! An uneasy feeling rose in the pit of his stomach as he stared at his sister. It was obvious he had not told her of their encounter, and his threats.

'I am thinking you married in great haste. If he did not seduce you, why was that? You would have won me over in the end, you know, and, as you say, you are of age. I could not have prevented it, anyway. But I would have liked to see you married at the house, with your friends about us. In mother's wedding gown. It was his doing, wasn't it? He wanted it kept a secret.'

'We both did,' Anne said, frowning slightly as she followed the two figures on the dance floor. Roy was smiling at something Frances had said. She had her head thrown back as she looked up into his face. How the brilliant red of her gown complemented the raven hair. On any other woman the vivid colour could have been too harsh, but not for Frances. She wore it well and knew it. Knew she had caught the eyes of many men as she passed. 'This is why we arranged this ball, Ewen, so that we could all come

together and do away with any feelings of mistrust
and enmity.'

'You ask too much!' her brother answered, his
mouth tightening. 'The Frasers and MacKenzies
have been enemies too long to be friends now.'

'Over what? This is our opportunity to end it.'
She could not understand his reluctance to bring
peace to the two families.

'Do you not know?' Ewen gave her a searching
look. 'It was a Fraser from Strath Spey that stole
the wife of Ranald MacKenzie. When the clans came
out in the '15 uprising, MacKenzie followed the man
on to the battlefield and killed him there. Two of
his brothers as well. That is why we shall be for ever
enemies. With his dying breath, Stuart Fraser swore
he was innocent of the accusation. MacKenzie cut
his throat as he uttered it.'

Anne lifted a hand to her mouth in horror, her
eyes rising to where Ranald stood smiling and chat-
ting to his guests. Yes, she believed it. The violence
that had possessed him then, now possessed her
husband. They were alike not only in looks, but in
temperament. Ranald had mellowed with age, Roy
had yet to do so. He had shown her he was unpredictable—and dangerous—and completely oblivious
to any opinions other than his own, where Mairi
was concerned. A chill began to creep through her
body, even though the room was exceedingly warm.
A coldness instilled by fear of the unknown. Something was terribly wrong. She sensed it and fought
to remain composed beneath her brother's scrutiny.

'I'm sorry, I thought you said he loved you. A
man in love has no secrets from his woman. What
else has he not told you, my dear? That he came to
see me in Inverness when his sister deserted me—threatened my life?'

'You turned her out of the house,' Anne whispered faintly. A confrontation between Ewen and her husband! Why had Roy not told her?

'A woman eight months gone with child? Nay! That is his story. The child was not mine, you know that, which is why she went. Left before its birth proved to me—and the whole world, the extent of her wantonness. My own brother . . . others . . . ' He broke off, veiling the satisfaction in his eyes as she paled even more. How many times had he told the same story to his friends. They all pitied him, as she had, and did now at this very minute. Poor Ewen! He was so word-perfect that there were times when he almost began to believe it himself.

'Go on.' Anne did not want to hear more, yet she knew she must.

'I do not think MacKenzie has been at all honest with you. Of course you were away in France when Mairi left, and we encountered each other. We did not part on good terms, did we, Anne? It was my fault. I felt—I know you did not mean to imply it either by word or inference, but I felt as if you blamed me for what happened. I beat her, I admit it. When I discovered she had—bedded—with James, I lost my temper and beat her. You know what happened, of course. She went to him. You saw them together in his room!' He ran a hand across his eyes with a sound resembling a groan and Anne laid her cheek against his arm, wishing with all her heart she had not left so hurriedly after James's death.

'If we had talked . . . ' she said brokenly, and his hand covered hers. To her relief there was no reproach in his tone as he answered.

'James was very special to us both. He destroyed me when he stole my own wife from under my very nose. Had it not been for Frances's understanding during those months after his death, I think I would have killed Mairi with my bare hands. Despite the unhappiness that woman had caused, Frances begged me to allow her to stay. She thought with James gone, our marriage might succeed, but . . . ' He shrugged his shoulders, conscious of her hanging on his every word. Every carefully spoken lie was intended to drive a wedge between her and the man who was a danger to them all—if he lived! 'Mairi took other men . . . and, in my desperation, I do not deny it, I turned to Frances for consolation. She gave it freely. She, too, had been betrayed. We drew strength from each other.' He paused, allowing his words to sink into her stunned brain.

'I do not think you know what you have done,' Ewen murmured.

Anne raised her head, her eyes troubled. So many thoughts crowding into her mind, demanding to be answered. Only Roy could do that—but would he? She would demand it of him. It was her right!

'I do not understand you.'

'I think you have been used, my dear.' He always talked to her in a fatherly way she thought, and her heart warmed towards him for his concern. Used? It was not possible. She would have known. A woman could sense these things in a man. Why then did she still feel so uneasy? 'What devious revenge he has planned, I know not, but married to you! Can you not see he intends to make you live a hell for what he believes I did to his sister!'

'No!' Anne cried sharply, and curious eyes turned in their direction. She fought back the tears. Roy loved her! He was different from other men, too arrogant by half and inclined to keep his own counsel, but such cold-bloodedness was not in him.

There was fire in his blood and in his temper when
roused. He could not have controlled himself with
her had he hated her so. And to exact the kind of
revenge Ewen was suggesting, he would have to hate
her with every breath in his body!

'Yes. How long did you know him before you
married? Three months? Four?'

'Four weeks,' she murmured, and he swore under
his breath. Now his suspicions were confirmed. Anne
was the weapon the MacKenzie had chosen to use
against him. Draw him out into a fight. Ewen was
no coward and despite his treatment of Mairi, for
whom he had never cared at all, he loved his sister
and the desire to protect her which rose in him now,
was far stronger than he had ever imagined possible.
If he could persuade her to return to him it would
solve everything. Frances would not like the idea of
sharing the house with another woman again, but
when she considered the advantages, of Anne's
return, she would accept it.

'The man was spawned by the devil himself. You
cannot stay with him. Leave with me—tonight.'

'If—as you believe—he has married me only to
get at you, he would come after me.' Anne forced
the words through stiff lips. She was no longer aware
of the gay music and laughter floating about her.
She heard nothing but Ewen's voice. He could not
be right!

'Have you not answered your own doubts, then?
He means to use you to reach me—believe it! You
know of his reputation surely—with the ladies of
Inverness? Yet from all those he knew—and knew
well from all I've heard—he selected you—Anne
Fraser. My sister . . . Four weeks, you say! He
must have struck up an acquaintance with you only
days after he threatened me. Would that I had taken

him up on his challenge that day, I could have
spared you this misery. I am willing to oblige him
at any time, now I know what he has done—and
why. I am no match for his blade, but at the end of
a pistol barrel . . . '

Anne became aware that the dancing had stopped
and that Roy was leading Frances to the floor
towards them. She felt the room spin giddily about
her. Tearing her hand free of Ewen's grasp, she
jumped to her feet to seek sanctuary in the Great
Hall where many people had begun to gather to
sample the excellent fare laid out on the long tables.
She glimpsed the look of surprise on her husband's
face at her sudden exit, but she was relieved he did
not attempt to follow her. She needed to be alone,
to compose herself before she approached him and
asked him to deny Ewen's preposterous accusations.
He would, of course. Roy loved her. Nothing could
change that. She sought to lose herself and her black
thoughts by dancing with whoever asked her.
Anything rather than face him at that moment. He
would laugh at her fears . . . no, he would be
angry, perhaps driven to seek her brother out and
demand an apology and that could lead to a fight.
Perhaps she should wait and mention it to him on
the morrow. It was not as if she believed Roy could
have been so cold-blooded as to deliberately entrap
her into marriage just to get at her brother. Had he
done so, he would never have given her his promise
not to be the first to draw his sword in anger. But
he had also said if Ewen challenged him, that he
would defend himself. Could he be hoping for that
on this festive occasion . . . hovering over Ewen
like a kestrel about to pounce? No! No! She was
mad to allow her thoughts to be tormented so.
Tomorrow she would tell him what Ewen had said

and they would laugh about it and dismiss it.

'What did you say to make Anne rush away like that?' Roy demanded, glowering at the man who rose to greet them, a smile lurking at the corners of his mouth. He did not attempt to hide his dislike now Anne had disappeared. 'If you have upset her . . .'

'You will what, MacKenzie? I see you wear no sword.' Ewen's fingers slid to the hilt of his own, his tone contemptuous. 'Are you expecting others to do your dirty work for you? Or are you a coward?'

More insults froze on his lips as three inches of shining steel showed itself beneath the lace ruffles of Roy's sleeve. The glittering eyes, full of hatred, challenged him to go further.

'If I had my way, I would drag you outside and finish you, Fraser. I promised my sister I would seek revenge for the falsehoods you have told about her and your inhuman treatment of a young girl you no longer wanted and cast aside like an old boot. And don't spout any more lies at me, for I know them to be totally untrue.'

'My sister will be interested to hear that,' Ewen murmured. 'The poor misguided woman actually believes you married her because you loved her, but we know otherwise MacKenzie, don't we? You wed her to get at me—well, here I am. You don't think I came alone, do you? I've fifty armed men outside this house. If I don't leave here alive, you will have a massacre on your hands. It bothers me not. I shall have the pleasure of killing you and taking Anne home where she belongs.'

'To live with you and your whore? The bitch that took Mairi's place?' Roy cast a baleful glare at the silent woman standing at Ewen's side. He sensed she was waiting for a fight to break out between them—he could feel her anticipation—the mounting excitement inside her. She didn't care for Ewen Fraser, he realised, any more than she had probably cared for her late lamented husband, James. A woman like her did not know how.

'You are ungallant, Mr MacKenzie,' Frances said quietly. If weapons were drawn between these two she fancied Anne's husband to win. He was part-man, part-devil when his temper was aroused, she suspected, the kind of man she liked to have round her, not weak and easily led like her present para-mour. 'However did you obtain such a reputation with the ladies, since you possess such ill manners?'

'Most of them were whores, like you,' came the cutting reply. 'And, like you, they were well paid.'

She gasped and stepped back, almost cannoning into Coll who had moved across the room to position himself directly behind Ewen. The brown eyes which regarded her, stripped her bare of her fine clothes and for a moment, she felt a chill of fear envelop her. This one would slit her throat without hesitation, for all his play-acting as a drunken fool. Against the two of them Ewen would stand no chance, he would never leave Tigh an Lóin alive. But, then—neither would she!

'You will apologise to the lady—or we go outside and settle this . . . '

'If there was one present, I would gladly do so.' Roy ignored the threat and returned the sgean dubh beneath his sleeve out of sight.

'I promised Anne I would not fight you here. There will be another time, Fraser, another place. I shall haunt you until death will be a release. Don't keep me waiting too long . . . '

'So much for your given word,' Ewen sneered, but the menacing voice, so velvety soft, yet with

murderous undertones, told him there was no escape
from this man's revenge. 'Anne will learn of your
treachery . . . '

'She will believe me, Fraser, I promise you that. I
can be most persuasive when I choose—and I happen
to love her. That is the only—do you hear me, the
only—thing that matters to her. She will accept your
death because it will be either you or me who returns
to her—and the odds, I think, are in my favour.'

'Good heavens, I do believe you are serious!'
Frances ejaculated. 'How extraordinary—to fall in
love with her after her giving witness against Mairi.
You do know, of course. It was Anne who told
Ewen about the little scenario between your sister
and James.'

Somehow Roy contained the red haze of hate
which rose before his eyes, the desire to hit this
woman who had struck at his one vulnerable
spot—to call for a sword and cut down his enemy.
Without a word, he turned and walked away from
them.

'How much does Anne know?' Frances asked,
when she had drawn Ewen away to a quiet spot.
She could still feel Coll's eyes watching them across
the room. 'What did you tell her? MacKenzie didn't
like the way you were both looking so serious. He
didn't like it at all. Perhaps we have a weapon there.'

'I'm surprised you noticed. You couldn't take
your eyes off him then—or just now.'

'Is my little Ewen jealous?' she laughed softly,
relaxing her body against his in a way she knew
always aroused him when he was in a foul mood. 'I
thought one of us should find out what is going on.'

'You heard what he said. He loves her. Not that
I believe it for a moment. He's using her, damn
him!'

'No. He's besotted with her. Haven't you seen the way he looks at her?'

'You are wrong. Old Ranald is terrified of more scandal; he would never have allowed his son to challenge me . . . People might have remembered another occasion when a MacKenzie and a Fraser fought. The simple solution was to marry Anne and bring her here. She's a hostage, don't you understand that?'

'Have you told her this?'

'No. She loves him, God help her! I tried to make her see what he is about, but it is she who is besotted. His hold on her is too great.'

'Then we shall have to do something about it, won't we? You—we—need Anne at home again with us, don't we?'

'If I have to kill him to free her, I shall. She is my sister, and I won't let anyone hurt her,' Ewen said harshly. 'Anyone at all. Understand that. What has to be done, will be achieved without one strand of her hair being touched. It's time we left. I feel as if there are a dozen dirks itching to sink into my back . . .'

'Just one—mine.' Coll stood before them as they turned, swaying slightly. Wine from the full glass clutched in one hand, spilled out over the skirts of Frances's gown.

'Look out, you drunken fool!' Her angry tone died abruptly as her eyes alighted on the three clansmen who had suddenly appeared at her side.

'Outside,' Coll ordered. 'Follow me at a distance. I don't want my brother or father to see what we are about.' His words were clear and precise, not the slurred, jumbled nonsense of an inebriated man. 'Hamish here will escort your woman, Fraser—first. Should your backbone not be strong enough for you to face me, instead of my brother. I'll not have you ruin his marriage. Escort the lady, Hamish. Keep a tight hold on her arm now, she looks a little faint. A breath of fresh night air will revive her.'

Ewen had no choice, but to follow in Frances's footsteps as she was propelled across the room towards the corridor. Coll led the way to a side door, reeling unsteadily and clearing a wide path through amused guests, who did not give a second glance at the people following him at a distance. The Frasers were here on sufferance and few acknowledged them.

CHAPTER SIX

FROM ACROSS the room, where she had been waylaid by one of Roy's maiden aunts, a terrible romantic whose questions about their hasty marriage flowed non-stop, Anne watched their departure with worried eyes. What was Coll up to? Where was he taking her brother and Frances? Was he forcing them to leave—or had Ewen voiced his intention of doing so and asked for Coll's company, so that there would be no trouble until they were safely out of the house? Why then had he not come to bid her farewell? Something was very wrong. Roy was drinking with friends and had not seen them quit the room, neither had Ranald.

As soon as she was able, without seeming rude to the old woman, she made her way after them, taking care that her exit was not noticed either. A servant at the main door told her that neither Coll nor her brother and his companion had passed him. Then where were they? Upstairs? But why? In another room? The door to the library was open, and she could just see a few of the guests who had adjourned to relax and enjoy quiet conversation away from the music and noisy chatter. None of the faces she sought was there. Outside, then . . . Her heart grew cold. Outside could mean only one thing . . . an argument—a fight!

She turned on her heel about to return to the other room to tell Roy, and then froze. If Ewen had spoken the truth about him—if he had only been using her, this was exactly what he had been hoping for. She would be playing into his hands if she appealed to him for help—signing her own brother's death-warrant. She had no one she could turn to—not in this MacKenzie stronghold. She was part of them, and yet she stood alone in this moment of crisis. Who would lift a hand to aid a Fraser?

She shivered as she stepped out of a side door into the cold night air. How quiet it was. Not a sound to break the stillness of the snow-laden court-yard. How silly she was, her nerves had been playing her tricks. There had to be a simple explanation for their disappearance—and then her eyes fell on the line of tell-tale footprints leading away from where she stood towards the gardens. They *had* come this way. More than three people too, at least five. Picking up her skirts she quickly crossed the court-yard. As she reached the trees which bordered the wild, rambling flower gardens, she heard the ominous sound of steel clashing against steel . . .

Despite the festivities, Coll had not consumed his usual amount of whisky that evening, but he had been drinking—and his reactions were beginning to slow. He swore as Ewen lunged at him and his sword barely missed his arm. The man was better than he had estimated. Roy could have taken him easily, but Coll was beginning to sweat freely. His shirt began to cling to his back despite the chill wind and flurry of snowflakes. If he got himself killed or injured, his brother would not rest until the Fraser was dead and his marriage to Anne would be at an end—the very thing he was trying to prevent.

'You are going to die by my hand, Fraser,' he said thickly. 'I'll not allow you to ruin my brother's life as you have my sister's.'

'So that he and Anne can live happily ever after.

Such brotherly love, such devotion,' Frances mocked from beneath the arbour where roses bloomed profusely in the spring and summer. 'Are you sure you are doing this for—him?'

'Hold your tongue, woman, or you'll share his grave,' Coll threatened, slipping on the treacherous snow-covered ground and falling to one knee. To his surprise, Ewen waited for him to recover his balance.

'I'm right,' she ejaculated triumphantly as she stared into his eyes. Instantly, Coll knew that she had successfully guessed the emotion he had been able to hide from his father and brother. If Anne's eyes had not been only for Roy, she would have seen it too! 'It's Anne! You are doing this for her. You want her for yourself! Two MacKenzies after the same woman.' She laughed, and his fury increased. 'You are fighting the wrong man! Surely it is your brother who should be here . . . '

'Damn you!' Coll's concentration was shattered by the revelation of his secret. He had vowed no one would ever know. In that brief moment as he glared at Frances, Ewen side-stepped from the path of his threatening blade, struck out and sent the weapon spinning from Coll's grasp.

'Kill him,' Frances breathed, as Hamish and other clansmen began to move forward.

'And have our throats cut by his men before we reach the gates? No, he shall be escorted out of here—our safe conduct.' The tip of Ewen's sword caressed Coll's exposed throat above the lace of his jabot. 'You are coming with us. Your brother will follow and I will kill him and free my sister. Within a week she will be back where she belongs with her own kin. Oh, I know you have more men hidden about the place, MacKenzie, but my men are just

outside the gates, within calling distance. One sound
from you will bring them in here. I shall allow them
their own—entertainment in the house before we
leave here and I then kill you *and* your brother.
Think on it before you open your mouth.'

'Put up your weapon, Fraser.' A figure detached
itself from the shadows of the trees behind Coll.
Frances took an involuntary step backwards at the
sight of Roy's murderous expression, the silent fury
lurking in those dark eyes as he stared, not at her,
or even Ewen, but the weapon menacing his brother.

Coll inwardly groaned, not for his own predicament, but for the worsening situation he had brought
about by trying to kill Ewen Fraser himself. And
how long had he been hidden while they fought!
What had he heard! Dear God, not that!

'And have your men cut me down?' Ewen gave a
brittle laugh. 'Call them out—I shall take your
brother first and then you.'

'I promised Anne I would not be the first to draw
my sword, which is why I am not wearing one,' Roy
retorted coldly. 'You are free to leave, and take
your—whore—with you. But the next time . . . '

'There will be no next time—only here and now,'
Ewen rasped. If there were more MacKenzies in the
trees and bushes they would have revealed themselves or he would have heard them. The fool really
had followed them alone. Ewen's face a mask of
hatred he lunged towards his enemy, the sword
arcing towards his throat. Roy flung up an arm to
protect himself, at the same moment throwing himself
backwards to avoid what could have been a fatal
blow. As it was the blade sliced across his arm and
a deep red stain began to seep through the blue
velvet of his sleeve.

'Roy—catch!' He did not want a weapon—he did

not want to fight—he had promised, but even as those thoughts ran through his mind, he reacted instinctively to Coll's cry, spun about his uninjured arm and caught the sword his brother had tossed to him. As his fingers closed around the hilt, he felt an awful coldness settle over him—had fate decreed he must kill Ewen Fraser here—tonight!

'You have drawn first blood, Fraser—and freed me from my oath. I swore I would kill you. I didn't realise how easy you would make it for me.'

'No, you would prefer a back alley so that you can tell Anne I was set upon and murdered by footpads, no doubt,' Ewen sneered.

'I can see what is happening for myself. At first I didn't believe you, Ewen. Forgive me, but I loved him so . . . ' Anne came tottering towards them like a ghost. Her body was numbed by the intense cold, her mind by what she had heard—and now saw. Roy—a sword in his hand, prepared to kill her brother. He had promised! Everything her brother had told her was true. He had married her to get to Ewen—not for love. For revenge! And she, gullible innocent, had fallen into his trap. And Coll was part of it, probably Ranald too. They had all lied and deceived her, conspired together to make her a tool by which they could get to her brother and she in her blindness, her love for Roy, had made it possible.

She felt weak. With rage, indignation, the pain of the rejection crushing her beneath its enormous weight. He did not love her. He had used her! She shook her head dazedly, unable to comprehend such hatred. She had never known love until she met Roy MacKenzie—nor this new terrible emotion which frightened her even more.

'Thank God you have come!' Frances cried. 'These MacKenzies have brought us here to kill us. Help us, Anne, for the love of heaven!'

Anne scarcely heard the plea, convincing though it was. Her eyes were riveted on her husband's bleak features. His gaze penetrated her very soul. What did he see there? Hatred—for her too? What else? He would have no use for her once Ewen was dead and his revenge complete. Her face was as white as the snowflakes settling about her shoulders as she fought desperately to gather her self-control. Deliberately she stepped closer to her brother, watched Roy's eyes narrow warningly and then with a deep breath moved in front of him, shielding him from her husband's sword.

'Stand aside. Anne, do you hear me. I did not want it this way, but I was provoked.'

' "I swore I would kill you. I didn't realise how easy you would make it for me." ' He swore vehemently as she repeated his words. They fell from her set lips like a death knell. 'I heard you . . . '

'And what did you see? And hear, besides that,' he challenged. 'Look at my arm. Your brother struck first. Coll will confirm that.'

'He is lying! They came upon us as we were leaving. Coll MacKenzie offered to escort us to the gate to avoid any trouble. And then he—your husband was waiting for us.' Frances lied easily and convincingly. If she and Ewen were to leave Tigh an Lóin alive that night, Anne had to believe the worst of her husband. Ewen had already sown the seeds of mistrust earlier and now she continued with the wickedness, secretly revelling in the look of agony on Anne's face. This love-struck idiot had unknowingly caused her many problems. To resolve them she had to be kept alive and return to Eskadale with her brother. There she could be dealt with in whatever manner was necessary.

'She lies,' Coll interrupted fiercely. 'It's true I was with them—I fought with your brother, Anne. I meant to kill him and save Roy this—this . . . but . . . '

'Now—or later, it had to happen.' Roy's voice was totally void of emotion. 'I was a fool to think I could get away with it.'

Anne gasped as if he had struck her. An admission from his own lips!

'He doesn't mean that. Not the way it sounds,' Coll said anxiously. 'This was my doing, Anne, believe me. I wanted to save your marriage. I knew if it ever came to a fight—and it would some day—and your brother was killed, you would never forgive Roy.'

'As I shall never forgive him for using me—lying to me.' Anne's voice was barely audible above the wind whistling through the trees. She had been too far away at first to hear what was being said and as she tried to approach closer, skirting thick rhododendron bushes, taller than she herself, her view had been obscured. She had come up behind her brother to hear Roy's fearful threat and see how purposefully the weapon he held was pointed at her brother. There was no doubt in her mind if she had not intervened he would have killed him there and then—still might unless a miracle happened.

'I love you, Anne. Believe me. If you don't, we have nothing.' Roy MacKenzie had never begged for anything from anyone in his life.

'Tell me—swear to me, that the past is over and done with, that you will never again raise your sword against my brother?' Anne demanded. 'If you love me—if I mean anything to you at all—you will do this and I will stay with you and perhaps we can salvage something from this—this near tragedy.' She was begging too, he realised. Begging him to remember how it had been between them, the tenderness, the sweet moments . . . the considerate way he had made love to her at the lodge that first night.

Coll held his breath as his brother wavered, prayed he would lie in order to save what little remained of their happiness and from there, perhaps build again, to make a secure future for them both. And then he looked into his brother's eyes and saw despair—indecision—acceptance—and knew he could not do it. Even for this woman he loved before his own life.

'I do love you. I would willingly prove it to you—but I do not make promises I cannot keep—in bed or out of it. I do love you, Anne. I always shall, no matter what happens between us now. You are my wife and unless your brother kills me, he will not take you from me. You have no say in the matter,' he added sharply as she opened her mouth to speak. 'Tigh an Lóin is your home and I am your husband. If you wish it to be any other way, then you have only to stand aside and let us fight. Your brother may be the better swordsman, though I doubt it.'

'How can you say you love me when you want to kill him?' she cried, unable to follow his reasoning.

'The one has nothing to do with the other. I love you and I married you. Ewen Fraser abused my sister and will die for it. If *you* love me, then you will accept I am capable of both hating him and loving you.'

'Did I not tell you Mairi was the only woman who meant anything to him,' Ewen sneered. 'He admits it. I see the way his mind works now, don't you? To marry you after false protestations of love, to bring you here, to heap this humiliation on your head before all his kin and friends—is this not what I am supposed to have done to his sister?'

'You go too far . . . ' Roy snapped, his fingers growing white around the hilt of his sword. 'You cannot believe that of me—to be so cold-blooded—so devious,' he appealed desperately to Anne.

'I saw a part of you I did not know when you faced your father over the jewels he wished to give me.' Anne's lips trembled visibly. She was swaying unsteadily—Coll thought she might faint—but she did not move from in front of her brother. 'Perhaps I never knew you. You are not the man I fell in love with.'

'My name is still MacKenzie,' he reminded her brutally, and she flinched at the taunt. 'As is yours now. You are no longer a Fraser.'

'Would that I was. I would give anything to turn back the clock. I wish I had never set eyes on you!'

'Then stand aside and your brother and I can finish what we have started. He may kill me and you will be free to go back with him.'

'No.' Anne's eyes blazed with defiant blue fire. 'You have a choice. Him—or me. Let him go, and—and I will stay with you—as your wife.'

The blood drained from her husband's face. He moved his injured arm, flexing the fingers which felt frozen, as was the blood which had soaked through the velvet sleeve. Stay! To turn from him when he tried to touch her, look at him with loathing in her eyes now she knew the truth. He had gambled and lost. She was no longer his. But she would stay, he would see to that—and the terms would be his. And as for her brother . . .

'You should not have forced the issue with me, woman. Take her, Coll!'

The last words came out like a whiplash. Before

she could grasp his meaning, Coll had flung himself upon her, plunging her backwards into the snow, holding her down, helpless beneath him with arms tightly around her. She screamed as Roy lunged forward, forcing Ewen to defend himself. The wind whipped away the distraught sound as if it had never been uttered. She fought against the arms which held her, abusively shouting at Coll, but he continued to hold her fast, without a word. All his attention was centred on his brother and the hatred on the dark face, the skilful way he thrust and parried, driving his enemy back towards the trees.

'No!' She screamed again as Ewen fell back against a gnarled oak and could go no further. This time it was Roy's sword against his throat. She could not believe this was happening. A few hours ago she had considered herself the happiest woman in the world . . . in love, with a wonderful husband. Now she felt betrayed, and used. In only a few minutes her whole world had collapsed about her.

'Put up your sword!' Ranald's vibrant tones rang out in the cold night air. 'Both of you, drop your weapons, or by heaven, son or not, I will have you cut down where you stand.'

Anne nearly fainted with relief as the old man came into her vision accompanied by a dozen armed clansmen and many guests, also with drawn swords or dirks.

'Stop him! Please. He is going to kill my brother,' she pleaded.

Ranald's steely gaze fastened on Roy's face, the returning arrogance as he faced his father, defied him, replacing the terrible look of hatred he had seen a moment before. Ranald's eyes fell to the blood-soaked sleeve and they registered momentary surprise. Roy was more of a match for Ewen Fraser, yet he was the one wounded.

'Put up your sword,' he thundered, as his son clung stubbornly to his weapon. Ewen's had been thrown aside instantly. An act which brought contemptuous looks from many of the men surrounding. 'So the word of a MacKenzie is his bond, is it? You gave *her* your word.'

'This is not Roy's doing, Father, but Fraser's,' Coll interrupted, as he released Anne and helped her to her feet. She pushed him away fiercely, her blue eyes blazing, as she ran to her brother's side. Roy's eyes followed her, but she did not see the pain mirrored in their depths for he quickly looked away and held out his sword to Andrew MacKinney who stood to one side of him.

'That's a filthy lie,' Ewen cried. He knew that every man looking at him wanted him dead. Only Ranald's fierce Highland pride, which would refuse to allow him to be killed while he was a guest in his house, could save his skin this night. 'He forced me out here. Mrs Fraser is witness to what happened. Do you think me a fool, Ranald MacKenzie to draw a weapon here!'

'And you must think I have some kind of death wish to try and fight you . . . ' Coll chuckled and his voice was suddenly slurred, his steps unsteady as he came forward to face his father. 'I'm too drunk to best him, Father. He came at me from behind while I was taking a little fresh air and disarmed me . . . '

'Coll, it doesn't matter now,' Roy said quietly. 'It's done. He provoked me, Father, and I fought back. If you had not come I would have killed him and not regretted it for an instant. It was for Mairi.'

'And what about your wife?' Ranald demanded.

Was his son mad to have risked the happiness of them all?

'Nothing has changed between us.' Roy did not look at Anne as he spoke. He dared not. He did not want to see the contempt and loathing in those eyes which had once looked at him with love. 'She is still my wife and will remain so, here at Tigh an Lóin. My love for her has not—nor will diminish. Neither will my desire to see her brother dead for what he did to Mairi. But I did not break my word to you—or to her. You should know me better than that.' He grimaced as he lifted his injured arm and a rumble of anger ran through the onlookers. 'I did not strike the first blow, nor draw first blood. Can you tell me you would have reacted differently had he attacked you—if you had seen his sword at Coll's throat would you not have gone to his defence?'

Ranald knew he too would have defended Coll, but he remained silent: one look of anger towards either of the Frasers and they would be dead within minutes. Beckoning forward two men, he ordered in a tone which brooked no argument,

'Escort the Fraser and the woman to their carriage. They are not to be touched.' The order was not well received, but Ranald was their chief and his word was law. Even so several looked expectantly towards Roy, as if hoping he might countermand the order. He had the feeling had he done so, they might have disobeyed his father and that he would not allow.

'You heard my father.' Roy frowned angrily as Ewen spun round on Anne and caught her hands in his, whispering, 'Come with me. He dare not touch you . . .'

Before Anne could answer, Roy stated, his voice as cold as steel, 'These men are my kin. MacKenzies. They would love to kill you. She stays. She is my wife and her place is here with me. Fret not, Fraser. I'll not wait until she is eight months with child before I turn her out.'

Anne's eyes turned to her husband, slowly, unbelieving of the words she had just heard. She did not realise that the anger he had been unable to vent on Ewen was now directed at her. It had reached a point where he could contain it no longer. So much for her great love, her protestations of undying loyalty, her resolve to stand by him no matter what happened between them. She loved her brother above him. He could not forgive her for that—any more than he could forgive himself at that moment for placing Mairi's happiness before his own. Love for his sister before that of the only woman he would ever love in his lifetime.

'Come to me when you can,' Ewen whispered as he bent to kiss his sister's cheek. 'If there was a chance here . . . but you know there is not. I shall free you, Anne, I promise. Free you from this house and—him!' A flicker of acknowledgment passed over her face, but she spoke not a word.

'Do not try my patience too far,' Ranald thundered. 'You have brought disruption to my house. Go now—if you wish to live.'

'Yes, go,' Anne whispered. 'I will not be the cause of more trouble—that is what *he* wants.' She did not look into Coll's troubled face, nor into the derisive eyes of Frances. Her gaze was riveted on the man she had married, the betrayer of her love.

'So much for the close blood-ties of the Frasers,' Roy taunted as Ewen turned and took the woman's arm and in silence they followed Andrew MacKinney towards the gate. Behind them the two clansmen ensured no one else attempted to follow.

'He has more sense than you give him credit for,'

Anne retorted, sudden life flowing back into her numbed body at the realisation Ewen was safe. Within minutes he would be with his own men, riding back to Eskadale. He could come for her, she knew, or rescue her from this predicament in some way—and she would go with him. She would not stay at Tigh an Lóin. 'At least my brother is a man! He has not hidden behind a woman's skirts in order to have his revenge. He will face you anywhere, any time you choose, my loving, devoted husband—and I hope I am there to see him kill you!'

'Anne, no!' Coll gasped. 'You don't mean that. You are overwrought. You love him.'

'Love!' She swayed back from both brothers like a sleepwalker, yet still in control of her emotions. Roy felt great pride swell inside him at her marvellous stand but then reality returned to wipe it away. She would fight him! He had not considered this! He had been so sure she would understand—accept what had driven him to his desperate deception—and had been prepared to wait for her to do so, however long it took. Conflicting emotions raged through him as he considered her. Hatred, anger, pride, the love he could not kill—that she could not even kill even when she looked at him as if he was the devil's own. 'You are a liar and a cheat.'

She flung the words at him with a defiance that even Ranald found surprising. She was no milksop. She would not grovel for his son's affections.

'Be careful with your words, Anne. Have we not hurt each other enough this night? Let it end here.'

'End here? It will not end until you have killed my brother and well you know it. You fool! You, arrogant, blind fool! Ewen did not come up to your sister's expectations and so she sought her pleasure elsewhere and in doing so, has ruined his life—and that of my brother, James. And now mine. That is the truth you refuse to accept.'

'Hold your tongue,' Roy threatened, stepping towards her, but she held her ground and a spasm of shock passed through his body as he realised she was not afraid of him. That made her dangerous—to him—and to herself! Did she want him to harm her so that Ewen would have a reason to call him out? She was out of her mind. Yet she had placed herself between him and her brother—defied the weapon menacing her. Protecting Ewen, as Roy was protecting Mairi. His clenched fist fell to his side and he did not touch her.

He was conscious of Ranald's eyes on him, beseeching him to have pity on her. Pity! She needed none of that. And for him to take her side! It incensed him. Why had he not sided with his own flesh and blood—his daughter when she had needed him?

'If you cut out my tongue, I will still somehow tell of what I saw that day. I have often wondered why you have never asked me about it. Now I know. Ewen you can discredit, because he and Frances are lovers. I don't deny it, nor does he. When his wife deserted him for others, he turned to her. She, too, had been deserted by her husband, if you remember?' She was totally without pity. She, who had tried to remain impartial in the conflict, now found herself throwing accusations, condemning where she had never done so before. '*I* saw them together. Your sister and my brother, James. Listen well, my husband and you, Ranald MacKenzie. I loved James above all people—even Ewen. We share much—that you in your hate and ignorance, would not understand—but with James . . . '

'When he died, a part of me died with him. I had

to get out of the house, away from Ewen and Mairi's constant bickering, away from Frances and Ewen seeking consolation together. And so I went to France for six months. When I returned—not to Eskadale, but to my own house in Inverness—your sister had left Ewen's house. As she was carrying the child of another man, I think him tolerant to have allowed her to stay until her eighth month.' She cried out, as Roy crossed the space between them and slapped her across one cheek. As she reeled backwards, he delivered her another blow which slammed her back against the gnarled oak where not long before he had held Ewen at his mercy.

He stood over her, hands clenched, prepared to deliver more should she malign his sister. Never before had Ranald and Coll and all the watching clansmen seen Roy so incensed, as he stood over Anne. Slowly, she raised her head and looked at him. The imprint of his fingers stood out against the chalk-whiteness of her skin. She was beautiful in her defiance and he shrank at what he was becoming in his quest for revenge. He loved her—how could he hurt her so cruelly, even in his anger?

'So much for the great love you bear me, Roy MacKenzie,' she scathed, still challenging him and he had to fight to contain the conflicting emotions inside him which would have made it so easy for him to strike out again at her—and so release the tumult tormenting his soul.

'I have said I loved you, woman. That is why I married you. That is why you will stay here at Tigh an Lóin with me—as my wife! I shall not say it again to you. If you wish to hear it you will go down on your knees and beg, do you hear me? You have had me acting like a love-sick calf since the first moment I met you. That is past now. I have your worth now—you lie like all Frasers to protect your own.'

'You will find you have paid a high price for your few hours of pleasure,' Anne returned dully. She began to shiver, from the cold and from the shock which had been thrust upon her, shattering her happiness. Coll stepped towards her, but one look from his brother brought him to a halt. He still did not know how much had been overheard of his conversation with Ewen Fraser. Roy was in a murderous mood. 'I shall pay an even higher one for not taking a lesson from my brother's misfortune. At least his marriage lasted three months . . . '

'No, damn you!' She had driven him too far! Coll was in front of his brother as he lifted his hand to strike that lovely face again. 'You have what you want. Be content!'

Ranald stared at his two sons, watching the conflict which raged on both their faces and knowing this was one time he could not intervene. Coll was showing more strength of character than he had ever thought possible—and was suddenly very sober! And Roy! His heart warmed to his eldest son. They were forever quarrelling about Mairi, but he had been prepared to sacrifice so much, and yet his father had not stood by him in his moments of agony. He would desert neither of them again. He was fast growing old and he allowed Roy to assume the full responsibilities of the estates without realising how his days were spent in endless torment. He wanted both his sons—he wanted his lost daughter—and he wanted most of all, for the frail-looking woman who faced Roy like a tigress at bay. Most of all he wanted her, for the strong bloodline she would give the MacKenzies. And he loved her too—as a daughter.

Roy's eyes narrowed as he contemplated father, brother, wife in turn, knowing to show weakness now before any of them, would be his undoing. It was to the latter he addressed himself, ignoring the other watchful eyes and listening ears.

'You will do to remember I have a short temper where Frasers are concerned. Our marriage will last as long as I want it to. Accept that, and save yourself further pain.' He stepped back from her, eyes now blazing. 'Go to your room and get out of that wet gown before you catch a cold. Your devoted husband will join you when I have made your apologies to our guests for leaving them this early, although,' and the heavy sarcasm in his voice brought a slow flush to her cheeks, 'a glass of whisky and the company of my father and brother are rather more to my liking than yours at present. Take her upstairs, Coll.'

Without a word Anne turned away from him and allowed Coll to escort her into the house. They entered through a side door and made their way upstairs by a servants' staircase which kept them away from the main house and curious eyes. Had she not seen the way Roy had reacted with her brother, listened to his devastating words out there in the snow, to which they had all been oblivious, Anne could have believed his concern for her was genuine. But of course it was not. He cared only that he might not be able to come to her bed and so provide his father with the grandchild he desired.

At a distance Roy followed. Ranald dispersed the men and slowly trailed in his son's footsteps. Roy watched as in the sanctuary of the library, fortunately now deserted, he went to the decanter and glasses on the table and poured out two large whiskies, pushing one towards his father.

'How satisfied you must feel over this night.' The words fell heavily from Ranald's lips and he knew he was inflicting more pain, but they had to be said. He did not like what he had seen emerging from his son—it was as if they were two different people—and yet he could not deny that he would have done the same at his age faced with the same dilemma. They were too much alike! 'You could have accomplished as much if you had seduced the poor child out on the moors.'

'No, I could not, because I was not planning for this night to happen as it has. Believe me, Father, I love her. Perhaps she will hate me for the rest of her life, but you will have your grandchild—and for what it is worth, I shall have her. I just didn't think . . . ' He bowed his head. Ranald came forward and laid a hand on his shoulder. 'I didn't think she would turn away from me. Not if she loved me.'

'What did you expect her to do when you try to kill her brother? Embrace you? Give her time. This will pass.'

'Time for the hatred to fester and grow—as mine has done,' came the bitter reply.

'Love can turn so swiftly to hate, given the right circumstances,' his father replied and Roy turned to stare into the suddenly grave features.

'One day you will tell me about Mairi,' Roy said quietly.

'Perhaps she is a love-child, perhaps not. I only know I loved her mother to distraction and when she took a lover, it broke me. Perhaps I was not gentle enough with her, though dear God, I tried to be. I am not a man to show his emotions, both you

and Coll know that. I could have driven her to
it . . . the night she came back to me . . . ' He
turned away, tight-lipped, and Roy knew he might
never know what had happened between them. Had
Mairi been born from that night . . .

Had it not been for the firm support of Coll's hand
beneath her arm, Anne knew her legs would have
given way beneath her as she climbed the stairs.
Outside her door he stopped and stared into her
face. He looked concerned, but she refused to accept
that he was. He was Roy's brother and had known
what was planned for this night.

'Don't fight him, Anne. He does love you. Accept
it.'

It was late by the time Anne stumbled into her
room, and she was glad Agnes had gone to bed. She
wanted no one to witness how she gave way to her
emotions when she was alone.

She swung round, surprised, as Coll stepped into
the room behind her.

'Leave me. Go back to him and tell him I am
safely locked up for the night . . . like the obedient
little boy you are,' she taunted indignantly.

'Anne, for God's sake! I admit I knew of his need
for revenge . . . but the way things have been
developing between you, I thought . . . ' Coll
floundered for words. They had seemed so happy
together, so content in each other's company! 'I
would not hurt you for the world.'

'You have his smooth tongue!' How she wanted
to trust him—or anyone!

'Don't be angry with me . . . ' He came close to
her. She could smell the brandy on his breath, and
froze, wondering what new indignity was about to

be thrust upon her. 'Anne, can we not be friends? You will need one . . . '

His arms closed around her without warning, his mouth sought and found hers, stiff with horror and disgust. She remained unyielding in his embrace, and when he drew back, she slapped him hard across one cheek.

'Now you can go back to your brother and tell him it did not work. I will not fall into your arms—or his—even to save my life!' she cried. 'And I began to trust you . . . '

'You should . . . it was not meant that way.' Coll backed away from her, a hand against his smarting cheek, his eyes bearing a look of rejection. 'I wanted only to let you know you still had a friend. And you have, Anne. If you need me, you have only to send for me.' He dared not say more.

'Get out!' She began to shake with rage and indignation. Was she to be spared nothing! 'And don't forget to lock the door . . . as he ordered you!'

Accept it! Accept what? The words screamed in her brain as she sank down on to the couch, the sound of the key turning in the lock echoing over and over in her brain. Accept the lovemaking of a man who detested her? To spend endless days a virtual prisoner at Tigh an Lóin, while Roy plotted the death of her brother?

How easy a victim she had been for him. How he must have laughed at her as they lay together. She buried her face in her hands, unable to bear those memories, which had once been everything to her.

He had said he would come to her. Her eyes flew frantically round the room, seeking something to push against the door. She found a heavy chair, and supported it against the wooden panels, with its back beneath the door handle. Let him try and disturb her now! And then she remembered the communicating door between their rooms, and ran to take out the key—only to discover it was not there. Someone, she could guess who, had been there before her and removed it. She had no way to prevent him from coming to her bed!

He would gain no pleasure from it, she vowed—if he had ever done so in the beginning. She would not allow herself one moment of pleasure as she lay in his arms. Her mind and body would reject him totally . . . but was she strong enough?

A long while later—she had no idea of time as she sat, head in hands, on the couch, her mind was still fighting against accepting the inevitable. Agnes had turned down the bed before she retired and laid out one of Anne's prettiest nightgowns on her pillow. She seized it and threw it into the furthest corner of the room, searched through the chest of drawers until she found a plain lawn one. She would never make herself attractive for him again!

Awkwardly, tiredly, she struggled out of her lovely gown and left it where it fell on the floor. The bed was cold despite the warming-pans, and she huddled beneath the covers in a miserable heap, her tears wetting the pillow beneath her cheek. Better to shed them now, she reasoned, while she was alone. When Roy came to her she would show no weakness, no affection, no tenderness. He had deprived her of everything except the breath in her body. He had killed everything she felt for him. In place of love, there was hatred. In place of gentleness, compassion— —there was only contempt . . . an urge to hurt him as he had hurt her. Yet how could she wound him? He had shown her, with the deviousness of his scheme, how ruthless he was, how immune to decent feelings. He was without honour!

And then, as she lay shivering in the huge bed, she remembered how Coll had seized hold of her and kissed her. It had not been a passionate kiss, meant to rouse her, to subject her to his will. Rather a brotherly kiss . . . and yet she had lashed out at him because she could not do so at his brother. Perhaps she had maligned him . . . yet he had known, he had admitted it. A friend, he called himself. If only she could believe that. How she needed one now! To be able to go to him and confide her fears, beg him to help her escape from Tigh an Lóin. If he cared for her at all, perhaps he could be persuaded to aid her.

A sudden thought struck her in the wake of this hope. She had seen Mairi and James kissing and had judged the girl's unfaithfulness by this one incident! If Roy had come into the room as Coll was kissing her—a gesture of affection, meant to offer comfort, would he have believed them innocent?

Had she seen James not offering love, but comfort, to a tearful, disillusioned girl whose marriage was falling apart about her ears? If so, then it was possible it *was* Ewen and not Mairi who was at fault—Ewen, who had lied to save his own face. Ewen who had driven his wife from the house with accusations which might not face up to close scrutiny. It had not mattered before because he had had her love—her trust—her complete loyalty . . .

Could she have been so blind? Ewen, not Mairi, seeking a way to end the marriage by any means possible? And in the background, Frances, hovering, ready to offer her own special kind of solace to him in his need. Frances and Ewen!

She had not been faithful to James, Anne knew,

but apart from one brief time when he had spoken of his determination to keep her, he had remained silent on the subject and refused to be drawn. His fierce pride would not allow him to turn her out of his house and so cause a scandal and bring dishonour on the house of Fraser. His name meant everything to him. No more would he have allowed Ewen to do it. Had he lived, she suspected he would have found a way to ensure Mairi remained his brother's wife. But he had not lived . . . a tragic riding accident had deprived him of his life.

Anne stiffened as she heard someone at the door. Outside, a man muttered an oath and moved away. Minutes later, as she sat upright, eyes wide with apprehension, Roy came through the door leading to her sitting-room. The bedroom was in darkness. She had needed no light to illuminate the room, for a full moon was shining through the windows. He came nearer to the bed, stripping off his coat as he did so, unfastening the jabot at his throat, the buttons of his shirt.

'Go away.' Somehow she managed to keep her voice level, as if she was in control of herself. Never had she felt less so. The thought of him touching her again sent her into near panic! 'Leave me alone! Have you not done enough to me already that you must heap further humiliation on my head?'

'You are my wife, and I expect certain—vows to be kept, whatever is between us,' he told her stonily, tossing aside the last of his clothes. 'I shall have you when it pleases me to do so, and if you are wise, you will not fight me.'

'You—You would force me to do your bidding?' she gasped, sliding across to the far side of the bed as he approached. 'You would not—could not . . . '

As she tried to clamber out, he threw himself

forward and caught her by the arm, dragging her back into the middle of the bed.

'If—If you dare to touch me again—I will kill you,' she swore, and he laughed in her face.

'Foolish Anne! Do you honestly believe you can sway me with such words—even a weapon? Do you want one? Here!' She found herself suddenly staring down at the dagger he had tossed on to the covers in front of her. Her fingers touched the cold steel and were quickly withdrawn, with his laughter echoing in her ears. 'You see! Brave words, but you lack the courage to carry out your threat. Like all Frasers, you do not have the courage of your convictions.'

'I married you, I went against my brother for love of you!' She flung the words at him furiously, and saw the broad shoulders lift in a shrug.

'It suited you to go against him. You didn't need all that much inducement either, did you?' he returned callously. 'He married in haste, too, did he not? You will live to regret it, if you fight me.'

His words broke the thin thread of her self-control. Without thinking what she was doing, she snatched up the knife, lunged at him with a cry. Heard Roy's sharp intake of breath as he averted the attack with a sharp downward movement of his hand that numbed every bone in her arm. The blade dropped to the floor.

'You bitch! So much for your great love! You are as treacherous as the rest of your kind. I must teach you never to be so foolish again . . .'

She tried in vain to avoid the hands which reached for her and cried out as her nightgown was pulled roughly over her head and thrown aside. She struck out at the face looming over her, raked at his cheeks with her nails, beginning to cry incoherently. He could not do this to her!

'Unless you want me to hurt you, be still,' Roy growled, burying his face in her loose hair as he coupled her wrists in one hand and the weight of his body stilled her frantic struggles.

'What do you care? Why should you consider my feelings now?' She was beyond reason as she thought of what he intended to do. Already the touch of him was making her recall how it had been before. Her love was too strong . . . too demanding of her. She could not fight . . . yet she had to do so to keep her self-respect. To do otherwise would be to proclaim how totally she was in his power.

'Damn you, I don't want to hurt you!' he ejaculated. 'But you are my wife, and I want you. You cannot deny me, I know it. I can feel it in you. Be still, you little fool!'

Anne twisted and writhed beneath him but he merely allowed her to wear herself out with her efforts. His free hand roved over her skin, igniting it with determined caresses that caused her to bite her lips to prevent herself from crying out and allowing her body to betray her.

At last, when she lay limp and spent, huge teardrops squeezing their way from beneath her tightly closed lids, he kissed them away, freed her wrists and said softly,

'I will never take you by force. You would like that, would you not? You could hate me then . . . run to Ewen and tell him how I have abused you.'

'I do hate you . . . and I will tell him . . . ' she threatened. 'Is this not force—rape? True MacKenzie style, from what I have heard?'

'Take care with your words, woman, or I might change my mind and show you what force is really like,' came the whispered warning from above her.

He took her in silence after that, subjecting her to the domination of his body with no thought for her own feelings. Yet, despite this, her body rose with his in the final moments before he rolled away and went to sleep, leaving her to lie awake and cry silently into the pillow, hating him—and herself for the love she could not kill. How was it possible to hate and love a man at the same time, she asked herself, as the first streaks of dawn penetrated the room.

Carefully she eased herself away from him, sat up to stare at the dark features beside her, so relaxed and boyish in sleep. He looked so peaceable. A stray lock of black hair curled across his forehead and she had to suppress the urge to push it away, as she had done so often before. She did not want to touch him ever again or have him touch her—reduce her to this low level. Yet if she remained at Tigh an Lóin, he could do what he wished with her and no one would question him.

CHAPTER SEVEN

QUIETLY ANNE STOLE from the bed, found her riding-apparel and dressed in the sitting-room. It was barely light and Agnes still snored in her bed when she looked in on her. Pulling a warm cloak about her, she slipped out into the corridor. No one was about yet. Like a shadow she negotiated the stairs to the Great Hall. Bodies littered the other rooms——guests who had decided to sleep where they had fallen rather than risk dropping from their horses by some frozen burn. Streamers hung haphazardly from the beams where someone had climbed up to try and rip them down.

An icy wind blasted her as she hurried to the stables and saddled the mare Roy had given her, knowing how capable it was of keeping its footing on the treacherous snow-covered ground.

She wavered as she mounted and her eyes fell on the finger where her wedding band should have been. She had removed it and left it beside the bed where her husband could see it when he first opened his eyes. Did he think he could subdue her by the force of his will? How little he knew of her. Anne did not consider herself a brave person, but neither was she a coward. She feared the other side of him, the black beast which had reared its ugly head and destroyed her happiness, but she would risk his enmity rather than stay and be ground beneath his heel.

She thought she heard a shout as she urged the mare out into the open, looked quickly around and discovered a sleepy-eyed stable-lad gawking at her. She ignored him. Through the gates, she galloped, under the noses of three dozing clansmen who had been left to guard the numerous carriages and fine-stepping horses which had come to Tigh an Lóin for the celebrations the previous day. She rode without thought of direction for a long while, afraid of pursuit, but when she reined in to get some bearings, she found the landscape behind her totally without other forms of life. As it grew lighter, the wind increased in fury, whipping away the cowl about her face, ripping the ribbon from her hair and tossing the curls about her cheeks in wild profusion until she was blinded. As soon as she had tucked them inside the cowl again, it was blown from her head, freeing her hair to whip and sting against her cold cheeks.

Which way? Inverness lay to the south—or was it east? The snow made it impossible to gauge where she was. If she could find the lodge, she knew the road to Inverness was but a mile away. A blur appeared on the horizon. It moved! Someone was coming after her! No, it was not possible. Wheeling her horse about, she plunged into the trees ahead and drew rein, watching. Closer, coming closer until she could make out a single horseman.

'No!' Her moan of distress was lost amid the howl of the wind. She would recognise that black horse anywhere. Roy! He *had* followed her. She rode like one demented, yet he closed the gap between them. The snow thrown up from beneath her horse's pounding hooves showered her clothes, and threatened to blind her as effectively as her hair had done. And then as she negotiated the bank of a riverbed, where icicles hung from the drooping trees like jewelled fruit, the mare missed her footing and stumbled, and she was thrown heavily to the ground.

Had the snow not broken her fall, she knew she would have sustained more than a bruised back. As it was, she lay stunned for several minutes, until as reality again threatened at the sight of the man bearing down on her, she clambered to her feet and looked around desperately for her horse. But before she could attempt to run to the mare she was thrown roughly to the ground again as Roy's stallion knocked her off her feet. This time she did not rise. She was winded, her head reeling, threatening to drag her down into the realms of unconsciousness. Hands grasping her by the shoulders pulled her upright and forced her head back.

'Are you hurt? Anne? Answer me, woman?'

'No.' She felt his body relax as she added with heavy sarcasm, 'I am undamaged. Still a negotiable item.'

'Damn you, you go too far.' Roy shook her until tears started to her eyes, then she was seized fast against his snow-covered coat and his mouth was bruising hers in a savage kiss that almost succeeded in doing what the fall had not. She lay limp, unresisting against him as he eased his mouth away. So terrible was her pallor, that he drew out the silver flask he always carried with him, full of usquebaugh and put it to her lips, ordering, 'Drink. You are frozen. You little fool, did you really think I would let you go? You could have been killed in weather like this . . . if you had not been able to get to your horse, or lost your way.'

'I care not what happens to me.' Her voice was hardly audible. She turned her face away so that he could not put the flask to her mouth again. Returning it to his pocket, he drew her to her feet, brushing the snow from her hair and clothes, pulling the cowl back over her dishevelled hair. 'You will be wet through by the time we get back to the house,' he growled. 'Now, do you come willingly, or do I tie you to your horse?'

Dull fire gleamed for a moment in the eyes which stared back at him, but she had no more strength to fight and reeled unsteadily to her horse, not even refusing his hand to help her mount. Taking the reins from her lax grip, he looked at her, considered the shivering form with something near to pity in his heart—but for a moment only. She would not run again—he would see to that.

'I should not have taken you like that last night.' The words did not come easily to his lips, but she looked so pathetic, so lost, and he was giving no ground by being kind.

'It is the only way you will ever have me,' Anne murmured. 'I will never willingly lie with you again.'

'Liar! You will not be able to prevent yourself. You could not last night, as I remember, for all your brave words and threats.' As if to prove to her how right he was, he leaned across and kissed her cold lips. Anne had no defence against this way of fighting and he chuckled grimly as an involuntary response softened her lips beneath his.

'You may be able to control my body, but not my heart—or soul. Those are my own. I hate you, Roy MacKenzie, do you hear?' She spat the words at him with false defiance, unable to bear the pain he had just caused her with his touch, slight though it had been. 'I loathe you with every breath in my body.'

His mouth tightened into a grim line. Turning their horses about, he headed them back towards Tigh an Lóin as fast as the unpredictable ground would allow.

'Take my wife upstairs, Andrew, and see her maid puts her to bed this instant. I do not want her catching a chill.' As soon as they were in the house, Roy's concern for her was shed like a cloak. Ranald came out of the library to meet them, with Coll close on his heels. It was the earliest either of them had been up and about for a good many years! 'I have brought her back,' he said to them. 'We had a slight—misunderstanding—but it is resolved now. Is it not, Anne?'

She raised dull, uninterested eyes to glance at him, and then into the faces of the other two men, and merely shrugged her aching shoulders. 'If you say so.'

'I do. You will not be going on any more of these early morning rides, will you?' Roy's voice had reached a dangerously low level.

'No. I shall do nothing that will give you any excuse to kill my brother. You will have to find some other way, Roy MacKenzie, for I shall be a model wife from this moment on. You will hear no word of reproach from me for your deceitful actions, the pain you have caused me . . . the love you have killed! You can do what you wish with me. Beat me, starve me, ignore me. The latter would be preferable, for I detest the sight of you! But if you come to my bed, I will not refuse you, although you will not find it satisfying to make love to a lifeless doll, for that is what I shall be in your arms from now on. I will not go to my brother for help. I will endure you until the day I die, but I will not be the cause of Ewen's death.' Lifting her head proudly, defiance now blazing from her strained features, she preceded the servant upstairs, with the regal bearing of a queen.

'By God!' Coll ejaculated. 'She's magnificent, even in defeat.'

'You talk like a fool,' Roy snapped. He was shocked by the vehemence in the words spoken to him. Glaring at his brother, Coll began to feel uneasy and spun around on his heel returning to the library, banging the door behind him.

Ranald was torn between following his son or going after Anne. Neither, he knew would thank him for his intervention. It was a battle of wills between two strong-minded, stubborn people and there could only be one winner. At that moment he did not care to wager who it might be. Resignedly he followed Coll into the library.

'I have sired a son without a soul,' he declared.

'Oh, Roy has a soul, Father, never fear. He could have let her run back to her brother, couldn't he? After all, that's what he wants—a reason to call out Ewen Fraser without causing you or the MacKenzie name any more humiliation. The way it will happen will be as much for you as it is for him, don't you see that? If only you were honest enough to admit to him you want the Fraser dead too! You could have saved a lot of this . . . no, don't look at me like that. There are times when I think your name means more to you than we do.'

'Coll!'

'You are getting old, Father. You want to live the rest of your days in peace. I understand that—but does it have to be at our expense? Do we have to watch every move we make lest we offend you? Roy is in love and it's tearing him apart. He cannot make the choice between wife and sister. Could you?'

'What would you know of love?' Ranald challenged.

Coll threw him a strange look. He had not slept

despite a fair amount of drink consumed after he
had left Anne. The memory of her lips imprisoned
beneath his would not leave him. For a moment
there was an unusually grave expression on his
young face. His eyes swept upwards, towards Anne's
room.

'You'd be surprised, Father. You really would,'
he murmured before leaving the library in search of
some breakfast.

As Ranald followed him, it was in his mind that
there was a possibility of both his sons being in love
with the same woman. Heaven preserve them all!

With the festivities over, Tigh an Lóin returned to
its normal quiet existence. Anne could have cried
with relief when the last of the guests departed.
Keeping up a continual pretence under their close
scrutiny was playing havoc on her nerves—yet
somehow she succeeded in convincing everyone she
was happily married and settled in her new home.

There were invitations to visit from many people.
She accepted as many as she thought prudent, realising Roy would probably restrict her movements
after her last escapade, but to her surprise he seemed
to agree with what she had done. She could come
and go when she pleased, he told her as they sat at
breakfast one morning, several weeks later. To
Edinburgh, his relatives in Oban, grandmother in
Kingussie—who had been too ill to make the journey
for Christmas—even to her brother. But if she did
not come back from any of them, he would issue his
challenge to Ewen Fraser and kill him without
compunction.

She was free—yet a prisoner. She saw pity in
Ranald's eyes as she rose and left them. Coll did not
look at her. She had scarcely said a word to him

since the night he had kissed her. It was proving an embarrassment to them both for she now realised he had indeed acted foolishly, but with kind intentions. Yet she could not bring herself to heal the rift and went her own lonely way day after day.

Roy came to her at night, but she never knew when he would climb into bed beside her, reach for her and demand without a word that she submit to him. She offered no resistance, bore his lovemaking in silence and, as she had hoped, his visits became less frequent, and he took to sleeping in his dressing-room. He had also begun to go out more, returning home in the early hours. He had a mistress in the village, Agnes told her, tutting and condemning the man who had abused her mistress with muttered curses under her breath. Anne found her language quite startling for an old maid!

Another woman! She found herself spending hours trying to visualise what she was like. The daughter of one of the estate tacksmen, Agnes said, a plain woman by all accounts, but free with her favours. He had gone to another! At first the news pleased her for it meant he would not bother her so often. She had come to dread it, for as desperately as she tried to remain unroused by his touch, he always succeeded in rousing her and in doing so, strengthened his hold on her. She loved him still! She could not believe it. Even now when she knew of his liaison with a strange woman, she wanted him still . . . hated it when he came to her and yet could not live without him doing so. She was in torment for days after the discovery of his unfaithfulness.

Gradually she began to believe this woman meant more to him than she did and she withdrew further into her shell of coldness. The silence and the tension between them mounted—and was only unleashed in nights of wild lovemaking which left her drained and bitter at the weakness which dominated her in the mornings which dawned afterwards. The moment they faced each other in the light of day, they were adversaries—enemies. Yet in the darkness, when he sought to lose himself in the mastery of her body, she was able to respond because he could not see her face—the torment in her eyes.

Towards the middle of February, Anne received an invitation to the wedding of a childhood friend, Sarah Keighton, to one of her Fraser cousins, Alan. The wedding was to be held at the family home of Drumnadrochit. She sat looking at the letter for a long moment, her mind beginning to race with possibilities. If she went, she would only be seven or eight miles from Ewen in Eskadale. Less than twelve from Inverness. She could travel there under the pretext of wanting to purchase some materials, having first sent Ewen a message to meet her at the house.

She had to find out what was happening and also put his mind at rest over her predicament. On no account was he to do anything which would antagonise the situation and result in a fight between him and Roy MacKenzie.

She chose an opportunity to broach the subject one evening when they were all in the sitting-room, enjoying coffee and brandies. Of late she had begun supervising the menus for the week, and Ranald was in a good mood after eating a late supper—a recipe she had remembered from France of chicken breasts soaked in butter and garlic covered in a rich pastry.

She had kept her word, and become a model wife. She ran the house more than efficiently and the servants were plainly relieved to go to her for their orders, rather than the unpredictable laird whose temper was never at its best first thing in the morning or late at night. Anne found them pleasant and willing to co-operate with her in new schemes. She spent the whole month of January redecorating the room in which they now sat. New cushion covers in bright velvets graced the chairs and sofa, re-covered in a bold print. The furniture, which she suspected had not been moved for years, was totally changed round, leaving free access to the french windows which opened out on to a walkway.

With the arrival of better weather, she took an interest in the gardens. Many more rose bushes and shrubs were to be planted and she spent hours on her knees beside the aged gardener, who found her a willing and eager pupil. If Roy disapproved of the way she spent her time, he never commented on it.

She looked across at the silent figure who sat with her letter in his hands. He was not going to let her go, she thought anxiously. There was a hardness about the set of his jaw as he considered the invitation—and the implications.

'Am I allowed to go?' she demanded quietly. She never raised her voice against him—had not done so since St Stephen's night when he had so cruelly claimed her. Anger did not affect him, nor tears . . . nor weakness. She had discovered a strength of character in her she never knew she possessed. It kept her going through the long days, made her put aside her problems and seek new interests, diversions to keep her occupied until the hours of darkness came . . .

'Drumnadrochit, is it? You could see your brother easily from there.' He looked up at her, the dark eyes gleaming suspiciously.

'I intend to go to a wedding, not a funeral,' she

replied. 'Send a man with me if you don't trust me, I care not.' She made it sound as if it was true, and Roy's brows drew together into a fierce frown. Should he let her go? So close to Eskadale. To Ewen Fraser himself. Wasn't this what he had been waiting for? Let her run to her brother. After a few days, he would follow and discovering that she was no longer at Drumnadrochit would give him reason enough to ride on to Eskadale—and demand her return. It would be refused, of course and then he could issue his challenge. Ewen Fraser at the end of his blade! How he had dreamed of the day. 'Of course you could always take me yourself, but the guests will be Frasers, and even you will not be able to kill them all,' Anne added sweetly.

'Let the girl go,' Ranald intervened. 'She hasn't been away from the house in months. She's not foolish enough to endanger the life of her own brother—she said so. And I believe her.'

Roy shrugged and handed her back her letter, hiding his apprehension.

'Go if you wish. How long will you be away?'

'Two days—three at the most.' Anne could barely contain her excitement. She was free to leave! Now if only she could convince Ewen of the futility of continuing this feud, she would have really achieved something worthwhile. She would have until the end of the week to prepare her moves. 'I shall leave on Friday.'

'Be back by Tuesday at the latest—or I will be riding to Eskadale,' Roy warned as she rose. There was no trace of alarm on her face as she looked down at him. What was happening to her? At night—on the occasions he visited her, which were growing fewer with each passing week, she lay like a lifeless object in his arms, forcing him to use every ounce of his skill and experience to rouse fire in her—he always succeeded, but not once had he been able to recapture the passion and tenderness they had shared at the lodge. Very often the sound of her sobbing quietly afterwards drove him from her bed. 'Take Andrew with you. There have been robberies on the road through Glencannich. Can you use a pistol?'

Surprised, she nodded. Andrew, his spy! No matter, she would find a way to see her brother even with him dogging her footsteps.

'I will give you one of mine for the journey. Keep it by your side until you reach your destination.'

On the morning she left Tigh an Lóin, he stood in the window of the library. He had not come out to bid her goodbye as Ranald and Coll did, nor had he spoken one word to her since coming into her room as she was dressing to give her one of the belt pistols she had purchased for him. It was loaded and primed, he told her as she carefully put it aside, together with the brass powder flask and small goatskin bag containing more lead balls and wadding. He was gone before she had a chance to thank him. His gesture had taken her aback. What devious scheme was taking fruit in his mind now for him to show such unexpected concern for her welfare?

She could feel his eyes boring into her back as she kissed Ranald on both cheeks and he helped her into the waiting carriage where Agnes sat disapprovingly. Was she making it so obvious that she hoped Roy would come out too, Anne thought, settling herself in a seat?

'Take care.' Coll leaned through the door, took her hand and touched her fingers to his lips with a smile that did not reach his eyes. Quickly she snatched it away, aware of the figure at the window, watching them. 'Are you sure you know how to use a pistol?'

'James taught me. I am quite a good shot. Well, I manage to hit what I aim at,' she replied, and he chuckled, lessening the awkwardness between them.

'Am I forgiven?'

'Yes. I—misunderstood.' Ranald had gone back inside so there was no one to overhear their conversation, except Agnes. She disapproved of Coll even more than Roy, with his easy-going manner and heavy drinking, his total refusal to accept responsibility of any kind. 'And I over-reacted. I'm sorry.'

'It isn't easy, is it?' he asked gravely and she shook her head, her eyes lingering on the library window. It was empty. He did not care enough even to watch her leave. Why then had he given her a weapon with which to protect herself? She did not understand him. 'Give him time . . . it cures all ills—deadens pain and makes the memory more acceptable to reality.'

'Sometimes I think you are not the fool you pretend to be,' Anne said quietly as he moved back and closed the door.

'I am but a poor Highland laddie bewitched by my brother's wife,' came the light-hearted reply, and she did not believe him for a moment. It was obvious to Coll she had not overheard what Frances Fraser had said and so put their close friendship on an awkward, if not impossible basis. But what about his brother? Did Roy suspect Coll's feeling towards Anne? Had *he* overheard Frances's words?

'What do the two of you have to blather about?' Roy demanded ungraciously as Coll returned to the house. He had come out of the library and was standing by the front door. Had he been about to interrupt their conversation, Coll wondered?

'This and that. You don't talk to her any more, brother. You should try it again—perhaps it will revive some of the old feelings between you. She's very lonely, you know.'

'You sound like Father. You would think it was my fault this has happened.'

'Isn't it? I did warn you one day you might have to choose between your wife and sister. And it is because things are the way they are between you that Father and I afford her our affection and treat her with the dignity befitting her position here as mistress of Tigh an Lóin. You still go to her at night, don't you?' Roy did not answer, the tortured look on his face was answer enough. 'Are you expecting her to suddenly forget what happened here? She has to learn to trust you again and if you don't help her, that will never happen.'

'Good God, man! I was almost on my knees to her that night. I told her I loved her—I proved it to her later . . . ' He broke off, a dark flush creeping over his cheeks. He was not a man to discuss his private life with anyone.

'She deserves better,' Coll said quietly. 'If she belonged to any other man, I'd take her away.'

Roy looked into the grave features and his eyes glittered dangerously. 'If anyone tries to take her from me, I shall kill them,' he answered bleakly. 'Don't even allow the thought to cross your mind . . . '

It was then Coll knew that he *had* overheard!

'Jealousy becomes you, brother.' He forced a smile to stiff lips. Nothing had ever come between them before to cause a really serious disagreement. He had never thought it possible. 'Why don't you try showing some of it in front of your wife.'

The wedding celebrations could not pass quickly enough for Anne, although she thoroughly enjoyed not having Roy's eyes following her every move. Andrew MacKinney, although he hovered close at hand, did not intrude in any way on her activities. He was as polite and helpful as he had been at the lodge during those idyllic honeymoon days which crept into her mind as she lay awake at Drumnadrochit after the bride and groom had slipped off on their own and the sound of laughter drifted up to the tiny room she shared with another guest for the duration of her short stay. She was as successful as she had been at Tigh an Lóin, at persuading everyone it had been a love-match between herself and Roy MacKenzie. There were frowns of disapproval from some members of the clan easily remembering past indignities they had suffered at the hands of the MacKenzies—in particular Ranald—but in the main, she was showered with good wishes and prayers for a family to bind them together.

A family! A child! More and more she was convinced she was enceinte, yet she dared not approach a doctor lest Roy hear of it. In Inverness she would seek one out to put her mind at rest. She could not be. She had heard of false pregnancies, caused by anxieties, problems . . . indeed she had her share of both. She was worrying unnecessarily. The fateful day over, she firmly refused offers to stay on, or visit aunts and uncles she had not seen in years and left for Inverness on Sunday morning. By midday she was installed once again in the Fraser house in Clathmor Street.

As the carriage had rattled over the bridge spanning the River Ness and into the regularly built burgh, she had found herself realising how little she had missed living here—despite everything. All the people she considered friends lived—or spent part of the year here, as she herself had done. There was a continuous whirl of activity: balls, town functions, hunting on the moors, tea-parties for the wives of the garrison officers. It was not a large place, but there was always something to occupy idle minds.

To her surprise, she came to accept that the only things she missed were the availability of good clothes and fabrics, and incidentals such as gloves and ribbons and French wine which she had come to enjoy during her stay in France. Tigh an Lóin was of course visited by chapmen, the Highland name for pedlars, but she had found their stocks inadequate for her needs. Many carried only the usual things like soap and candles, tobacco and dried fruits, needles and pins, but no fine silks for new dresses or bright ribbons for her hair. She would purchase what she needed on Monday before starting back for home.

It had been easy for her to send a messenger to her brother's house, decoying Andrew away on a false errand. She would use the same ruse when it was time for Ewen to arrive, she decided. Andrew MacKinney must know nothing of what she was about or he would report to Roy and her attempts to avert a disaster would have been all for nought.

She tried not to analyse why she was doing this. It was to save her brother from being killed, she had told herself time and time again on the journey—but always another reason jostled at the back of her mind, to save the life of her husband also. Roy was a master with a sword, with pistols too, but so was Ewen with the latter. If these weapons were used, either, or both might be injured—fatally wounded. She must prevent it at all costs. She prayed Ewen would accept her plea, understand her dilemma and do nothing . . .

She lived beneath the roof of a man who she believed hated her, yet came to her bed in an attempt to drive her from the house seeking sanctuary with her brother—his sworn enemy. She had not weakened so far, nor would she, whatever he did to her. The life she led was a private hell of his making, but she could not leave. Only his death would free her from the bondage he imposed. She prayed at night for her love to die and give her blessed relief from the torments of mind and body, but it remained as steadfast as it had ever been—hidden from his sight until the end of her days. He thought he had killed it and she allowed him to believe the lie for in its way it offered a strange kind of protection. He no longer mocked the moments they had shared at the lodge. In pretending she cared nothing for him any more—and had even grown to hate him, much of his power over her had diminished. Only at night as they lay together, did the truth rise up in the darkness to taunt her. She would never stop loving him! Sometimes the knowledge was terrible to bear.

She ate very little of her dinner. The sight of the food, appetising though it was, made her stomach churn unsteadily. She went up to her room to rest, for she found the journey had tired her. Agnes was left with instructions to wake her well before six, when Ewen was expected. Was she pregnant? Again the thought haunted her. Or had she merely eaten too much rich food the day before.

'Mistress Anne, wake up. You've a visitor downstairs.' She had fallen into such a deep sleep that Agnes took several minutes to rouse her.

Anne sat up, brushing the hair from her eyes. She felt as if she could have slept for another four hours.

'Who? No one knows I am here.' Suddenly her heart almost stopped beating. Roy! Oh, no, not him! Had he followed her, expecting to find her with Ewen? He would too, she thought with rising alarm, for the clock showed five of the hour. He would be here soon.

'You'll not believe it. It's her, Mairi MacKenzie, as bold as you please—and with a babe too. The hussy! I tried to turn her away, but she insisted, and that MacKinney man has taken her into the parlour.'

Anne could not believe her ears. Mairi—here! They had not seen each other in—how long was it now? Agnes stared at her in amazement as she jumped to her feet, smoothing down the creased skirts of her travelling gown before she headed for the door.

'You don't intend to see her?' Agnes asked, shocked.

'I don't know why she has come, or how she knew I was here . . . but I'll see her. It's time she knew how I feel about her scandalous behaviour.' She had left for France a few weeks after she learned that Mairi was going to have a child and had not seen her since. All of eight months, counting the time she had been married to Roy, she calculated.

She had changed. Anne saw that instantly. She was thinner, the large brown eyes more prominent in the fine bone structure. She did not look as if she was destitute, Anne thought as she stepped into the room and regarded the figure before her in a plain gown of saffron velvet, a dark brown woollen cloak thrown back about her shoulders. In a chair in front of her, the curly-haired baby playing contentedly with a noisy toy was equally well clothed. She had soon found someone else to care for her needs, Anne thought, hardening her heart.

'You wish to see me?' she said. 'I marvel at your nerve, Mairi—after all you have done to my family.'

'Coll has told me of your marriage,' Mairi replied in a quiet tone, not rising to the taunt. 'You are to be congratulated on your excellent choice, although I believe it has already turned sour on you—as mine did.'

'You are remarkably well informed.' Coll again! Anne inwardly bristled at the declaration. Whenever she began to accept him as her friend, something like this came between them. 'You are staying in Inverness? Does Ewen know?'

'No, and he must not be told. Roy opened up our house here for me. I have been staying there since before he wed you.'

'How long before?' Anne forced the words through stiff lips. She had always suspected that Roy knew of his sister's whereabouts, now the proof was hers. It brought her little satisfaction to know the double-game he played with her was far more devious and calculating than she had at first believed it to be.

'A day—no, two. He took me completely by surprise. I thought he would stay at the house with me, as we had not seen each other for so many months, but he left me with Coll—and the next thing I knew, he had—married you.'

'After finding you . . . listening to your lies,' she accused. 'Do you know why he married me? Not because he loves me. He wants to kill Ewen—because of you. My God, how can you stand there with that innocent look on your face when you have already been instrumental in causing the death of my brother, James—and might be the cause of Ewen's death too.'

'No!' Mairi cried, her face paling at the accusations. 'I was fond of James . . . and what he felt for me was not love, but pity. He knew what was happening under his own roof, but he loved Frances too much to stop it, for it would have meant sending her away. Then, Ewen married me and he thought for a while they had separated, but that was their intention. It took only one short month before she was back in Ewen's bed and James and I became soul-mates in our desperation. Soul-mates, Anne—as you and I were in those early days, before you went away . . . hating me, believing the lies which had been told to you.'

'I went away because I could not bear to see you growing fat with a child not fathered by your husband,' Anne retorted. Why was she even bothering to defend herself? *She* was not in the wrong. 'Because of you, I now live in hell, do you know that?'

'Coll told me,' the other replied nodding her head. 'Roy is wrong to hurt you as he does, but the wounds Ewen inflicted on me have gone deep. He was incensed with rage when no one would defend me—not even my own father. He has always been my champion, even when we were children.'

'Defend you—against the truth. You cannot fight that . . . ' Anne broke off, beginning to sway. She had grown exceedingly hot, yet there was no fire in the room and she did not even have a shawl about her shoulders.

'Are you ill? Sit down, let me fetch you something to drink . . . '

'There is fruit juice on the table.'

For several minutes after she had drunk the contents of the glass Mairi handed her, Anne sat with eyes closed. Gradually the faintness passed and she opened them again on to the anxious face hovering over her.

'Please go! We have nothing to say to each other.'

'Very well. I will accept that you do not believe me . . . that Roy has hurt you too much for us ever to be friends again, but before I go, I must show you why I came.' The girl picked up the gurgling little baby and came back to where Anne sat, a hand against her throbbing head. 'Look, Anne MacKenzie—does your brother Ewen not have a mark like this? Did you ever see another like it?'

Anne could not contain the gasp which escaped her lips, for beneath the curly brown hair on the tiny head was a birthmark, somewhat resembling a misshapen crown.

'The child is Ewen's,' Mairi said, covering its head again with a blue bonnet. 'I am not the whore you think me. He lied. The child cannot be James's, for he did not have a mark like this. He told me that only you and Ewen possess them . . . and now Ewen's son.'

Instinctively Anne's fingers lifted to her own mark behind her left ear. It was true. The baby had been fathered by Ewen . . . yet he had denied it to her—to everyone. Why?

'Roy—has seen this? Yes, of course he has.'

'The day he found me. Do you accept now I have not lied?'

'And from you he came straight to me, begged me to marry him. Oh dear heaven, the man was truly sired by Dhommil Dhu! To use me so . . . knowing I loved him.' Her composure faltered and she bit her lip to keep back the threatening tears. If Ewen had lied about the child, what else had he lied about? She raised questioning eyes to Mairi's face, said quietly, 'Will you ring the bell by the fireplace. We will have a cup of tea while we talk.'

'I have not come to cause you more pain, for if

we do talk together, that is what I will do. I have
done what I came to do. Perhaps it is better I leave.'

'No, I want to hear everything. I have to be
sure . . . I am sure . . . ' She shook her head still
stunned by the unexpected turn of events. For so
long she had believed Ewen—trusted him implicitly.

Over a tray of tea, and hot buttered scones, they
spoke of things she had never thought to speak of
again. Mairi talked of those first few happy weeks
after her marriage, before she came to realise that
not only did Ewen not love her, but had taken his
brother's wife as his mistress. The affair had started
long before Ewen and Mairi had married. He had
shattered her perfect world as callously as Roy had
shattered Anne's when he told her the true reason
for their secret elopement.

As Anne listened ashen-faced to the girl's story,
the long days of humiliation spent beneath Ewen's
roof, watching him with another woman, with only
James's friendship to make life worth while, his
constant accusations of unfaithfulness, in order to
cover his own philanderings—even to the extent of
accusing his own brother, Anne realised that she
had never really known Ewen.

'I watched them together,' Mairi whispered, tears
smarting in her eyes with the pain of it all. And then
the baby whimpered and she gathered him to her, a
smile breaking through her sad features. 'She had
only to crook her little finger and he was at her side.
I stood no chance against her. If I thought he had
loved me, just a little, I would have fought him, but
he grew to loathe me, to treat me as an object of
derision. *She* made sure of that. I could do nothing
right. She ran the house and I was never consulted
on anything. When James was killed . . . I knew
I had lost him for ever.'

'I know he quarrelled with Ewen the morning he went riding . . . and did not return.' Anne forced her mind back to that terrible day. 'Ewen made me believe it was over you . . . and Frances was in tears while they were absent from the house, saying James had told her himself you were his mistress.'

'I do not blame you for believing their lies. They have told so many—so well. And why should you not take his part against me—a Fraser!'

'That was not the reason, and well you know it,' Anne said quickly. 'I had seen you with James—and misunderstood. I admit that now. There was a time not many weeks ago, when I could have found myself in the same predicament, had I been found with—with Coll. He had kissed me, he was only trying to be kind, but I was angry and I misunderstood—I struck him. I have often wondered how Roy would have reacted had he come upon us? I should have talked to you more.'

'I should have tried to make you believe me—instead I gave up. Ewen killed whatever I felt for him in six months. I became an unwanted embarrassment to them both and so they sought to be rid of me.'

'By driving you from the house.'

'That was Frances's doing. Ewen knew what she was about, of course, but he was far too weak to go against her wishes. The servants, like everyone else, believed the worst and treated me like—like a contagious disease. Frances never lost a moment's pleasure telling me how people were talking about me—how my father had refused to mention me and only Roy still called me sister. How she gloated over that, knowing I had nowhere to go if I left the house. You had gone to France and so there was no one to challenge her authority.

'She hates you, do you know that? She is a little

afraid of you, I think, because you are so strong. I knew if I stayed, they would take my baby from me. It was all the proof I had of my innocence. I told Ewen I would go to Roy. I knew he would believe me. That was when Ewen beat me for the second time. I left the house the next morning with Frances watching. I was not allowed to take anything with me, not even a change of clothes. She gave me a handful of coins and told me to find a man to father my bastard. She knew it was Ewen's child—I swear it! She knew, and he did also.'

'Don't distress yourself any more, please,' Anne begged. 'You must come back to Tigh an Lóin with me. We will face your father together.'

'No! I could not bear to see the same questions in his eyes,' Mairi faltered, rocking the baby against her breast. 'I am safe here in Inverness.'

Anne's head jerked up in dismay as she heard a carriage draw up in the road outside. She blanched visibly.

'Ewen! I'd completely forgotten that I'd asked him here tonight. I had some silly notion of trying to prevent him fighting with Roy. If it were not for the possibility of Roy being hurt, I think I would go ahead and let them meet, after what you have told me. Oh, Mairi, how could I have been so blind to your plight?'

'They were kin—you were too close to accept that Ewen could be so evil. Had he not met Frances, we might have stood a chance. I would like to believe it, anyway. I would have made him a good wife. I loved him above my own family.'

'As I love your brother,' Anne whispered. She had admitted it to herself at last. Nothing had changed. She would do anything to prevent more unpleasantness. Perhaps if she talked with Ranald, convinced him his daughter had been the victim of a cruel plot to discredit her. 'Quickly, upstairs! Go through the kitchen as soon as he is in here with me,' she added as she heard the voices coming closer. Mairi snatched up her gloves and fled into the other room. Closing the door behind her, Anne turned to greet her brother, forcing a smile to her trembling lips, and found herself facing James's widow!

'My dear, how well you look. Marriage agrees with you.' Frances considered the startled young woman before her and then dropped into the nearest chair. Anne felt herself grow cold as her gaze fastened on the tea tray and the two used cups. 'Have you been entertaining? Your husband is here with you?'

'As it is obvious that you have read the note I sent to Ewen, you know he is not.' She could not hide her dislike of this woman, but Frances merely smiled at the frosty note in her voice. 'Where is he? Why has he not come to see me? Does he not realise how important this is?'

'He has other—business in Edinburgh. He will not be back for at least a week. He asked me to come in his place and bring his apologies. You can tell me what the great mystery is, surely. Ewen and I have no secrets from each other.'

'Partners in evil as well as partners in bed,' Anne snapped, and Frances's smile vanished. Her full red lips pursed thoughtfully as she considered the words and all traces of friendliness were wiped from her carefully powdered features. 'Don't bother to deny it. I know everything. I find it hard to accept what you have done to an innocent girl . . . but I know it now to be the truth. I have seen Mairi's child. He carries the birthmark that both Ewen and I possess. It cannot be doubted.'

'So, little Mairi still intends to cause trouble?

Foolish girl. How unpleasant it will be for you, Anne, to hear of James's infidelity with her. She is out of the same mould as her mother, of course, despite everything your husband has done to cover up the fact. Ranald accepts she is a whore . . . and the rest of his family. You would be wise to do the same.'

'I am not Mairi. I am not frightened by your threats,' Anne retorted, defiance burning in her blue eyes. She gained courage as she went on, remembering how lovingly Mairi had held the child to her, even though he shared the blood of a man who had maligned her unjustly, sought to degrade her and install another woman in the place of his unwanted wife. 'Perhaps it is as well Ewen did not come tonight. I do not think I could have kept my temper. Tell him I will do everything I can to keep Roy MacKenzie away from him—and my consideration is for my husband, Frances, not my brother. I will side with him no longer in this matter.'

'Then you, too, must accept the consequences for your foolishness.' Frances rose to her feet, smoothing down the skirts of her velvet gown. The heavy cloak she wore was heavily trimmed with sable fur, the cowl framing her beautiful face. Her eyes were derisive as she turned towards the door. 'I shall not stay longer. Ewen shall have your message.'

'No doubt you will elaborate on it to suit your own purposes.'

'That is quite possible. This is not the end of it, you know.' The malevolence which blazed from her face was so unexpected, Anne found herself taking an involuntary step away from her. 'We have gone too far to stop now. We shall stop Mairi—and you, if you continue to interfere. James thought he could outwit us too, the fool—and look what happened to him.'

She was gone before Anne could recover her stunned senses. James! But it had been a riding accident . . . his horse had thrown him and he had hit his head rendering him unconscious before he rolled down an incline and drowned in the shallow waters of the loch. At least, that had been the verdict of the inquest. Murder! Was that what Frances had been implying? James—murdered, because he was in the way?

'I heard . . . ' Mairi came flying into the room to take Anne in her arms. 'We all did.' Behind her came Agnes, clutching the baby to her—and Andrew MacKinney, his expression grave.

'Ay, mistress, we heard,' the maid said bitterly. 'And did you see the look on her face? She means you harm, mark my words. We must get out of here . . . tonight . . . '

'Where will I go?' Mairi whispered. 'They could have men watching the house when I return. I must protect my baby. He is all I have . . . '

'No, you have me—and Roy and Coll and your father. I will make him accept you,' Anne vowed. 'You will be safe at the lodge until I have spoken to him.' She turned to Andrew MacKinney. 'Will you support me in all that I tell him, Andrew?'

Her look challenged the man. He nodded. She did not stop to consider her husband's reaction to her change of attitude. Her present concern was Mairi and the child.

'Good. You have things back at the house, Mairi, that you will need. Andrew will fetch them. We leave first thing in the morning.'

'I am afraid . . . you do not know what they are capable of doing,' Mairi said, the fear mirrored in her eyes. Anne slipped an arm about her shoulders and hugged her reassuringly.

'What can they do? The carriage will stop for no one until we reach the lodge—and I have a pistol should there be trouble of any kind. I will not allow them to hurt you again. It is my sincerest wish that I see that woman burn in hell for what she has done . . . ' Anne declared vehemently. Was not her own marriage in ruins because of Frances's treacherous lies? She saw a smile touch Andrew MacKinney's thin mouth at her brave words.

'I too, am armed, should we be accosted. We shall give them a good fight. It is time, is it not?'

'Are you sure it was Mairi you saw?' Frances demanded of the young, thick-set man who sat opposite her, leaning forward so that his legs deliberately pressed against her own. She did not rebuke him for his boldness, but she had other more important things on her mind at that moment than making love, even though he had proved himself to be the most virile of the lovers she had taken to her bed over the past year. Ewen was a mere shadow in contrast—but Ewen had inherited a great deal of money on James's death and until she had laid her hands on more than she had to date, she would not abandon him. Besides, there was the question of the new will. The lawyer who had dealt with it, luckily an old admirer, could be relied on to keep silent only so long as she paid him—or Anne too died, thus transferring everything to her brother, as the original will had stipulated. The meddling little fool had grown sure of herself under Roy MacKenzie's guidance, but she was still floundering in the dark, unaware James was the key to the whole business. James who had sought to get back at his wife by changing his will and leaving everything to his sister instead of his brother, Ewen, as had been originally intended . . . before he became aware his wife was unfaithful to him.

Anne did not even know she was a wealthy woman—and would never discover it. If she had to be killed, then so be it, and Mairi alongside her. She laid a ringed hand on the man's arm and stroked the smooth material of his jacket. Taking it as an invitation, he leaned forward still more and she allowed him to steal a kiss. As he became more insistent, however, she drew back with a soft laugh.

'Later, my impetuous boy. We have plenty of time with Ewen away until the end of the week. First, you must do a little errand for me . . . Have you men you can trust?'

'If I pay them enough. Shall I come to you afterwards?' He was not more than twenty, Frances mused, as she studied the swarthy features—with the instincts of a born killer. She had found him very useful. He obeyed her without question and as a reward was given access to her bed whenever it was possible to do so. Ewen was fast becoming superfluous in the light of this new and totally satisfying relationship.

'My door will be unlocked.'

CHAPTER EIGHT

JUST BEFORE nine o'clock the following morning, Mairi left the house wearing some of Anne's clothes, accompanied by Agnes who carried the sleeping baby boy well wrapped up against the cold and hidden beneath a shawl in a basket. Andrew also left with the occupants of the coach so that it would appear to anyone watching, that only Anne and her servants had left. If Mairi's arrival had been noticed, and Anne suspected it had, it might be construed that the girl was still in the house, awaiting their return.

A horse had been saddled for Anne at the back of the house. She hoped to slip away unnoticed and meet the carriage well outside the town limits.

She waited a full fifteen minutes after it had left before she ventured out herself. As she went to pull herself into the saddle, as sharp pain tore through her side. She clung tightly to the pommel, faint and weak for several minutes. Had she caught a chill? She had been shivering a great deal during a sleepless night, but her skin burned to the touch. A slight fever, nothing to be alarmed about, she reasoned, trying to mount again and this time succeeding. Although, again she experienced the stabbing pains in her lower abdomen as she did so.

For a minute she sat to compose herself before starting off through the cobbled streets towards the Firth. She kept a steady pace, not wanting to draw attention to herself. It was fortunate that at this time of the morning everyone was too concerned

with their own business to give much notice to a
passing rider. She had a woollen cloak swathing her
body for it was a dull, damp morning with dark
clouds in the sky which threatened rain. She would
be lucky to reach her destination without getting
soaked, she thought as she heard a rumble of thunder
in the distance.

A mile out of Inverness, the carriage waited
beneath some trees, with Andrew MacKinney
anxiously scanning the road for Anne. She suspected
his relief was as great as her own as he helped her
to the ground, steadying her as she swayed.

'Are you ill, my lady?' She noticed a subtle difference in his tone of voice and had done since she
declared she would fight to protect Mairi from her
own brother. They were allies now, instead of
enemies. If only she could share the same with Roy.
At least it would be a beginning.

'No, tired, that's all. I could not sleep last night.
I have not been followed, of that I am sure. Let us
leave this place quickly.'

'Mistress, you look like a ghost!' Agnes declared,
taking one look at her frightful pallor, as she seated
herself in the carriage. 'What's wrong?'

'Nothing, don't fuss.' Her tone was sharper than
she intended and Agnes drew back into her seat, a
hurt look on her face. Mairi said nothing, but she
sensed something was very wrong indeed. As the
journey continued she was conscious of Anne biting
her lip in pain when the carriage jolted over uneven
ground or lurched unsteadily into pot-holes in the
road.

Under Andrew's careful directions, the driver
turned from the main road on to the muddy cart-
tracks which meandered through wooded areas and
pleasant little glens dotted with stone walled crofts
with thatched roofs of heather and fir. These people

were strangers to her, Anne realised, as she glanced out of the window trying to judge how far from the lodge they were. At least another hour—or more, she estimated. Her discomfort had not lessened, but at least it was no worse, she thought thankfully. As soon as she reached Tigh an Lóir she would go to bed and rest, perhaps send Agnes to the village for the woman there who was knowledgeable in the art of healing with herb medicine. She was overtired and feeling the strain of the past months. Perhaps things would be easier for her with Mairi's return. It would be pleasant to have another woman to talk to and she felt she had much to make up for her treatment of the girl. And, of course, there was the baby to be taken into consideration. Once Ranald knew the child was fathered by Ewen, Mairi's rightful husband, Anne suspected he would welcome his daughter home again. He would have the grandson he longed for to bounce on his knee while she would endeavour to achieve that same aim, no matter how scathing Roy's comments on her change of heart.

She had been wrong and was willing to admit it. When he discovered she had not intentionally lied about Mairi and James together, would he find it in his heart to forgive her? She doubted it. The hurt had gone too deep. Her rejection of him was too final, too damaging to his fierce MacKenzie pride. She sighed wearily and wrapped her cloak more firmly about her as a bout of shivering racked her body. She tried to doze, but the ride was too uncomfortable and each time she managed to relax, the pains returned to stiffen her limbs, momentarily depriving her of breath.

'You are not at all well,' Mairi declared, spreading a rug across her lap. 'You must ask Roy to send for the doctor as soon as you get back to Tigh an Lóin.

Make sure she does, Agnes. I'm sure she has a fever.'

'Tomorrow it will have passed. All I need is sleep,' Anne insisted, but deep in her heart an alarming thought was making itself apparent. She closed her mind against the pain—and what it could mean if her calculations had been correct, shutting her eyes to avoid further conversation.

A sharp report brought her bolt upright in the seat, her fingers seeking the pistol Roy had given her which rested in the pocket of her skirt. Following in the wake of it, a cry—like a man in agony. Agnes screamed as a dark shape fell past the window, and crossed herself. Anne's horrified eyes saw the body of the coachman sprawled in the road behind them. She knew instinctively that he was dead. He came from the village and had a wife and six children, she remembered as she thrust her head out of the window, desperately trying to see what was happening.

'Inside,' Andrew yelled, snatching a look over his shoulder as he struggled to retain control of the team. The reins had fallen from the lax hands of the coachman as he pitched headlong from his seat and he was desperately fighting to reach them again. As if aware they were running free, the horses increased their pace, threatening to upset the carriage and spill everyone out on to the ground.

Horsemen! Three horsemen coming up behind them. Without delay Anne cried,

'On to the floor, both of you. We are being attacked.' She slid down beside Mairi, tugging the pistol free from her pocket. Another shot, a hoarse command for Andrew to pull up the carriage or be killed. Her heart lurched in fear as he obeyed, but then remembering he too, was armed, she assumed he thought it best to tackle their would-be assailants while he could take steady aim. It was sensible reasoning. She could not have hit either of them travelling at that fast pace.

They were dressed in well-worn clothes, she saw, as they rode by the window. Three pairs of cold eyes surveyed the women huddled on the floor. Anne kept the pistol well concealed beneath her cloak until they had passed and then she began to lift it cautiously, in readiness.

'It's them. What now . . . ' They were speaking to a fourth man out of her view. She craned her neck to try and see his features, but he was well out of they way. They spoke as if they had been waiting for this very coach! Dear God, had Mairi been right? Had she been followed by Ewen's men bent on silencing her, depriving her of the source of proof she had as to her innocence! These men had a look about them that made her shiver. Ruffians who would do anything if the price was right. Had Ewen stooped so low because of his love for one woman?

'You have your orders. Kill them all,' came the harsh command.

Agnes fainted at the words. Mairi thrust herself over her baby, beginning to sob. Kill them! Ewen was her brother! He would not send men to murder her . . . but Frances would! If it was made to look like an accident, Ewen would never know the truth. Had James been killed in the same manner, without his knowledge—without his involvement? It was the only answer. She would not accept her brother to be a cold-blooded murderer of his own kin. She heard a shout of rage from above, Andrew! Another shot and one of the men who had stopped them, slowly keeled sideways on his horse and fell to the ground. Another—and then a terrible, unnerving silence. Muttered voices, too low for her to catch what was being said. Was Andrew dead too?

Gripping the pistol firmly, she cocked it, pointing it at one door. If they came to the other, would she have time to turn and fire? As the thought passed through her brain, the door in front of her was wrenched open. Agnes's inert form was pulled out and dumped unceremoniously on the ground.

'Now, my fine beauties. Which one of you is next?' Anne was aware of the aroma of stale ale and wine on the man's breath as his hands reached for Mairi's shivering form. As he grasped her by the hair, dragging her, still clinging to the child, to the edge of the floor, she took aim and fired into the leering face, which disappeared in a hideous bloody distortion of what it had once been.

Before she could reload, someone cursed her close by. The door against her back opened without warning and she screamed as she was hauled from the carriage and sent reeling to the ground several feet away. She landed with a sickening thud which robbed her of breath. The pain seared her body like tongues of fire as she lay unable to move. A man then moved into view above her while another stood watching the scene from beneath a tree.

She did not know him. The young face was cruel. The eyes without pity as a low moan escaped her lips. Yet even as she realised he was about to kill her, she prayed that Mairi would take this opportunity to escape and hide herself with her baby. And then her eyes fastened on the trews he wore . . . her brother's colours! Fraser colours! It was true.

'If you kill me you will be found and hanged,' she cried as he bent over her, pushed aside her cloak and ran a calloused hand over her breasts, squeezing them beneath the material of her dress. Oh no! She almost fainted to think he might first rape her. 'My husband will never rest until he has found you.' Roy—care what happened to her?

The man chuckled. It was the most spine-chilling sound she had ever heard. There was a ripping sound as he fastened a finger in the neckline of her bodice and tore it open to the waist. Her shift was treated with the same brutality. Her nails raked at his face as his weight descended over her and she realised he was too strong for her to throw off. His face blurred before her tortured vision . . . she felt herself slipping away from the peril which threatened her into a blackness which offered blessed relief from the pain and humiliation he intended to subject her to.

And then without warning she felt a rush of cold air upon her cheek. Another curse . . . she knew that voice and the vehement oath. Through bright tears flooding her eyes, she saw her attacker sprawled on the ground, nursing a bruised chin. She knew the arms that went around her, cradled her against a leather jerkin and sobbed his name over and over again.

'Anne! For the love of God, woman, look at me! Has he harmed you?' Roy demanded. He had been staying at the lodge in her absence, unable to bear the emptiness of the huge canopied bed at Tigh an Lóin. He would never know what had made him turn his horse on to this track when he had intended to return home. It was a miracle! He did not question further, nor did he contemplate what would have taken place had he not come upon the carriage when he did.

She shook her head, unable to speak for tears. He crushed her against him and she felt him tremble as he did so. Then he was putting her gently aside, rising to his feet with drawn claymore to face the man on his knees in the dirt. She realised the fourth man had disappeared!

'Get up. Or I will kill you as you are now,' he thundered.

Anne had been horrified by the indifference with which her attacker meant to rape her. He was not drunk, nor looked or smelt as if he had been drinking. He had been ordered to kill her and was merely allowing himself a bonus by forcing himself on a pretty woman. She had no doubt she would have been killed with the same indifference . . . the same pitiless manner. She saw no mercy on her husband's face as he moved towards him and closed her eyes, shutting out the noise of clashing steel by thrusting her hands over her ears as she crouched on the ground, praying for it to end.

Mairi's voice penetrated her reeling senses, brought her back to reality but for a moment only. She found herself lying in the carriage with Agnes patting her hand and weeping over what had almost taken place, raining curses down on the head of the man who now lay dead beneath the trees.

Half in, half out of the carriage, Roy knelt by Anne with Mairi facing him on the seat, her face as bitter as the reproach which fell from her trembling lips. There was a streak of blood across his forehead.

'She saved our lives! Is there no compassion left in you? Not only are you a fool, Roy MacKenzie, but you are blind too! Can you not tell when your own wife carries your child . . . '

Anne relaxed, allowing the blackness to creep over her again. She was too weak to fight it and it would bring peace from the terrible pain which now consumed the whole of her body. A child! She had been right to be afraid. She was going to lose Roy's baby!

'You must believe me, it is the truth. The child is proof. Look if you do not believe me! Ewen betrayed her. His men tried to kill us! Please, take her back and love her as she deserves.' Anne clung tightly to the hand holding hers, desperately fighting against the laudanum which threatened to drag her down into the realms of sleep. She could not sleep yet! Not until she had made him listen!

Already the events in her mind were becoming confused. She remembered Mairi—the attack on the coach, the hands of the man who had tried to rape her—but much that had taken place before that was unclear, no matter how hard she tried to focus her thoughts. Sleep was stubbornly claiming her.

Ranald had been at her bedside when she recovered consciousness. Agnes was also hovering near by, but there was no sign of the face she sought and hope died within her. She was too weak—too miserable even to cry in this final moment of rejection. Yet when her eyes came to rest on Ranald's anxious features, she sought to right some of the wrongs her brother had brought about. She seized his hand, driven on by the knowledge of her discovery in Inverness. To try and absolve Mairi in his eyes.

'You have the grandson you have always yearned for . . . ' she whispered. 'I wish I had been the one to give him to you, but perhaps it is a selfish thought. Who better than your own daughter to give you your heart's desire.'

'Hush, child. You must rest, not talk this way and excite yourself,' he begged, a break in his voice at the sight of her tortured face. He had not accepted her in the beginning because she was a Fraser and he had a long memory. She was not the wife he would have chosen for his eldest son, but in the months she had been beneath his roof, she had conducted herself with great pride which endeared him to her. In the face of his mistrust—he had found himself accepting her as the new mistress of Tigh an Lóin. She was the replacement for the daughter he had lost. He realised now how wrong he had been to afford her this status. She was someone in her own right—not to be confused with Mairi.

Lost! No, he had abandoned his daughter. He acknowledged it now. Unable to bear the scandal which accompanied the dalliance of an unfaithful wife, he had turned his back on her, rejected her—refused to acknowledge she existed. The scars left by the adultery of his wife would never heal and had been instrumental in ruling his conduct towards the daughter she had borne him.

Mairi had her mother's gentle ways. That had not helped to endear her to him. Her eyes—her colouring—it was like looking at a mirror image! But he had never been able to accept she was of his blood. He had killed the Fraser lover and two of his kin in a blind rage and never spoken again to the fragile woman who had been led astray in a moment of weakness.

Passion, was how she had described it! A moment of passion! Something he had failed to rouse in her despite the birth of two fine sons, despite the love she had for him. He had struck her on that day—and then afterwards ignored her presence in the house. Yet when she died some six months later, he discovered an empty void in his life which could not be filled—or replaced with another woman.

How deeply had these events affected Roy—and Coll, he wondered now?

'She is asleep,' Agnes whispered. Carefully, Ranald released himself from the fingers entwined around his and laid the cold hand on the covers. The shaded lamp beside the bed threw soft shadows across the face of the sleeping girl. He stepped back, not wanting to leave her, and knowing he must. She was as close as a daughter—and yet more . . . how she had intruded into his world without him ever being aware of it. As she had done with Roy, he suspected. Now, what use were either of them to her?

With a heavy heart he left the room and rejoined those waiting for him below.

'How is she?' Roy came to his feet the moment his father appeared. He had been perched on the arm of Mairi's chair. Coll stood by the fireplace. No one had been attempting conversation.

Ranald looked into the taut features without compassion as he sought the comfort of the nearest chair.

'Why ask? Go and see for yourself. See what you have brought her to—you and that brother of hers!' he returned drily. 'Pour me a drink, Coll—if there is anything left.' He eyed the depleted decanters and knew that both his sons had been drinking heavily since he quit the room an hour ago. Both of them seeking to drown the voice of conscience—and he was little better, he thought, raising the glass to his lips and draining it without appreciation. 'She's sleeping. There's nothing we can do for her. She is in God's hands. Only he can give her the strength she needs to live. The loss of the child has drained her . . .'

He heard a savage expletive explode from Roy's lips. He had not known! He stared at his eldest son, watched the colour mount in the dark skin as Mairi and Coll too, turned to stare at him. He had been blind—that was the least of his faults. No! They were all to blame! Poor Roy! So strong when it came to defending his own family ties—so weak when it affected his heart. Ranald did not like to dwell on the past with its bitter memories, but he found himself doing it now and it brought him closer to the girl who lay upstairs—wishing she could die.

How he had loved his wife. He was not an ardent lover, but he had thought them well suited. Yet she had looked at another man—lain with him. Why? He had made no secret of the fact he wanted heirs and she had given him two stalwart sons, but that was not the only reason he went to her. Had she wanted something more? Had the Fraser given it to her? Or in that wild night when she came back to him, begging his forgiveness and he had raped his own wife—had Mairi been sired? Now, when Anne lay so ill upstairs—a woman used . . . was Roy not following in his footsteps?

'She will not die,' Roy said and they all turned and looked at him.

'Have you not done enough?' Coll said, and the black eyes turned on him, terrible in their destruction. 'Let her die in peace.'

Roy glared at him for a full moment, the slitted gaze unnerving and yet on his brother's face he saw something he had not bargained for—defiance—allegiance to his wife!

'No!' The word came out in a defiant negative. 'Do you really believe I will allow her to die?'

'Your revenge, my brother,' Coll murmured. 'How sweet it must be.'

Roy was almost upon him, clenched fist raised before his face, when Mairi ran between them, pushing the younger man back.

'Stop it, both of you! If you care, either of you, use your breath to pray for her,' she cried.

'She will not die,' Roy repeated tight-lipped. 'If—if she does, I will be gone from here one minute after she is laid in the ground. I will kill Ewen Fraser and you will not stop me—any of you!'

'If we lose her, my son,' Ranald replied, rising to his feet to confront his two sons, 'I will be riding beside you with Coll alongside us both. And men from Tigh an Lóin behind us. Her death will not go unavenged. Fraser and his whole household will die by our swords and the house will be put to the torch so that nothing remains of his infamy!'

'So, at last you believe,' Roy said slowly.

'Like you, I am a stubborn man. Ay, I accept Mairi was not to blame. I have had my daughter returned to me, but in bringing it about, you may have lost the woman you love.'

'It would appear we MacKenzies love not wisely, but too well, eh Father?' Roy said, but his eyes were on his brother as he spoke the words.

'Go to her,' Mairi pleaded, touching her brother's arm, not understanding the strangeness of the way Coll and Roy regarded each other. 'Let her know how much you love her. Make her believe it.'

'It sounds so easy when you say it,' Roy said, wishing he knew how to reach his wife. She hated him. Wished him dead! Had he not heard it from her own lips?

'You forget I know what she is going through,' Mairi cried in a distraught tone. 'Much as I love you, it would be very easy to despise you for hurting her so cruelly.' Picking up her skirts, she ran from the room.

'Mairi—wait!' Never had he imagined such scorn from his beloved sister. Ranald laid a hand on his arm and motioned to the chair behind him.

'Sit down and let us wait for the doctor. Perhaps there will be a change for the better.'

Roy slumped into the seat, refusing the glass Coll held out to him. With a shrug he drank it himself, despite his father's glower. Did none of them realise how deeply he too, was suffering?

'You underestimated your little Anne. I did warn you,' Ranald said.

'I never intended using her against her brother,' Roy retorted angrily. 'I wanted her so much, can't you understand that? I'd have sold my soul to the devil to have her.'

'We have all made mistakes. You with Anne Fraser—and I . . . ' He paused, deep lines of pain furrowing his brows. 'Mine was with my own daughter. She was right, the situations are alike. I do not believe that is of your doing. Anne loved you enough to risk her brother's anger and marry you—and Mairi risked mine. Your scheme went wrong because you failed to realise this girl is too proud to run to her brother and ask for help. She preferred to suffer alone, as Mairi did.'

'But the child?' Roy protested, the strain beginning to tell in his expression. Never had Ranald seen him so drawn. 'Why did she not tell me?'

'And give you another weapon to use against her brother? Do you not think the similarity between her life and Mairi's did not cross her mind?'

'Good God! I love her! I never intended all *this* to happen!'

Roy lowered his head into his hands. He felt suddenly very drained and alone. She could not die! She was his whole life! Ranald stared at his son for a long while and then lifted his eyes to the empty space on the panelled walls. As in other rooms, all portraits of his daughter had been removed and stored away in an attic. Tomorrow they would all be cleaned and replaced.

'Mairi was always too proud—too stubborn . . . '

'It runs in the family, Father. Unlike forgiveness,' Roy flung back harshly.

'As I said, you may have lost your wife. Through the loss I shall have regained a daughter.'

Roy stared into his father's face. He had fought so long to achieve this moment, yet compared to the struggle going on upstairs, it was unimportant. He watched his father ring for a servant, listened in amazement as Ranald ordered,

'I want all the rooms which the Lady Mairi once used to be opened at once. Lay fires and see everything is clean for her and her child. Be quick about it,' he snapped as the girl stood open-mouthed in the doorway.

'At once, sir.' She dropped a curtsy and scuttled from the room eager to spread this astonishing piece of news throughout the house.

It was almost two hours before Mairi reappeared. During the whole of that time, Roy had not moved from his chair, nor Coll from beside the whisky decanter which was now empty. His mood of depression had worsened. A dozen times it had been in his mind to go up to her. But what if she rejected him? Sent him away with hatred in her eyes, her voice. Damned him to hell for the agony she had been through because of him?

Mairi tiptoed into the room, aware of Ranald dozing by the fire. But she had not gone two paces before her father sat upright in his chair, demanding,

'Well?' It was the first word he had spoken to her since she came back into the house. Roy came to his feet, his eyes searching his sister's colourless cheeks. He feared the worst.

'She—she has a fever. She recognises no one. The doctor thinks there is no hope!' she faltered and broke. 'Oh, Roy, she's dying. She has lost the will to live.'

'Nonsense. She is far stronger than any of you realise. You are tired, Mairi. Go to bed. In the morning you will see she is better.'

Mairi looked from her brothers to the face of her father, her lips moving soundlessly. No words would come. Coll rose not very steadily to his feet and put his arm around her.

'Don't argue now, little one. There is always tomorrow to do that,' he murmured.

She started towards the door, turned back to look at the silent man in the fireside chair. With a sob, she flung herself into the arms which lifted slowly to offer her comfort—and to welcome her home again. It was several minutes before any of them realised that Roy had left the room.

Somewhere in the house, a clock chimed the hour of two. The doctor stepped back from the bedside and closed his black bag, flexing his aching shoulders as he turned to stare at the man who had been standing in the shadows for over an hour.

'I've done all I can. I'm sorry. She will not respond. Without the will to live . . . ' He shrugged, embarrassed and slightly perturbed by this man's unnerving presence in the room. He did not speak, or move, just hovered out of sight, watching, listening to the wild ramblings of the feverish woman tossing and turning in the bed. She was quiet now. It was almost the end he thought, but he did not say so for as Roy moved into the candlelight and he saw the glitter in those black eyes, words failed him. He was not a superstitious man . . . but to look at him now, he could almost believe the devil had come to claim another victim. 'She—She is in God's hands . . . '

Roy smiled humourlessly as he crossed himself and hurriedly left the room.

'In God's hands—and mine,' he whispered as he bent over the bed.

The dream world induced by the heavy dose of laudanum administered to her, to dull the pain following the loss of the baby, was so beautiful, so tranquil, Anne did not want to return. Her mind

and her body were at peace at last as she drifted
from one memory to another. She felt no bitterness,
or anger towards anyone. She was at peace and soon
she would allow herself to approach the dark void
opening up in her path, allow herself to be drawn
down into the inky blackness where she would be
forever at peace.

But for a moment longer, she wanted to enjoy the
touch of Roy's lips against her feverish cheek, her
mouth. Why did he not allow her to tell him she
loved him still? Each time she tried to speak, his lips
would silence her. He was so gentle with her, whispered such sweet words in her ear as he had done
on their wedding night as they lay together in the
lodge. That was where they were now, she realised,
opening her eyes on to a darkened canopy above
her. The lodge! The only place she had been truly
happy with him.

With a sigh she turned her face into his shoulder
and his arms closed around her holding her tightly
against his chest. She was secure again, unafraid. If
God chose this moment to take her, she would not
mind . . . such a perfect memory to linger in her
mind in her final moments. She had no doubt she
was going to die. Although her body no longer felt
on fire, stabbed with a thousand red hot needles
each time she tried to move, she knew she was very
weak. Besides what did she have to live for? Roy
detested her! Ranald bore her presence in his house
under duress. Coll pitied her and believed it to be
true love. Better to leave this ugly world behind. She
wished she could have borne the child though.
Perhaps had Roy seen it, he might have loved it as
he was unable to love her. That would have been
something worth while.

Her drugged mind fought against the urge to cling
to him one last time. He was only a figment of her

tortured imagination, conjured to mind in her final
desperate moments. Yet . . . if only the man in
reality could be as wonderful as the dream image
who held her, begged her to live for his sake, in a
voice quivering with emotion. He loved her, he said.
How often had she heard the same words from
Roy's lips in other dreams which did not come true
either. Love her! He hated her. She was Ewen
Fraser's sister. An object of contempt. The weapon
he had chosen to exact his revenge on the man who
had discarded his sister after months of humiliation
and degradation.

He loved her! He whispered the words against her
hair before pressing his lips to hers, instilling in her
a momentary desire to grab hold of the thin thread
of life still remaining in her body and make this
ecstatic moment come true.

How tender was the look in the black eyes so very
close to her face. How she thrilled to his touch, the
sincerity in his voice. Even in her weak state, her
lips gave him answer. It was the last thing she
remembered before opening her eyes on to a room
where the first pale grey shadows of dawn were
stealing through the uncurtained windows to lighten
the shadows about the bed.

The dream was still vivid in her mind. And she
was still asleep, she thought, turning her head slowly
upon the pillow for she could see Roy's face close
to hers, feel his hand cupping her breast, burning
her skin through the material of her nightgown. The
other was about her shoulders, amid the abundance
of thick red curls.

When she became aware of her surroundings again,
it was fully light. The rays of a watery sun coming
through the windows, slanted across the foot of the
bed. There was no one beside her! She was quite
alone in the huge bed—in the room itself. She

realised she no longer felt so hot and uncomfortable and her head had ceased to ache. She was drowsy, but aware of the emptiness inside her resulting from the miscarriage. Yet she knew she no longer wanted to die. The sunshine was like new life flowing into her . . . that and the remembrance of the softly spoken words which had given her such joy and peace of mind.

And then her sleepy gaze fastened on the deep indentation in the pillow beside her and colour rose in her wan cheeks. He *had* slept beside her. It was no dream!

In the days and weeks which followed, however, during a slow, but steady recovery back to health, Roy visited her very little and never hinted by his manner or a careless look, that he had been with her. He had brought her back to life, but acknowledged it not. Disappointed, hurt by the fierce pride in him that made it impossible for him to admit he loved her to her face, Anne found the days beginning to drag. She lost interest in all about her and began to grow thin from her continual refusal to eat properly. Why had he not let her die—and freed them both? Agnes lost patience with her—Mairi pleaded in vain for her to rise from her bed and assume her responsibilities in the house. What did it matter if she showed herself, Anne returned with a shrug, there were two women now and only one could successfully be the true mistress of Tigh an Lóin.

Even Coll visited her, to be promptly ushered out by Mairi upon a visit from Ranald. He had no more success than anyone else. The girl who lay before him was still a shadow of the vital creature Roy had brought home that first day, who had endeared herself to all with her willingness to be part of their

world. With a sigh he turned and left the room
without speaking to her.

Without warning, Roy appeared in her bedroom one
morning as Anne was picking uninterestedly at the
small plate of coddled eggs Agnes had brought her.
Slices of toast were growing cold beside it. She
wondered when the kitchen would realise how limited
her appetite had become and stop sending her food
she had no intention of eating, no matter how
appetising they made it appear.

She knew he had been away from Tigh an Lóin
for several weeks, staying with friends near Loch
Maree. Coll, too had been absent from the house,
but from the way Mairi had spoken, she gathered
they had not been together. Her heart leapt at the
sight of the tall figure who came to stand at the foot
of the bed and she hated herself for the momentary
weakness in her that made her pleased to see him.
Then, as she lifted her eyes to the angry features,
she knew it was no social call to enquire after her
health. What did he care? He had grown tired of
telling her she mattered to him and had begun to
treat her as little more than a stranger. Not once,
since St Stephen's night, had she heard one endear-
ment fall from his lips.

'What the devil do you think you are playing at?
Are you determined to stay in this bed for ever? The
servants have something better to do than wait on
you all day long.' Unconsciously, she drew herself
back against the pillows, steeling herself against the
contempt in Roy's voice. 'I have received an excellent report from Doctor MacInnis. There is no
reason why you should not be up and about, taking
the air to put some colour back into those cheeks.
Riding again . . . '

Had he come to her with a different approach,

Anne knew she would not have been able to refuse him—but to order her from her sick bed!

'Need I remind you I have just miscarried?' There was no friendliness in her voice and she watched him stiffen.

'No, you need not. Nor have I overlooked the fact you thought fit not to tell me of your condition.'

'I was not sure.'

'You risked your life . . . and your brother did the rest. I shall add the crime of murder to my list. The murder of my son!'

A boy! She would have had a son. Agnes came into the room and snatched up the remains of her breakfast.

'Why don't you go back to where you've been these past weeks,' she challenged, 'and leave the poor lamb in peace. You've not had a thought in your head for her before now . . . '

'You have half an hour to get up and get dressed . . . in something suitable for a christening,' Roy said stonily, ignoring both the interruption and the baleful looks directed at him. Anne thought she felt like throwing the remnants of her chocolate at him. 'I shall come back for you within that time. If I find you still abed, playing the invalid, I shall drag you out by the hair and dress you myself,' he added threateningly, and Anne stayed the hand moving towards the china cup and saucer.

'I have already told Mairi, I cannot—cannot attend the christening. I am not strong enough. I swear it.'

'She was disappointed at your refusal. I have told her you have changed your mind. She wishes us to be godparents, heaven knows why, we have little to offer each other, let alone an innocent babe, but we will accept because she asks it of us. This afternoon the family will be united in the family chapel. All of

the family, Anne. Do I make myself quite clear?'
Roy strode from the room.

'The bully! The inhuman brute!' Agnes fumed as
she pushed aside the bedclothes. But Anne knew he
meant every word and was quite capable of carrying
out the threat. 'You cannot go out, mistress. You
are so pale and thin . . . '

'Perhaps he is right! Lay out the blue silk, the
dress in which I was married. He wants me to look
presentable, well, he can find no fault with that one.
And accessories . . . Oh, look at my hair!'

She stood before the looking-glass in despair. Six
weeks of virtual self-denial had left its mark on her.
The red hair was dull, lacking its usual brilliant
lustre. Her skin was chalk-white, cheeks thin and
pinched. Was this really her!

'I cannot show myself like this. Quickly, find some
cream and brush these tangles from my hair . . . '

At least he had roused her, Agnes thought, as she
deftly wielded the brush on the unkempt locks, even
if it was for the wrong reason!

Roy surveyed her in silence when he returned,
scrutinising every aspect of her appearance until she
wanted to scream at his disinterested calculation of
her face and body.

If he recognised the gown, his expression did not
betray it. It clung more loosely than before to lithe
hips, and curving bosom, but the shower of frothy
lace hid this well enough. He frowned at the loose
cloud of hair which framed the pale face and she
held her breath waiting for him to comment, but
said nothing.

He escorted her to the sitting-room where the
french windows were thrown open to admit the
warm spring sunshine. She stood for a while admiring
the flowers beginning to blossom from their winter
shells. Their perfume floated about her. She felt a

hand brush her arm as Roy thrust a glass of sherry in front of her, saying quietly,

'Is it not good to be alive? Breathe deeply, smell the fragrance of your efforts. The garden has never looked like this in April. You have given it life. Enjoy what you see—what you have.'

She turned to go back inside, but he was blocking her path. She put aside the sherry without touching it and the refusal to join him brought a bitter smile to his lips.

'I have reassured Father and the others that we are—reconciled.'

Anne caught her breath at the words. What was he insinuating?

'You gave me back life, but it was not of my choosing.' She forced the words through stiff lips. Why could he not have left her alone? Was his mistress so unsatisfactory that he now sought his wife once again in an effort to appease his father? She had lost the child . . . Ranald would want another. She felt faint to think of Roy making love to her again, solely for that reason . . .

'I thought you were too drugged to be aware of my presence that night.' He gave her an odd smile.

'You do not deny it?' she gasped.

'Why should I? You wanted to let go of life . . . I was determined you would hold on. I have my reasons.'

'Reasons which involve Ewen and Frances, no doubt.' She tried to push past him, but his hands locked on her shoulders, biting into the soft skin until she winced. Immediately they loosened, but he continued to hold her.

'No. As a matter of fact, they concern you—and me.' Roy's voice had become quite strained. He had not calculated for the confrontation between them to be so soon. He had intended taking her away

from Tigh an Lóin for a while, so that they could
be alone to resolve their differences. He knew he
should not have touched her. Now he ached to kiss
those quivering lips, sweep her into his arms and
conquer her as he had done so often before, but he
knew to do so might lose her for ever. He could feel
her trembling beneath his hold and a wave of disgust
washed over him. Instead of love, he had instilled
fear. And he would pay dearly for what he had
done.

'You did not have to say all those . . . things
you did.' Anne tried to look at him, but his eyes
burned into her very soul. He would see the love she
still had for him unless she kept her face averted.
She heard him swear softly as she bowed her head,
refusing to look at him. She did not want to be used
again. To die that kind of death would be a hundred
times more agonising than the one she had just
escaped.

'Did I not?'

'You did not mean them. You—you could not.'

'Then I shall have to prove to you somehow that
I did.' An urgent note crept into his tone, confusing
her with its sincerity. Roy's eyes flickered towards
the door, praying they would not be interrupted
until this issue had been settled between them.

'You are a past master at deception.' Still she did
not look at him—dared not! 'You have tricked me
too often before, fool that I am.'

'I can lie with my mouth—my eyes—the way I
look at you.' He was forcing back her head, eyes
blazing now as he saw sudden hope rise—then die
in her expression. He would make her believe! He
had to! 'But not with my body—or my heart. No
more can you. I shall take you to the lodge and
prove it to you.'

'No!' The cry torn from her lips by his words told

him all he hoped to hear. Not fear of him—but of herself had made her remain in isolation, avoiding contact with him lest her body weakened as it had so many times before when he touched her. 'I will not—be used again!'

'No, you will not. By me—or your brother.' His fingers touched her cheeks and were abruptly withdrawn as if he could not trust himself to allow the intimacy to develop and deepen at this time. He wanted her alone at the lodge where he could bend her to his will again, Anne reasoned, and knew she would be helpless to prevent it.

If he loved her, why did he not kiss her, hold her as he had that wonderful night, convince her with his touch, not meaningless words? Would she believe him so soon after the mistrust and enmity between them? Was his suggestion to be alone again not better? Or was she falling once again into the spider's web, this time perhaps, not to emerge?

'You are aware, of course, the men who attacked you were Ewen Fraser's men?' She nodded miserably. 'And you defended him!'

'He is my brother. I defended him as fervently as you—you fought for Mairi,' she retaliated, two spots of colour beginning to burn on her otherwise colourless cheeks. 'What do you intend to do about him now?'

'I have not made up my mind. Only his death will bring about peace, but I have promised myself I will do nothing more to cause you grief—or pain.'

'You cannot hurt me any more,' Anne replied, hiding the surprise she felt at his words. Had she not been a victim of his deceit before, she would have sworn he spoke from the heart. 'You have destroyed everything I felt for you. My brother has deprived me of the relationship we once shared together. I have nothing . . . I want nothing, from either of you.'

'Then that is my loss.' Roy stiffened as he heard the sound of voices, the click of the door opening. In a low tone which only reached her ears, he added very slowly—and with great conviction, 'Our positions are now reversed. It should amuse you—or at least give you satisfaction. I love you. If you have nothing to give, so be it, but I will not let you go, Anne. I will never set you free. You will belong to me for ever.'

Ranald and Mairi made such a fuss of her that Anne was brought near to tears. Roy stood nearby watching them together behind a closed expression. He did not come as close to her for the rest of the afternoon as he had done for those few minutes in the sitting-room. He loved her. She was afraid to accept he spoke the truth, but each time she thought of the tremor in his tone as he spoke the words, her heart leapt and a tiny flame flickered again in the cold ashes of her love. No, never cold. They smouldered waiting to be ignited. And she was sure he knew it. He had not accepted the lie she told and once they were alone together at the lodge, he could prove it.

It was what she wanted. Her heart cried out to give him what he desired, to end the conflict between them. Each time she looked at him, she found his eyes on her, questioning her refusal to accept what she had been told. She gained no satisfaction to think their positions might indeed be in reverse now. His love rejected, scorned out of hand, to die beneath her withering contempt! If she did not accept he truly cared for her, then she had nothing. The emptiness inside her would fester and grow until it consumed her and they ended their days in utter misery. She was tired—beaten. She no longer wanted to fight him, only to love him and be loved in return.

John Robert Henry Michael Fraser cried all the
way through the baptismal service until Anne held
him, with Roy standing so proud and erect at her
side. This should have been their child being anointed
with holy water. A hand was laid on her arm and
she gained comfort from the pressure of the strong
fingers which gently squeezed. He too had felt her
loss. Her battle was over. In that moment she knew
she would be whatever he asked of her, go wherever
he ordered, remain by his side until the day she drew
her last breath. He would not let her go, he had
said. The words roused excitement inside her as she
handed the gurgling baby back into his mother's
arms. Stepping back, she lifted her eyes, wet with
tears, to her husband's face.

'I shall send Andrew ahead to the lodge to prepare
it for us,' Roy said quietly as they stood together in
the Great Hall, Coll fumbling clumsily with the cork
of a bottle. Only at the last moment did he avert a
disaster and drowned a nearby maid instead of Mairi
and the baby. Everyone of the household was gathered to drink the health of Ranald's grandson. All
the men had been consuming ale or whisky for most
of the morning, Anne thought as the Laird and his
youngest son embraced each other. All except Roy,
who was never far from her side. Whereas before he
would have been in the thick of it, with his glass
raised and voice as high as his father and brother's,
he now seemed content to remain in the background
and allow others to do his celebrating for him.

'No, I would rather you did not do that,' Anne
said, remembering Roy's remark.

'As you wish. But I've not used it since—that
day . . . I stayed there while you were in Inverness, but not since.'

'Why? While I was away?' Anne looked at him

curiously. She was more tired than she would admit to anyone, not wanting to spoil the festivities. She hoped she could soon slip away to her room and the welcome comfort of her bed.

'Perhaps I wanted to be close to you in that great old bed, as I was on our wedding night,' came the outrageous reply. 'We will leave in the morning. On horseback. I will tell father to expect us when he sees us. He has some idiotic idea in his head that I should court you all over again . . . even marry you here in the chapel as I deprived you of a decent wedding before.'

'I should like that,' Anne said softly, sudden warmth springing to her eyes. 'I should like that very much indeed, Roy Mackenzie.'

'Then you shall have your courting—and your wedding . . . But first, I shall have you all to myself for a few days, to settle any doubts in your mind,' Roy said, lifting her fingers to his lips. For a moment she thought he was going to kiss her before everyone, tensed herself expectantly for the touch of his mouth and was bitterly disappointed when he drew back, wicked lights glittering in his eyes. 'I will not keep you waiting long, I promise. Before you stand beside me again and say your vows, I will be sure you are mine and you will know I am yours!'

This was reminiscent of her wedding day, Anne thought as Agnes helped her dress in a feverish haste the following morning. She donned a plaid woollen skirt and a silk blouse, topped with a dark jacket, which curved into her narrow waist. Her hair was caught up in a dark ribbon.

'Ay, he will like the look of you,' the maid said as she turned to her for approval. 'Are you sure you know what you are doing? After all he has put you through. The loss of the babe? The humiliation?'

'You asked me that once before, if you remember,'

Anne told her, a soft smile touching her mouth. She had slept well and there was more colour in her cheeks than Agnes had seen in many weeks.

'Ay, and you did not listen to me then either,' she returned sourly. 'He's up to his old tricks and you'll suffer for it.'

'I love him. That is all I know—all I care about. I must take the chance that he has spoken the truth.'

'Him! In love!'

'He has changed . . . I can sense it. I cannot live without him and I don't intend to try. Mairi is home again and Ranald has his grandchild. Even Coll is walking around with a very satisfied look on his face for some reason we have yet to discover.'

'Perhaps he's found himself a lass.' Agnes was no fool. She had sharp eyes and very keen ears and like most of the servants she was aware of the devotion of young Coll to his sister-in-law. Unlike the others, she was shrewd enough to read something else into that unexpected alliance.

'For his sake, I hope so. Wish me well, Agnes. I will be back in a few days and then you will see how right I am to take this second chance being offered to me.'

'If you come back with a long face and tell me he's playing you for a fool again, I'll poison the black-hearted rogue,' the maid retorted with great vehemence—and she meant every word!

Roy was waiting outside with two horses already saddled. On a pack horse beside them, was a small valise containing her change of clothes and several large bundles. Anne looked at him questioningly.

'Would you not have me do my courting in style?' he asked, helping her to mount.

'I want no fancy words or meaningless gestures,' she said and the black eyes narrowed sharply, but he did not rise to her cautious tone. 'Where are

Mairi and your father? Are they not to bid us farewell?'

'I have left a note for Father to explain our unexpected departure. Like you—and my dear sister, he would be most suspicious of my—shall we say—change of heart. But then he does not know it is love not hate that rules it any more. Like you, he would question if I have one,' Roy answered as he swung himself into the saddle and gathered the reins to him. His attention arrested by a rider coming towards them, he broke off, and she also turned curiously towards the oncoming figure.

'It's Coll! Has he been out all night?' Perhaps Agnes was right—he had found himself a lass.

'And where are the two of you off to like a pair of lovers?'

Anne pursed her lips at the mockery in his voice as he dismounted before them. His jacket was open despite the crispness of the early morning breeze, his bonnet set at a jaunty angle. She could smell the brandy on him even from where she sat.

'Anne and I are seeking a little peace and quiet at the lodge. We will be back in a day or so. And you, brother?' Roy eyed him with some amusement. He had not managed to discover who was his brother's latest sweetheart. Coll was very secretive about this one. It was a relief to him to know there was another woman in the background, however. His association with Anne had begun to both irritate and worry him. He knew it to be sincere, but that made it all the harder to accept for Coll was not the one to indulge in anything other than the lightest of flirtations, despite what he had overheard. 'By the brandy fumes about you, I'd say you have had a far from peaceful night.'

'You are looking at a very sober man. I spent last night at the house of my future father-in-law—on his insistence,' Coll returned with a wide grin.

'Are you telling us you are about to be married?' Roy sat back on his horse, his mouth gaping. He had not envisaged this drastic step. 'Who to?'

'Judith MacPherson.'

'The Earl of Mhor's ward!' Roy's incredulity grew. 'Man, she's an heiress in her own right.'

'I thought I should continue to live in the custom to which I have become accustomed. Did I not tell you I would only marry a woman who could support me in grand style? Her dowry alone would keep all of us at Tigh an Lóin for a whole year. The marriage contract was drawn up last night over a cask of the finest brandy I have ever tasted. Roy—oh, Roy, will we have some times together when it is all mine. Upon my marriage, I assume control of all my bride's wealth and property and upon the death of the Earl, his vast estates also become mine. What say you to that?'

Roy could only shake his head, speechless at the announcement. It was Anne who leaned towards him, her hand outstretched.

'I am so happy for you, Coll. You will be sadly missed by all the village lasses, for you leave many a broken heart behind you.'

'And some I did not even make an impression on,' came the quiet reply as he drew her down to him, offering his cheek for her congratulatory kiss.

Roy was conscious of his brother's whole body stiffening as her lips brushed his skin—of his fingers flexing over her arm, barely touching it—as if he could not bare the contact. As she drew back, their eyes met and locked—in silent understanding—acceptance passed between them.

'Be happy, brother.' Roy clasped Coll's hand in a bruising grip.

'Will you dance at my wedding? In three weeks,

there is to be a betrothal ball to put me on show for all her family—God help me. You shall both meet her, then.'

'Try and keep me away! Does Father know?'

'I am about to break the news to him. I have the feeling he will be quite proud of this scatterbrained individual on his achievement. The old Earl has taken quite a liking to me . . . looks on me like a second son, he said last night. He was tight, mind . . .'

'And—do you love this Judith MacPherson?' Anne asked quietly, aware no mention of the emotion had so far been made in the conversation.

'We are—suited to each other,' Coll said, stepping back from the horses. 'And the way I look at it, we have all the time in the world to grow to know each other—to fall in love. I mean the kind of love that will still be with us when we are in our dotage.' He surveyed them with a slow smile. 'Think on it, my children—all the time in the world.' Despite the mock gravity in his voice, something told both Roy and Anne that he was in deadly earnest—offering them wise advice.

'What is it?' Roy drew rein as he became aware Anne was not keeping pace with him. The lodge had come into their view and she was dropping back. It had seemed so simple, the answer to all their problems, Anne thought, but now, seeing the place again, remembering how it had been between them here, she was growing apprehensive. 'If the place means as much to you as it does to me, you will not be of faint heart now,' he added and she spurred her mount to canter with his.

The place was damp, darker than she remembered, even on this sunny day. She had enjoyed the ride and it had brought a bloom to her cheeks. But there was a wariness lurking in her eyes which took Roy aback. Did she have doubts, still? If she asked it of him he would go down on his knees with his protestations of love, but he knew she would not. How could there be love between them if there was no trust?

'I'll light a fire, it will brighten the place and warm it for us for tonight. The evenings are still chilly. You should have let me send Andrew ahead.'

'No, we will manage.' Her smile was half-hearted as she entered and looked around her. He noticed her gaze lingered on the door leading to the bedroom and quickly eased himself past her with the valise and full saddle-bags.

'Would you like to see what is left in the cellar by way of wine? We cannot have a courting without that, can we? I'll find some wood. The ride has made me ravenous. I suggest we have an early dinner.'

'And then, Roy? Afterwards?' Anne asked quietly, and a dark eyebrow rose at the nervousness he heard in her tone.

'You sound like a bride . . . a shy, skittish little creature about to meet her doom at the hands of the strange man she has been bound to in wedlock. It is not like that between us, is it?' Her silence brought a tightening of his lips. 'Whatever happens—if anything happens between us again, will be of your choosing. I have no intention of rushing you—or dragging you into the bedroom and ravishing you. My patience—God help me—will be infinite.'

He was gone so long that Anne had found some cloths and dusted the eating area, laid it with fresh white table linen and was delving into the contents of the saddle-bags when the door opened again and he came in with armfuls of wood.

'What has Katie provided for us?' he asked,

kneeling before the hearth. Within minutes there
was a crackle of flames and he rose with a nod of
satisfaction. He had asked the cook to scour the
pantry for something special.

'There is enough food here for several days.' Anne
had envisaged two, three at the most. Now she
realised he had estimated much longer. His smile
mocked her nervousness as she took out two jars of
fruits, pickled in brandy, joints of venison, ham and
other salted meats, biscuits, a large fruit cake and
an enormous wedge of cheese.

'Everything else we need is here.' He eyed the
bottle of wine on the table and one of port. As he
reached for the former and began to open it, she
gathered up most of the food and turned away. 'I'll
find a home for this, we aren't going to eat it all at
once.'

The enormous kitchen had plenty of cupboards
and cool stone cavities for the meat. She lingered as
long as possible away from the other room and
expected something to be said when she reappeared,
but Roy was busying himself setting up a spit for
the meat. There were two glasses beside the open
bottle, but neither had been filled. Somewhat hesitantly she poured the wine and was sure she saw a
flicker of pleasure in his eyes as he looked up and
accepted the glass she offered. He sat back on his
heels, watching the heat begin to force the juices
from the piece of venison.

'Do you want to talk?' he asked quietly and she
shook her head. 'We must—sometime. I offer no
excuses for the way I have behaved, Anne—I am
not that kind of man. I did what I did, believing I
was right . . . and I was.'

'Yes.' Begrudgingly she admitted it. 'About
Ewen—but not me. Never about me.'

'Will words take away the pain—erase the loss of our child?'

'No. Only time can do that . . . at least I pray it will.' She sipped at her wine and curled up on the sofa as she had done that first night. But on that previous occasion she had been innocent, unawakened, his pawn. Roy turned and stared into her doubting features, made no attempt to touch her and so further heightened the tension growing inside her. If he had grabbed hold of her, made her his wife again, at least she would have had something to reproach him for, but his manner was faultless, his behaviour impeccable.

He cooked the food like an experienced chef, served it to her in great style and with a panache that brought a smile to her face, despite all her misgivings. He *was* trying. She could do no more than acknowledge his efforts. But she could not relax, despite the wine which accompanied the meal.

'Damn it, must you sit there looking at me as if you expect me to jump over the table at you?' Roy demanded harshly. 'If I had known it would be like this, I would not have suggested we come here. I cannot wipe out the pain and misery I have caused you. I only wish I could, but I am begging your forgiveness. I swear to you now, I will never by word or deed bring you such grief again.'

'Please—do not make promises you cannot keep. Your hatred of Ewen has not changed. You cannot tell me truly that it has.'

'No,' he admitted. 'And I will not lie. But you will not be involved, nor any of my family. I accept I must find another way to end it.'

'Can you not—let it end without killing him?' she pleaded. 'He has lost a wife—albeit he did not love her, but he must have felt something for her in the beginning . . . and he has lost a son, too. He is in

the clutches of an unscrupulous woman who will
use him until she tires of him. You did not hear the
way she spoke to me in Inverness. I believe my
brother is paying a terrible price for his misguided
love.'

'As Mairi did. As you did.' Roy thrust his glass
away from him, knowing he must not get drunk.
Yet he felt it was the only way to obliterate the
memory of what had happened. She was slipping
away from him, he could feel it! What do I have to
do to convince you of my love, Anne? Take you to
bed?' Instantly she flinched away, even though the
table separated them by several feet. 'You hate my
touch, I know. Yet there were times . . . '

'I don't hate it.' The words were out before she
could contain them, but she was glad. 'I only wish I
did. I have no defence against you, Roy, surely you
know that by now? You took my love and used
it—used me, but you did not kill it. It would be
better if you had, for then I could truly hate you.'

'What are you saying.' He was staring at her as if
unable to accept what her words could mean. He
had hoped . . . but her attitude had been so cold,
so distant since her illness. 'You love me, still?'

'God help me, yes! And that is why as much as I
want to, I will not fall into you arms. I cannot trust
you . . . I am afraid,' Anne cried and the tears
she had held back as she spoke were unleashed
down over her cheeks. She ran from him then into
the bedroom, slamming the door after her. He did
not follow.

For hours she lay across the bed, but he did not
even open the door to ask how she was feeling. It
was the truth, she was afraid of him. Afraid to trust
in this love of his that would lift her to the moon
again and just as easily, grind her under his heel
when it suited him to do so. When the first afternoon

shadows lengthened across the room, she rose and went to the valise on the chair and began to unpack it.

Roy did not look up when he heard the door open quietly. He knew she must be standing in the doorway looking at him, but he remained with his head resting on his hands, staring into the dying flames of the fire. He had gambled—and lost. She would never belong to him again. He had no intention of asserting his authority over her, those days were gone. If only they could be buried along with the hatred and mistrust. She loved him . . . and feared him. Dear God, what a terrible vengeance he had wrought upon an innocent girl! Tomorrow he would take her back to Tigh an Lóin.

He heard a rustle of soft material and out of the corner of his eye saw the hem of a burgundy coloured gown and a slender foot thrust into a leather slipper. Wondering if he was dreaming, he lifted his eyes to the figure standing close at his side and his eyes widened—in disbelief—apprehension as he saw she had put on the very same robe she had worn that first night. Her hair was loose about her shoulders like tongues of fire. Slowly she sank to her knees beside him, reached out with a trembling hand to touch his cheek.

'What game are we playing now?' he asked harshly. Did he think he could look at her like this and not touch her?

'The game of love,' Anne answered, her eyes brightening as his hand closed over hers. 'If that is what you want.'

'I will not take you that way again.'

'Will you send me away, then? I do love you, with all my heart and soul and nothing you ever do will kill what I feel for you, but I am afraid. You cannot blame me for that,' Anne whispered. She heard his sharp intake of breath as she leant against him boldly—inviting him to put his arms about her and take what she offered. Her warm breath was against his cheek, her breast pressing against his arm. 'Whatever our life together is like from this moment on, hell or heaven, I want no other man to hold me. I am willing to take the chance. You said you would never let me go. I hold you to that.'

'And you will never have cause to regret it.' He gathered her against him, his mouth claiming her own in a gentle, tender kiss, yet it burned her lips for she could feel the suppressed passion within him.

'My husband,' she whispered and saw his eyes were misty with tears as he lowered her to the floor beneath him. Tears! For her! 'I will never doubt you again . . .'

'I will give you no cause,' Roy swore as he opened the robe and lost himself in the worship of her body, pouring into it all the love he had denied her—and himself too long. She kissed the wetness from his eyes, loving him all the more for this moment of weakness he did not attempt to hide—or deny.

His hands once again had their own very special magic as they caressed her, as did the lips that grew more searching, more demanding, until she clung to him with a cry and begged him to take her and end the long, bitter months of estrangement. To lift her to the ecstatic heights she had known before in his arms. This time it would be different for them both for they would go on forever reaching those dizzy peaks.

As the sky darkened outside the lodge, the three men who had been waiting in the trees for the same length of time as Roy and Anne had been within, moved from their cover and hastened towards the door. They had been waiting weeks for the woman to leave Tigh an Lóin. It was a nuisance that she was not alone, but it was not important.

Dozing in Roy's arms, Anne saw them first as she sleepily raised her head wondering if the fire was still alight. It mattered not if it had gone out for she was warm and comfortable and in no hurry to move. She screamed at the figures crossing the floor towards them and Roy, his brain still fogged with sleep, had hardly begun to rise before he was struck down. She was dragged to her feet, her wrists tied roughly behind her back. As she began to struggle one of the men growled warningly,

'Come quietly, or I'll kill your man.' A keen-bladed knife was thrust towards Roy's throat and instantly Anne submitted, knowing she would do anything, go anywhere to save her husband's life.

One of the others had the decency to close her gaping robe and fasten it while her cheeks blazed with colour. Her mind went numb as she was lifted and carried unceremoniously outside and propped in front of him astride his horse. She knew who her captors were, for the answer lay in the predominantly red plaids, striped with green and black. Fraser men! Her brother Ewen's men! She was being taken to him . . . and when Roy came after her with his men, then the bloodshed would begin in earnest . . .

She could hear the sound of voices raised in anger from below and knew her brother had returned to the house. He had been away when she had arrived, bound and near fainting from the ride which had threatened to break her back. Her pleas to slow down had been ignored and she had been threatened with a gag if she continued to annoy them.

She had been left in a room at the top of the house. Part of the rooms her mother had once used. They were in near decay now. No repairs or decorating had been done in the two years she had been away. The once bright little sitting-room was drab and so dismal, a lamp had been left burning for her on a table by the door. Where had all the money gone, she wondered as she stared at the paint peeling from the walls, the dusty uncared for furniture. In her mother's day it would have gleamed. Even after her death when Anne had taken over the running of the house and sought to instruct Mairi, it had always been well looked after. The girl had shown an eagerness to learn and take on her full responsibilities as Ewen's wife in those early days before all the accusations began: before the death of her beloved James, now shrouded with suspicion: before Frances had decided to assume the role she had delegated to others in the past, treating Mairi as an outsider, an inferior: before she had gone to France and the final drama had been played out beneath this roof resulting in Ewen's wife fleeing for her life to the sanctuary of Inverness.

And then a drama of a different kind had begun, when Roy discovered her there and sought not only to protect her, but to revenge himself on all those who had maligned her. She, Anne, had become innocently involved in his scheme. Two years since she had set foot in this house. Five months since she married Roy MacKenzie! She felt suddenly old as she contemplated what had passed in that time . . . and very afraid as the voices grew louder, angrier . . . approaching the door behind which she was imprisoned. Ewen and Frances! Arguing about her!

Slowly she came to her feet, unconsciously smoothing back the tangle of red curls from her face. What madness had prompted Ewen to have her brought to the house by force? She had not heard a word from him since the night in Inverness when Frances had visited her in his place and she had come to wonder about her brother's involvement with the woman. For love of her, he had misused and abandoned his wife, decried his son—what man of sound mind did that? Even after she had left him, he had hunted her like an animal, but why? She could not understand why it was so important for him to retain a hold over Mairi. She wanted to be free of him and it would cause a scandal once she proved the child she had with her belonged to him—her rightful husband. All Ewen's accusations—and those of Frances, which not only confirmed, but added to Mairi's apparent infidelity, would be proved false, but scandals were soon forgotten.

She could understand his chagrin having gone so far in his affair with Frances, but to think of harming his own wife and son, for she was sure that was what he meant to do—appalled her. And now she had been taken forcibly from the lodge, from the arms of her husband, and subjected to a tortuous ride—and imprisonment—like Mairi! There was something more! She did not know what . . . but there was something more!

'Anne—my dear child, you look . . . ' Ewen halted on the threshold, staring at the figure before him with horrified eyes. Anne's robe was creased and dirty, her hair in disarray and the marks of the ropes which had bound her could be plainly seen on her white skin.

'I have been abducted from the side of my husband, bound and thrown across a horse like a sack of grain.' Her voice was cold, the blue eyes chillingly so as she stared at him—and the woman who appeared behind him. 'I will not speak to you with *her* in the room.'

'Anne, for the love of heaven, I know not what

has been happening!' Ewen spun around on Frances, his face working angrily. 'You said she had come of her own free will! In a robe, and naked beneath! You lying bitch! Once again you deceive me.'

'Only because you are too weak to take on these responsibilities for yourself,' Frances spat in an authoritative tone that confirmed all Anne's suspicions. Here was the strong one—the instigator of all Mairi's troubles—and her own. Her brother was in love . . . he would do anything for this woman. Anything! She felt very cold, remembering the cloud surrounding James's death. She swayed and immediately Ewen was at her side, guiding her to a chair.

'Have someone bring us wine,' he ordered.

'Suddenly you are master in this house,' Frances hissed and the venom in her voice brought Ewen wheeling about, his hand upraised to strike her, but another figure appeared at her side, a young man whose hand was on the sword at his belt. Anne recognised him immediately as the fourth man from the attack on the coach. She fell back into the chair as he smiled in her direction, vividly remembering the horror of the hands that had fumbled at her bodice, torn it open and sought to rape her while he had watched and done nothing! Frances, not her brother had sent the men to kill her and Mairi. She was sure of it now. Obliterate them from the face of the earth so that whatever they knew would go with them to the grave. But what was it she knew—or Mairi knew, that Frances considered so damaging?

'Until the day your—paramour—sinks a dagger into my back ay, I am still master here, woman, and you are little more than a paid whore who is long past her best—so get you gone and send someone to me or do we have our reckoning now?' Ewen threatened. He stepped towards the two people, his fingers reaching for his own weapon.

A smile masked Frances's features as she stayed the hand beside her, saying quietly, 'As my lord wishes. We will await you below. There are things to be discussed—make the most of the time you have with your sister.'

'What—What did she mean?' Anne whispered as the door closed behind them. Ewen laid a finger against his lips and waited a few moments, before crossing to the door and opening it. The corridor outside was empty. A servant appeared before he could close it with a tray bearing wine and glasses. After he had gone, he closed the door and poured large measures for them both.

'Drink it,' he advised.' You are not going to like what you hear.'

'If you are about to tell me that Mairi is not the adulteress you have proclaimed her, you can save your breath,' Anne said, drinking deeply. The heady wine restored her flagging spirits and gave her a courage she knew to be false, but at such a time, any kind was welcome.

'So you know?'

'Everything! You have a son, Ewen. Have you no wish to see him? Acknowledge him?'

'She would not allow it,' her brother replied, slumping into another chair and she looked at him in astonishment.

'She? Where is your backbone?'

'You sound like James . . . he called me a weakling too that day . . . struck me . . . God help me I did not mean to kill him, Anne.'

She flinched so violently that the blood red wine spilt over her robe, staining it. Her eyes widened as she stared down at the damaged material. It was like an omen. Blood would be spilled today . . . but whose?

'Why do you look at me like that?' Ewen demanded. 'You said you knew! Oh, my God, you did not! How could you . . . ?'

'Tell me. Perhaps we can resolve together what haunts you,' Anne whispered, but he shook his head. 'Please, Ewen. She is not all-powerful. Roy will help, if I ask him . . . '

'It is well between you, then?' Her brother's eyes were dull as he looked across at her, as if the life has suddenly gone from him.

'It is now. Why did you send those men to kill me—and Mairi when we left Inverness?' She had to hear the denial from his own lips. 'I sent you a letter, but *she* came in your place and said you were too busy to come to me. Does she dominate every moment of your life, every thought, every breath?'

'Does Roy not do the same with you?' Ewen asked and she nodded, understanding the fires which raged in him. It was the same for them both. She regretted nothing now she had lain in Roy's arms again and experienced the depth of his love, but Ewen . . . he had nothing, she suspected and her heart went out to him despite all that had happened between them. He was of her blood, she would not desert him.

'I want to know about James, and why you have maligned your wife so cruelly, disowned your own son. I have just lost a child, Ewen—it was a boy. You do not know the agony I have been through. Before it is too late, tell me, let me understand . . . '

Ewen rose and refilled his glass. She hesitated, then allowed him to refill her own. She was terribly afraid, not of him, but of the vengeful woman below and the smiling young man with her who had death lurking in his eyes.

'You killed James . . . your own brother! Tell

me it is not true! It cannot be!' She thought she
knew everything! She knew nothing!

'It was an accident, dammit! I rode after him. We
had quarrelled that morning . . . about Mairi. He
knew what I—we were doing to her—and why. We
hoped she would run home to her family, to that
brother of hers that adores her—but she was stubborn.'

'She loved you . . . '

'She did not tell you about James . . . about
that day?' he asked slowly and she shook her head,
steeling herself against the new grief she knew was
about to come her way.

'She overheard me talking to Frances. After that,
it was not so simple. We could not let her go, could
we, to tell the authorities I had killed my own
brother? I rode after him . . . caught up with him
beside the loch. We argued, you know how quick-
tempered I am.' He turned away from her, his face
twisted with emotion. She half rose from her chair
to comfort him, then stopped herself. He had killed
James! Her cheeks were ashen as he continued, 'He
said he had changed his will after he discovered that
Frances was my mistress. I would never inherit his
money and property—this house, to squander it on
a worthless woman. It would go to you, my dear
sister. You are mistress here, no other. You didn't
know that, did you? You are rich, Anne! Beyond
your wildest dreams. James invested well. He had a
shrewd brain . . . and he knew you would care
well for that which he gave you.'

'Me!' she gasped. 'I don't understand. Why was I
not told?'

'Do you think Frances wanted to be deprived of
her money—her position? She knows the lawyer who
handled James's affairs and . . . manages
him . . . as she manages me and others, I have

come to realise,' Ewen retorted. 'You left for France the day after the funeral assuming, as we did then, that I would inherit. It was not to be. No one knows, however, we have kept James's secret. Until now . . .'

'You killed your own brother and made it look like an accident and then took the inheritance he had intended for me?' Anne said in a hollow voice. Never had she believed Ewen capable of such treachery.

'Exactly. Frances handled everything. Unfortunately Mairi overheard us talking that day when I came home. She knew I had killed James.'

Anne was white with disbelief as she said, 'She said nothing . . . do you realise that? To this day, she has told no one of what she heard. Oh, Ewen, how she must love you still. I cannot believe we are of the same blood.'

'Would you not kill to protect him—Roy MacKenzie?' her brother demanded and she nodded, her face flushing with colour.

'I would . . . and I will, if you raise a hand against him. You, or that butcher sent to murder me!'

'What are you talking about? What man?'

'With Frances. He and some others waylaid the coach when I was returning from Inverness to Tigh an Lóin. Mairi and the baby were with me. They had orders to kill us. One tried to rape me before he killed me . . . had Roy not arrived. That one with Frances now—stood watching.'

'Holy Mother of God! Anne, I know nothing of this!' Ewen went down on one knee before her, tried to clutch her hand, but she pulled it away.

'Then why am I here if it is not to be killed—and bring Roy and his family into a trap? I love him, Ewen—above all things—above you! I will not allow

you to murder him as you have murdered James
—with or without her help!'

'You believed that of me? Have we drifted so far
apart? Were we always so close . . . ' Ewen began
and then sitting back on his heels he regarded her
with what she considered to be a very strange expression on his face. Desperation, coupled with a kind
of resignation! 'No, close as we were, it was always
James you turned to for help or advice. *I* came to
you. You had the strength I lacked. When events in
this house sickened you, you went away . . . '

'How I wish I had not,' Anne whispered and he
hesitantly touched her hand. 'If I had stayed. Oh,
Ewen, perhaps I could have stood against Frances
where you could not . . . '

'Nay. I am weak, I admit it . . . but I am not a
murderer. It was an accident,' he insisted. 'I would
have gone to the authorities, but she persuaded me
otherwise . . . as she has persuaded me to many
things of late. But, sweet sister, believe me—you
must! I knew nothing of the letter you sent to me
from Inverness. She kept it from me. She taunted
me that now you had Roy MacKenzie you no longer
needed me. I came to believe it.'

'If only you had contacted me . . . or I had
you, earlier. But after St Stephen's night, I was
afraid to. You must know that, Ewen. Roy truly
loved me when he married me, but he also wanted
to kill you. I almost lost him through his hatred.
Am I to lose you?'

Ewen swore. She laid a hand across his lips,
silencing him.

'Do not take on so. We have our love and it will
sustain us . . . but I lost my baby after your men
attacked the carriage. No! Her men! The man with
her now was their leader. I know you would not
send men to kill your own son and he is indeed your

flesh and blood—he bears the same mark as we do.' With a groan he laid his head in her lap, reminiscent of past days when he had come to her seeking comfort, reassurance and she, not knowing the strength in her, had given it as love and devotion to her own brother. Without it, he would have fallen totally beneath the spell of a strong, ruthless woman. Anne knew what drove him now—and understood.

'You love her above all, I know,' she said, gently stroking his hair, 'as I love Roy, but we no longer seek to destroy each other, Ewen. He loves me. I was in his arms when those . . . those men tore me away. Do you know what will happen now? He will guess who has taken me. Blame you, and come here. I will not let you kill him.'

'No more will I allow it.' Ewen raised his head and stared into her set features. 'You should see yourself now. So determined. So sure of yourself. So like James. I was always the misfit!'

'No! You never gave yourself a chance.'

'I never will now.' There was a finality in his tone that took her aback. She watched him rise and cross to the window. For several minutes neither of them spoke. 'You have been here over three hours. It will not be long before he comes for you.'

'And what then?' she asked in a hushed tone and he smiled into her ashen face, a softness in his eyes she had not seen in many a month.

'You will not suffer because of what I have done, nor will he. I detest the man, but if he loves you, then I shall give him the chance to love you—the chance I never had . . . never gave Mairi. If *she* had not been here . . . '

'You would have been happy,' Anne said, nodding. 'And you would have had a fine son. Will you let me tell her it was not her fault.'

'If you wish . . . she hates me too much to care.'

'If that was the truth she would have betrayed your secret long ago. She kept silent for love of you, and almost died for it at the hands of your mistress's new paramour. Oh, Ewen, can you not break free of her?' Even as he turned and looked at her, she knew he could not. No more could she break loose from Roy. They were as one, for better or for worse, for good or for bad. 'Why am I here? What is her reason for my abduction?'

'To have you sign papers which would turn all the estates and money over to me, as if James had never made a new will,' Ewen said dully, his expression growing thoughtful.

Anne seized on the suggestion. 'Then I will do it. Do you think I want to see my own brother indicted for murder? Take it all, I want nothing. I have all I want.'

'And I believe you. How lucky you are. If only it was that simple. I think she means to dispose of me soon. I have become a liability. I still have a conscience, you see, and it bothers me more with each passing day. She is without a conscience, without a heart, or a soul. She was sired by the devil himself.'

'Even Dhommil Dhu is not that evil,' Anne returned with a humourless smile. 'Leave her then.'

'And go where? Don't you understand, woman . . . I can't leave her! God help me, I can't!'

'Then you must continue to be part of her evil schemes, or be a man.'

He stared at her through narrowed eyes and for a moment it could have been James standing there before her, daring her to speak to him in such a fashion! It was in him, but was it too late!

'Or end it—for both of us, so that we can do no

further harm to anyone. I will not let her go, Anne. I will not let her go.'

'Ewen, let me sign whatever papers you have, please,' she begged, afraid of this strangeness in him. 'Before Roy comes. Let me go!'

'Ay, before he comes . . . there must be no more killing.' He turned towards the door. As she came to her feet to follow him, it opened and Frances stood there, the man at her side smiling as he looked towards the two figures in the room, death mirrored in his eyes.

'You have gone soft,' the woman hissed, eyes glinting with malice as they came to rest on Anne's defiant face. 'She has talked you round as I knew she would. No matter, we are prepared. Have you the papers, Malcolm?'

'Ay, my lady. As you dictated them. Ready for signing.'

Frances took several sheets of parchment from his hands and tossed them down on to a table.

'All you have to do is sign your name, Anne, and then you are free to leave here.'

'As I was in Inverness. You sent men to kill me . . . and when that failed, you had them lay in wait for another suitable opportunity.'

'Yes, I did, didn't I?' Frances's face twisted into a smile and Anne felt her brother tense. 'What a cosy little scene we interrupted. Your husband must be out of his mind with worry by now, considering the *déshabillé* in which you were taken,' Frances laughed, eyeing her crumpled robe.

'An act of love is something you would not understand.' Anne's voice was like iced barbs, penetrating to the heart. 'We have survived all you have done to Mairi and to me and Roy. I shall bear another son and this time your hired murderers will not take him away from me. They did not take

Ranald's grandson from him, did they? Mairi is safe and will remain so. You cannot touch her.'

'But I have you! Roy MacKenzie may follow you, I hope, of course, he does. I shall let Malcolm have you before you have—your accident!'

'No!' Ewen said and she looked at him with wide-eyed mockery.

'Suddenly you have a backbone? For what? You have no say in this, she knows too much.'

'You have done more than enough to ensure your own existence. This is my sister . . . and you will not touch one hair on her head or I will kill you.'

'You!' Frances exploded into laughter. Malcolm stood at her side with a hand on his sword, and Anne knew what he was thinking, a chill of fear running through her at the expression in the cold, pale eyes.

'Ewen, take care,' she begged. 'She cares not for your life.'

'I know it, but if I am to die, then I shall take her with me . . . ' Ewen cried and launched himself at Frances. He had not gone three paces when the hilt of Malcolm's sword felled him to the ground. Frances said quickly as he turned on Anne,

'Not yet, you fool! First she must sign the papers or we kill them for nothing.'

'No!' Anne backed away from the figure approaching her defiantly. 'I will sign nothing—not now. It will all come out, you know. Mairi will not keep silent when I am dead. You will be exposed for what you are.' Roy, oh Roy, where are you? she cried in silent terror.

Malcolm's eyes flickered past her shoulder to the window and as he stiffened, hope rose inside her. She wheeled about and a cry escaped her lips at the sight of the horsemen approaching.

'You will gain nothing from harming either of us

now, Frances,' she said triumphantly. 'My husband has come for me and he has brought close on thirty MacKenzies with him. Save yourself while you can.'

'She's right,' Malcolm growled moving back towards the door. 'I'll saddle two horses. We can be away from here long before they reach the house.'

'And where will we go without money?' Frances demanded contemptuously. 'Keep you head or you'll be of no further use to me. We shall be here when the MacKenzies arrive. They will find me in a state of shock after witnessing how Ewen killed his own sister when she would not sign these papers . . . I tried to stop him, but . . . ' Lifting a hand to the shoulder of her gown, she fastened her fingers on the thin material and ripped it savagely, exposing the rise of a full breast. She pulled the pins from her long hair and shook it about her shoulders. 'I shall convince them I tried . . . but it was you, my trusted Malcolm who laid low the mad dog, and saved my life. Unfortunately you were too late to save Anne. Kill her and then finish him and when I bring them rushing up here, be sure you are convincing.'

'Ewen was right after all—Dhommil Dhu did sire you,' Anne breathed, her eyes wide with fear. On the floor, Ewen groaned and Frances stepped back through the door.

'Do it now and make some noise about it to convince the servants,' she ordered, closing the door quickly behind her.

Anne's fingers closed about a small statuette on the table beside her. With all her might she flung it at the window and as Malcolm's hands went instinctively to his face to shield it from flying glass, she thrust him back against the wall. She prayed frantically that the sight and sound of an object hurtling through the air, together with the screams which followed, would bring Roy even faster to her side.

A blow from behind all but stunned her as she slipped to her knees, splinters of shattered glass sinking painfully into her legs and hands as she slowly sank to the floor. Malcolm reached for her throat. His fingers went around it, shutting off her breath. As her senses began to reel she watched him slowly draw the dirk from his belt. He was going to cut her throat! No, she could not die now, she had too much to live for. Roy was so close . . . No! No!

Behind them, Ewen came up on to his knees, fighting his way through a haze of pain. Blood streaming from the head wound almost blinded him. He wiped it away with his sleeve, fumbled for his own weapon. His fingers had no strength in them . . . his vision was blurred. Thank God the swine was too occupied with torturing Anne in her last moments to sense his furtive moments. Leering at her, as he held her nearly senseless in the grip of one powerful hand, he was waving the blade to and fro before her wide-eyes, revelling in the agony she was experiencing as it drew closer to her throat.

Ewen's blade sank deep in to his back. Anne was thrown backwards onto the floor, sobbing with terror, gasping for air, pinned beneath the prostrate body which suddenly fell upon her. She could hear someone swearing, but it took her several minutes to realise it was Ewen, as he tried to pull the man off her. Sick with revulsion, she added her strength to his to free herself.

'It's over . . . hush, lass, don't greet. I'll not let her harm you either,' Ewen whispered as she sank against him, spent and tearful. 'By the sound of those horses, your man is below. Frances will be greeting them. Let's give her a surprise, shall we? Can you walk?'

She nodded, not yet able to find her voice. She raised trembling fingers to her bruised throat, shuddering as she stared down at the dead body at her feet. Ewen had saved her! Wordlessly she laid her lips against a bloodied cheek in gratitude. He was swaying too, she noticed, as unsteady as she was herself. Blood was oozing from the gash on his head, but he would not let her tend him. First, he had to get her to safety, back to the man she had married and then he would settle with Frances and end it once and for all.

The sound of voices came to them as they reached the top of the staircase. Ewen drew Anne back into a recess as Frances came hurrying up, with Roy immediately behind her, sword drawn. The sight of his tortured face tore at her heart.

'Hurry, for the love of God! He has gone mad . . . Had my servant not intervened, he would have killed me also. She may still be alive . . . '

'She is still alive, you lying bitch. But no thanks to you. Your lover is dead, and now I will settle with you,' Ewen cried in a terrible voice. With a scream, she turned and ran from the man who looked at her with murder in his eyes, from the dishevelled girl at his side, from Roy MacKenzie whose sister she had tried to destroy and from his father and the other clansmen from whom she knew she would receive no mercy.

'Roy, stop him, he will kill her!' Anne whispered, sagging in her husband's arms where Ewen had thrust her. He was running after Frances before either Ranald or Coll had a chance to stop him.

'She said he'd killed you . . . Oh, my love . . . ' Roy's lips cut off her frantic plea. 'I've been in torment since they took you. I recognised the plaid, so I knew it was Ewen's men. Every mile we rode, I had your face before me. If anything had happened to you . . . '

'Ewen saved me. Frances was going to have us both killed. She is behind everything . . . Ewen was her pawn . . . he loved her too much to break free of her—until now.' Somewhere along the corridor, a door slammed and Roy's head jerked up, his mouth tightening.

'Our men are all about the place, they won't escape us. He is mine, do you hear, Father? Coll? No man touches Ewen Fraser but me.'

'No, you don't understand. Listen to me,' Anne pleaded.

'Anne, there is blood on you. Are you hurt, girl?' Ranald demanded.

'Glass . . . from the broken window . . . My hands are cut too, but . . . '

With a low oath, Roy gently took them in his, and wiped away some of the blood. He had been so relieved to find her alive, he had not noticed anything other than her face wet with tears.

'I thought it might have been you who attracted our attention, but then that woman said you were dead, murdered by your own brother. What devilry is there we don't know, my love? You say he saved you from her?'

'She ordered a man to kill me. Afterwards, he would have killed Ewen too. Go after them, Roy, I fear for what he might do, not only to her . . . '

'Ach! There's no great hurry, they can go no further than that room yonder. Be still, woman and let me bind these hands. You are more important to me than they are at this moment,' Roy chided, with a roughness of tone that told her he was having difficulty in holding back his emotions.

'There was a time you would not have admitted that to me,' Anne whispered, fresh tears springing

to her eyes at the confession. He lifted her injured
hands to his lips for a brief moment.

'And a time you would not have believed me, had
I the courage to say it,' he returned. 'Those times
are past for us . . . '

'What are you doing?' Frances whispered, her eyes
dilating as Ewen closed and locked the door after
him. She had come into the wrong room in her
haste. This one was where Malcolm lay. She did not
give him a second glance. There was no escape
except through the door where Ewen now stood,
staring at her as if he had never seen her before. The
blood from the gash on his head had dried on his
face. As she watched, he lifted a finger and touched
the red streaks, a smile masking his face. It was the
most terrible thing she had ever seen for there was
death in his grimace—death without mercy! 'Unlock
it, Ewen—please! We can go out through my sitting-
room,' she implored.

'No! You are going nowhere. No more am I. It
ends here.'

'Fool! Coward!' She looked around for a weapon,
but even as her eyes fell on Malcolm's dirk lying on
the floor, Ewen anticipated her move and scooped
it up out of her reach. 'You would dare use that on
me!' She spat the words at him when the blade rose
before her eyes. 'You are nothing but a weakling—an excuse for a man. Without me to tell you
what to do, you cannot think for yourself. Like that
one, at your feet. You need me . . . we need each
other. It was good for us before, wasn't it? With
Mairi gone, we shared so much more.'

'I gave and you took . . . We shared nothing,'
Ewen said bleakly. His hand trembled. He wanted
her dead. He had to kill her before she tainted more
lives with her evil, but to sink the dirk into her

breast. He shuddered and she laughed out loud.

'It's not so easy, is it, little man?' she taunted and his fingers tightened purposefully about the hilt again. She evaded him as he stepped towards her, tripped over the dead man on the floor and fell heavily. As she went down, her fingers clutched for support at a nearby table, sent it crashing to the floor, scattering ornaments and the papers— smashing the oil lamp and sending red hot oil flaming over the carpet. She screamed as flames licked at the hem of her gown, began to beat at them frantically with her hands.

'Ewen! Help me!'

She became aware he had moved back from her and was leaning against the far wall. The paper on the floor flared to life between them, flames licking hungrily over the linen cloth and over Malcolm's body. It dawned on her suddenly that he was not going to help her!

Coll lifted his head and sniffed the air. Simultaneously, his father and brother became aware of the odour creeping towards them.

'Fire! Oh, dear God, what has he done?' Anne cried. 'Help him, Roy . . . help him . . . '

'Stay here,' he ordered, putting her to one side, but she ignored the order and limped painfully after them as they ran towards the door where smoke was seeping through cracks and from beneath the oak panels. There was a terrible fear in her heart. She called her brother's name, but there was no answer and the sound which came from within chilled her to the bone. It was a roar like a rushing wind, but she knew it was not that, but the awesome sound of flames crackling and comsuming all in its path.

'Help me, Coll,' Roy shouted and together they put their weight against the door. It shuddered, but did not give way until the third attempt and as it caved in, the intense heat drove them back. Roy looked into his wife's agonised features and turned to rush into the inferno, but Coll grabbed his arm and held him fast.

'Don't be a fool, man. Can't you see nothing can survive in there. Look!'

In the centre of the room, the fire was hungrily sating its appetite on the two objects, no longer recognisable as human beings. One lay inert, the other still moved and still screamed. And against the far wall, barely distinguishable through the smoke and searing redness, a face distorted by the tremendous heat. Without fear, without a sound, Ewen Fraser waited to meet his creator and account for his crimes. The horrific scene was too much for Anne to bear. She swayed, her eyes closing. Roy swept her up in his arms and quickly carried her from the house.

The fire raged unrestrained. The MacKenzie clansmen had alerted the servants and helped them to safety, but on the orders of Roy MacKenzie himself, no attempt was made to bring the blaze under control. It was late afternoon before it was cool enough for anyone to venture inside the smoking ruin. Anne refused to leave until she heard from her husband's own lips that Ewen was dead, even though she knew no one could have survived the terrible heat and flames . . . and she had seen that he had been making no attempt to save himself—or Frances. He could not leave her—yet nor could he live with her any longer. Mairi was vindicated. James's death avenged by the very brother who had taken his life.

Roy came to her, through the billowing smoke haze which still hung low over the ruins, carefully picking his way over the charred beams which had once supported the first floor.

'He has made his peace with Mairi—and you—and

me,' he said, gently drawing her to her feet. She clung to him trembling, gaining comfort from his words for his thoughts were hers also.

'An act of absolution for what he did—with Frances's help.' There was so much more to tell him, but she was tired and shocked and wanted nothing more than to be held in his arms for a very long time.

Roy carried her to where the clansmen waited with their horses. She turned her face into his plaid as he swung himself up behind her. His clothes were heavy with the odour of smoke. His lips touched her cheek, followed the path of a tear to her lips. The tender kiss lifted a little of the weight from her heart, for it was more eloquent than any words. In silence he turned his mount round and they rode away from the gutted house without a backward glance.

Pack this alongside the suntan lotion

The lazy days of summer are evoked in 4 special new romances, set in warm, sunny countries.

Stories like Kerry Allyne's **"Carpentaria Moon"**, Penny Jordan's **"A new relationship"**, Roberta Leigh's **"A racy affair"**, and Jeneth Murrey's **"Bittersweet marriage"**.

Make sure the Holiday Romance Pack is top of your holiday list this summer.

AVAILABLE IN JUNE, PRICE £4.80

Available from Boots, Martins, John Menzies, W. H. Smith, Woolworth's, and other paperback stockists.

Mills & Boon